John Bruce, John Manningham

Diary of John Manningham,

of the Middle Temple, and of Bradbourne, Kent, Barrister-at-Law, 1602-1603

John Bruce, John Manningham

Diary of John Manningham,
of the Middle Temple, and of Bradbourne, Kent, Barrister-at-Law, 1602-1603

ISBN/EAN: 9783337018603

Printed in Europe, USA, Canada, Australia, Japan

Cover: Foto ©Raphael Reischuk / pixelio.de

More available books at **www.hansebooks.com**

DIARY

OF

JOHN MANNINGHAM,

OF THE MIDDLE TEMPLE,

AND OF BRADBOURNE, KENT, BARRISTER-AT-LAW,

1602-1603.

EDITED FROM THE ORIGINAL MANUSCRIPT BY

JOHN BRUCE, ESQ.,

AND PRESENTED TO THE CAMDEN SOCIETY BY

WILLIAM TITE, ESQ., M.P., F.R.S., F.S.A.,

PRESIDENT OF THE SOCIETY.

WESTMINSTER:
PRINTED BY J. B. NICHOLS AND SONS.
M.DCCC.LX.VIII.

TO

THE COUNCIL AND MEMBERS

OF

THE CAMDEN SOCIETY.

GENTLEMEN,

When you did me the honour to appoint me President of your most useful Society as the successor of the Marquess Camden, I felt anxious to express my sense of that honour by some appropriate acknowledgment.

I at first thought of printing a MS. from my own library, but, not finding one that seemed exactly suitable, in my difficulty I applied to my old and valued friend Mr. Bruce, and he pointed out to me Manningham's Diary in the British Museum as possessing a varied interest in the literary world which was likely to commend it to your notice. I willingly adopted his suggestion; and I owe to him my sincere acknowledgments for the pains he has bestowed in seeing the work through the press, and in prefacing it with an interesting essay.

I have now to offer you this copy of Manningham's little book, and to assure you how sincerely I am

Your obedient and obliged servant,

WILLIAM TITE.

42, Lowndes Square,
3rd October, 1868.

*

PREFACE.

The original of MANNINGHAM'S DIARY, which is here printed, is No. 5353 in the Harleian collection of MSS. in the British Museum. It is a diminutive 12mo. volume, measuring not quite six inches by four, and containing 133 leaves. The handwriting, of which an admirable representation is given in the fac-simile prefixed, is small, and in the main extremely legible; yet in some few places, from haste in the writer, from corrections, from blotting, from the effects of time, and from other obvious causes, difficulties have occurred in a word or two, which, even with the assistance of gentlemen most skilful in reading the old hands, have not been entirely overcome. The few instances in which the collater has been baffled are indicated by marks of doubt.

The first historical writer who noticed this little volume for a literary purpose was Mr. John Payne Collier. In his Annals of the Stage, published in 1831 (i. 320), Mr. Collier quoted from this Diary various passages connected with his special subject, and drew attention to the principal personal facts disclosed by the writer respecting himself, namely, that he had many relations in Kent, and had probably been a member of the Middle Temple.

The late Mr. Joseph Hunter was the next writer who used the work for an historical purpose.[1] With his well-known fondness for genealogical inquiries he applied himself to determine who the writer was whom Mr. Collier had designated merely as a barrister.

---

[1] See his Illustrations of Shakespeare, i. 365.

In this inquiry Mr. Hunter was completely successful. Pursuing the clue given by the mention of relationships in Kent in the various ways which would occur to a person skilled in such investigations, Mr. Hunter fell upon a track in which coincidences between the facts stated in the MS. and those elicited by his own researches followed one another so rapidly as in the end to leave not even the shadow of a doubt that the desired result had been obtained.

We shall briefly indicate the course by which Mr. Hunter arrived at his conclusions. It looks easy enough after the end has been attained, but it will be borne in mind that inquiries of this kind are extremely discursive. The statement of a few leading facts upon the establishment of which the final conclusion is arrived at, gives no idea of the time lost in investigations which are merely tentative. In all such inquiries we are soon reminded of the pretty passages which, after turnings and windings almost *ad libitum*, are ultimately found to lead to nothing.

Besides cousins of at least seven different names who are alluded to by the Diarist, several of them in connection with Canterbury, Sandwich, and Godmersham, there is one whom he specially commemorates as "my cousin in Kent" (p. 19), and whom he frequently vouches by that designation, or merely as his cousin, as his authority for information which he chronicles. This cousin was evidently the writer's most important connection—the great man of the family. To visit him and his somewhat wayward second wife was the principal object of the Diarist's journeys into Kent. It also appears that this cousin was a man advanced in life,—roughly stated to be 62 years of age in March 1602-3, and that he resided at a place called Bradbourne, in the neighbourhood of Maidstone. This last fact led directly to the identification desired.

Bradbourne was easily found. It has been for centuries a family seat in the parish of East Malling. Hasted has represented the house in one of his pictorial illustrations pretty much as it yet exists. It has been shorn indeed of many of the noble trees, of the deer, and of some of the other aristocratic adornments with which the county historian surrounded it, but it still stands a stately old-fashioned red-brick mansion, probably of the date of the reign of Queen Anne. Long before that period the same spot was occupied by a previous residence of a county family. From the time of the Protectorate it has belonged to a branch of the old Kentish stock, the Twysdens; and before they purchased it—"in the reign of Queen Elizabeth," as Hasted remarks[1]—"it was in the possession of a family named Manningham."—Manningham! Our diarist slightly alludes to a cousin of that name, " G. Manningham, deceased."[2] The clue was vague, but at that little chink there entered light sufficient to guide the researches of an antiquary.

The inscriptions on the older monuments in East Malling church are printed in Thorpe's *Registrum Roffense.*[3] To them Mr. Hunter had recourse, and with good success. Amongst them he found one upon a monument[4] still standing on the north side of the chancel of the church to a Richard Manningham, evidently a person of importance in that neighbourhood. It is not stated in the inscription that he was the owner of Bradbourne, but he lived at the time when our author paid his visits thither, and his age, as given on the monument, although not coincident with that stated by the Diarist,—for the monument declares that Richard Manningham died on the 25th April, 1611, in his 72nd year,—was sufficiently near to stimulate to further inquiries. But without following Mr. Hunter step by step it will be enough to state that from the

[1] Vol. ii. p. 215, ed. 1782.
[2] P. 108.   [3] Lond. 1769, fol. p. 793.
[4] The inscription is surmounted by a bust of singular coarseness, evidently the work of some country sculptor, and executed in the worst taste and manner.

inscription he went to Doctors' Commons, where, under the vicious system of mismanagement which then prevailed, he was one of the favoured two or three who were permitted to use the testamentary records, whilst all other inquirers were excluded with a most offensive disregard of courtesy. The will of Richard Manningham helped on the inquiry very considerably. It was further advanced by an heraldic Visitation of Kent, and was finally and triumphantly concluded by an inspection of the register-books of the Middle Temple.

Without derogating in the slightest degree from the merit of Mr. Hunter's investigations, or desiring to deprive his memory of one atom of the credit which attaches to it on that account, we prefer to state the facts respecting the Manninghams in words of our own, which will enable us to weave into the narrative some additions to the results of Mr. Hunter's inquiries.

About the middle of the sixteenth century the Manninghams were a numerous family of the middle class,[1] branches of which were scattered about in various parts of England. The Richard Manningham of the monument at East Malling was born at St. Alban's; Robert Manningham, descended from a stock which removed out of Bedfordshire into Cambridgeshire, lived and died at Fen Drayton in that county; George Manningham dwelt in Kent, and from the marriages of his female descendants in that county there probably sprang the numerous cousinred of the family to which we have already alluded. Their *status* in Kent before Richard Manningham settled at Bradbourne may be inferred from one fact which appears in the Diary, namely, that George Manningham was bound as surety with William Somner, father of the well known antiquary of

---

[1] " *Honestâ natus familiâ* " are the words of the inscription to Richard Manningham, the very words used also as descriptive of the descent of Sir Thomas More on his monument in Chelsea church; *familiâ non celebri sed honestâ natus*. (Faulkner's Chelsea, i. 207.)

Canterbury, for the father's performance of the duties of the registrarship of the Ecclesiastical Court, in which office he preceded his son.

Richard, Robert, and George Manningham are all stated to have been relations, and probably they all stood about upon a par in worldly circumstances, but Richard pursued a way of life which enabled him to shoot ahead of all the members of his family. Of his youth we have no particulars, but he was well educated even according to present notions. He united an acquaintance with modern languages to the share of classical knowledge taught in our old grammar-schools, and is commemorated as having spoken and written Latin, French, and Dutch, with freedom and elegance, and and as having been able at the age of sixty-two to repeat *memoriter* almost the whole of the first and second books of the Æneid.

Brought up to some branch of commerce, he was a member of the Mercers' Company of London, and in his business days resided in the metropolis, but age found him with a competency, and brought with it some customary infirmities. He retired from London, purchased the quiet sheltered Bradbourne, and passed the evening of his days in occupations in which literature bore a considerable share.

He was twice married; the first time to a native of Holland, a family connection of the Lady Palavicini, afterwards wife of Sir Oliver Cromwell, the uncle of the future Protector.[1] This marriage was a happy one. The lady survived the purchase of Bradbourne,[2] and was buried in the church of East Malling. Richard Manningham's second match was with a Kentish widow. The traces we find of her in the Diary do not leave an impression that she added much to her husband's happiness. She is not alluded to in his will.

---

[1] Diary, pp. 49, 51.

[2] The last notice we have of her is under the date of 1595, when her husband, "at her request and for her sake," lent her kinsmen, Arnold Verbeck, Abraham Verbeck, and

We may therefore conclude that she died between 1602 and 1611.[1] There is no mention of issue by either marriage.

Childless, solitary, and infirm, Richard Manningham was in no degree misanthropic. Out of his abundance he applied considerable sums in charity, and for the benefit of his kindred, and at an early period looked around for a Manningham who might inherit the principal portion of his property and carry on his name. His choice fell upon John Manningham, a son of Robert of Fen Drayton, and his wife Joan, a daughter of John Fisher of Bledlow in the county of Bedford. That person is our Diarist.

Richard Manningham carried out the obligations of this adoption in the most liberal way. It is obvious from the Diary that John Manningham, whom Richard Manningham designated by the several titles of " cousin," " kinsman," and " son in love," received a generous education of the best kind. He was intended for the practice of the law, and on the 16th March, 1597-8, was entered of the Middle Temple, as the son and heir of Robert Manningham of Fen Drayton, gentleman, deceased. John Chapman, probably the same person who is mentioned in the Diary as one of the cousins who lived at Godmersham,[2] and John Hoskyns, were the members of the Inn who were his sureties upon his admission.

On the 7th June 1605, having kept his exercises and been on the books for the needful seven years, he was called to the degree of

Goris Besselles, merchant-strangers, 400*l.* which remained due with all interest upon it up to the 21st January 1611-12, the date of his will. He forgave his debtors the amount, provided they paid 40*l.* a piece to Margarita and Susanna Verbeck, daughters of Arnold, and to the testator's niece Janeken Vermeren, daughter of his first wife's sister, within twelve months after his decease.

[1] The registers of East Malling do not begin until 1640. We beg warmly to acknowledge our obligations to the Rev. W. L. Wigan, the rector, who in the kindest manner searched from 1640 to 1660 for entries relating to the Manninghams, but without finding anything about them.

[2] Diary, pp. 108, 111.

an utter barrister; whether afterwards advanced to the dignity of being permitted to plead in actual causes in court does not appear.

Whilst in the Temple he had for his chamber-fellow Edward Curle, son of William Curle, a retainer of Sir Robert Cecil, who procured him to be appointed one of the auditors of the Court of Wards. Several persons of this family are quoted in the Diary, and the close relationship of chamber-fellow ripened not merely into lasting friendship with Edward Curle, and with his brother Walter, who afterwards became Bishop of Winchester, but into affection towards their sister Anne. John Manningham and Anne Curle were married probably about 1607. A son was born to them in 1608, who was named Richard after the *quasi*-grandfather at Brad- bourne. Two other sons were subsequently named John and Wal- ter, and three daughters, Susanna, Anne, and Elizabeth. Where John Manningham lived after he quitted the Temple, whether in London with a view to practice at the Bar, at Hatfield which was the place of residence of the Curles, or at Bradbourne with his "father in love," then a second time a widower, does not appear.

On the 3rd January 1609-10, the old merchant proved the reality of his assumed fatherhood by executing a deed of gift to John Manningham of the mansion-house of Bradbourne and the lands sur- rounding it in East Malling, and two years afterwards, on the 21st January, being, as he states, "in tolerable health of body in regard of mine age and infirmities," he made his will. It confirmed, "if needful," the deed of gift to John Manningham, appointed him sole executor, and with some slight exceptions and the charge of a con- siderable number of legacies, most of them tokens of remem- brance, gave him all the residue of his property. The multitude of the old man's legacies and not less so their character tell of his continuing interest in the connections of his past life. They read like the last utterances of a warm and affectionate spirit casting back its glance upon those from whom it was about to, part ; whilst his adjuration to his adopted son to discharge the amounts with punctuality, although deformed by the verbiage of legal formality, and smacking a little of the mercantile estimate of the indispensable importance of payment on the very day, is not devoid of real solemnity.   Omitting some of the tautologous expressions it reads thus:—" I charge John Manningham, by all the love and duty which he oweth me, for all my love and liberality which I have always borne [to] him and his heretofore, but chiefly in this my will, that he pay every legacy within six months after my death, those excepted that are appointed to be paid at certain days, and those to be duly paid at their days appointed, as my trust is in him, and as he will answer afore God and me at the latter day !" Nor is the pious close of the document without a share of true impressiveness:—" Having thus, I thank God, finished my will, and set an order in my worldly affairs, I will henceforward await God's will to depart hence in peace, most humbly beseeching him that when the day of my dissolution shall be come, I may by his grace be armed with a true and lively faith, firm hope, and constant patience, and be ready to forsake all to go to my blessed Saviour and Redeemer Jesus Christ.   Amen, good Lord !"

He had not long to wait. His will was dated, as we have remarked, on the 21st January, 1611-12. On the 25th of the following April, [1] Richard Manningham entered into his rest, and John Manningham into possession as adopted heir. On the following 1st of May he proved the will of his "father in love" at Doctors' Commons.

The few particulars we have been able to gather of the course of this family after the death of Richard Manningham are little more than a brief register of dates. On the 16th April 1617, William

---

[1] The year 1611, given on the monument as that of the death, is contradicted by the date of the will and other circumstances. It should have been 1612.

Curle the father died. He was interred in Hatfield church, where a monument commemorates his fidelity as a public officer, his good-fortune in his children and friends, and his calm and happy death.[1]

In 1619, John Philipot, York Herald, made a Visitation for Kent as Deputy for Camden, the Clarencieux. On this occasion John Manningham registered his arms and pedigree. It is observable that he did not introduce into it the descent of his cousin Richard Manningham from their common ancestor, nor even his name. If the Visitation may be depended upon we may infer that be-tween the time when the return was made and the 21st January 1621-2, when John Manningham made his own will, he lost his daughter Anne by death, and his youngest son, to whom he gave the name of his brother-in-law Walter, was born. Before the same day his other brother-in-law and chamber-fellow Edward Curle had also died. The last trace we have found of him is in 1613.

In the will of John Manningham to which we have just alluded, and which it will be observed was dated like that of his predecessor on a 21st January, he described himself as of " East Malling, esquire," and devised Bradbourne and all the lands derived from his " late dear cousin and father in love " Richard Manningham," who for ever," he remarks, " is gratefully to be remembered by me and mine," to his widow for life and after her decease entailed the same on his three sons in succession. He gave to his daughter Susanna a marriage portion of 300*l*.; to Elizabeth, 250*l*.; to the little Benjamin of his flock, the young Walter, anything but a Benjamin's share of 100*l*.; and to his executors 20 nobles a piece; all the rest of his personalty he divided between his widow and his eldest son. He named as executors Dr. Walter Curle, who had then ascended upon the ladder of preferment

---

[1] " *Verâ fide Christianâ* " are the words of the epitaph, which were deemed an authority by the Index-maker for Clutterbuck's Hertfordshire, ii. 370, for entering a " Christiana Curle " in his list of names.

to the Deanery of Lichfield, and John Manningham's cousin, Dr. William Roberts of Enfield. The Will was proved on the 4th December, 1622, by Dr. Curle alone, Dr. Roberts having renounced.

Two further facts bring to an end the brief glimmerings we have been able to discover respecting the third generation of the Manninghams at Bradbourne.

Bishop Walter Curle made his will on the 15th March 1646-7, and left to his nephew and godson Walter Manningham a sum of 50l. To the boy's mother—" my loving sister Mrs Anne Manningham," the Bishop left " a piece of plate of twenty ounces."[1]

Nine years afterwards the "loving sister" had followed the Bishop into the better land. Where she was buried does not appear, certainly not at East Malling. Bradbourne then fell to the second Richard Manningham, who sold it in 1656 to Mr. Justice Twysden, in whose family it still remains. Thus drops the curtain upon the connexion of the Manninghams with East Malling.

Other persons of the same name appear in the succeeding century, one on the episcopal bench as Bishop of Chichester, from 1709 to 1722, and his son Sir Richard Manningham as a distinguished physician and discoverer of the fraud of Mary Tofts the rabbit-breeder, but their connexion with the subjects of our inquiry does not very clearly appear.

Turn we now from the Diarist and his family to the Diary. It was written by John Manningham whilst a student in the Middle Temple, and runs through the year 1602 down to April in 1603. Occasionally, as we have remarked in one of our notes, some few of the entries are out of chronological order, either from mistake of the binder or irregularity of the Diarist. In some cases it clearly arose from the habit of the latter of making his entries in any part of the book where there happened to be a vacant space. The consequences

[1] See Lansd. MS. No. 985.

are of so little moment that we have thought it best in printing to follow the order of the original MS. as it now stands.

Chronological sequence is the less important as the book is scarcely what is generally understood by a Diary. It is rather a note-book in which the writer has jotted down from time to time his impressions of whatever he chanced to hear, read, or see, or whatever he desired to preserve in his memory. The result is a curious patchwork. Anecdotes, witticisms, aphoristic expressions, gossip, rumours, extracts from books, large notes of sermons, occasional memoranda of journeys into Kent and Huntingdonshire, with some little personal matter of the true Diary kind, are all thrown together into a miscellany of odds and ends.

Our Diarist could not have lived in a better place than in an Inn of Court for the compilation of such a book. The common dinner and the common supper, the less formal gatherings at the buttery-bar and around the hall fire, and in the summer time the exercise taken in the pleasant garden—an indispensable accompaniment of an Inn of Court—brought together multitudes of the "unbaked and doughy youth of the nation," full of life and spirit, most of them under training for legal practice or public business, and sparkling with all the freshness and volatility, the exuberance and glow which distinguish the opening of young wits. This was the very place to furnish materials for such a note-book as we have described. Among such companions the *bon mot* of the bar, the scandal of the Court, the tittle-tattle of the town, were the very *pabulum* of their daily conversation. A witty sarcasm would tell among students not "past the bounds of freakish youth" with infinite effect, and it mattered little—such was the universal freedom of language and manners in those days—how literal the expression, or to what kind of subject it related. Perhaps even additional zest was given to a pithy speech by its want of reserve in relation to transactions which we have come to regard as better left untalked about. Neither was there

found any greater difficulty in writing about such matters than in
speaking of them. The line of stars which occasionally will be
found stretching across our page indicates the occurrence of passages
which principally on this ground we have deemed it unadvisable to
print.

The time in which our Diarist wrote was distinguished by one
event of surpassing interest—the death of the great Queen who had
ruled the country for more than forty years. In reference to that
event he possessed peculiar opportunities of acquiring information,
and what he has told us is essentially of historical authority. His
channel of communication with the Court was Dr. Henry Parry,
subsequently Bishop of Gloucester and afterwards of Worcester,
at that time one of her Majesty's chaplains and on duty in that
character at the Queen's death. On the 23rd March 1602-3, the
rumours respecting her Majesty's health were most alarming. The
public were even doubtful whether she was actually alive. In
satisfaction of his curiosity our Diarist proceeded to the palace at Rich-
mond, where the great business was in progress. He found assembled there the Archbishop of Canterbury, the Lord Keeper, and
others of the highest official dignitaries. The Queen still lived, and
the ordinary daily religious services were still kept up within
the sombre palace. Dr. Parry preached before the assembled visitors,
and our Diarist was permitted to be one of the audience. The
sermon was as little connected as could be with the urgent circumstances which must have drawn off the thoughts of his congregation, but in the preacher's prayers both before and after his discourse
he interceded for her Majesty so fervently and pathetically, that
few eyes were dry.

Service over, Manningham dined in the privy chamber with Dr.
Parry and a select clerical company, who recounted to him the
particulars of the Queen's illness; how for a fortnight she had been
overwhelmed with melancholy, sitting for hours with eyes fixed

upon one object, unable to sleep, refusing food and medicine, and until within the last two or three days declining even to go to bed. It was the opinion of her physicians that if at an early period she could have been persuaded to use means she would unquestionably have recovered, but she would not, "and princes," our Diarist remarks, "must not be forced." Her fatal obstinacy brought her at length into a condition which was irremediable. For two days she had lain "in a manner speechless, very pensive and silent,"—dying of her own perverseness. When roused she showed by signs that she still retained her faculties and memory, but the inevitable hour was fast approaching. The day before, at the instance of Dr. Parry, she had testified by gestures her constancy in the Protestantism "which she had caused to be professed," and had hugged the hand of the archbishop when he urged upon her a hopeful consideration of the joys of a future life. In these particulars our Diarist takes us nearer to the dying bed of the illustrious Queen than any other writer with whom we are acquainted.

Dr. Parry remained with the Queen to the last. It was amidst his prayers that about three o'clock in the morning which followed Manningham's visit to the palace she ceased to breathe.

For the last few years the public mind had been disturbed by claims put forth on behalf of a multitude of pretenders to the now empty throne. The people had been bewildered and alarmed by the production of no less than fourteen different titles advanced on behalf of a number of separate claimants. A strong impression prevailed that on the Queen's death a struggle was inevitable—that the long peace which the country had owed to the Tudors would come to an end with them. The vacancy had now occurred, and every one was anxious to know in what manner the claimants would prefer their claims, and who would arbitrate amongst their clashing interests? Above all things, as likely to involve the most important changes, what course would be taken by the Roman Catholics? It seemed a great opportunity for them, so great that no one imagined they would allow it to slip past.

The statements of our Diarist at this time are of particular interest. The ministers of the late Queen acted with equal promptitude and prudence. Sir Robert Cecil had settled the matter long ago, and all his fellow-ministers now concurred in what he had done. Not an instant was lost; at the very earliest moment, at day-break, in less than four hours after the Queen had ceased to breathe at Rich-mond, a meeting of the Council was held at Whitehall. A procla-mation already prepared by Cecil, and settled by the anxious King of Scotland, was produced and signed. At 10 o'clock the gates of Whitehall were thrown open. Cecil, with a roll of paper in his hand, issued forth at the head of a throng of gentlemen, and with the customary display of tabards and blare of trumpets proclaimed the accession of King James.

"The proclamation," remarks our author, "was heard with great expectation and silent joy, no great shouting." At night there were bonfires and ringing of bells, but "no tumult, no contradic-tion, no disorder in the city; every man went about his business as readily, as peaceably, as securely, as though there had been no change nor any news of competitors." The quickness and unanimity of the council, combined with the popular feeling in favour of King James, fixed him at once in the new dignity. Opponents were over-awed and silenced when they found that the supporters of the King had as it were stolen a march upon them, and that, although he himself was absent, his friends were in possession of all the powers of government on his behalf. The previous agitation subsided almost instantly. The disturbed sea rocked itself to rest.

From this time general anxiety was directed towards the North. "The people is full of expectation, and great with hope of our new King's worthiness, of our nation's future greatness; every one promises himself a share in some famous action to be hereafter

performed for his prince or country." The anticipations which
the people framed for themselves from the change of sex in their
new governor, from the change of age, and from the ambition which
they imagined would be developed in him by his transference from
a small rough unsettled country to one which by forty years of
steady government had acquired a unity, a solidity, a definite and
noble position among the nations of the world, of which all true
Englishmen were proud, have no where been brought so clearly
before us, as in the pages of our Diarist. Such anticipations were
like the fire of brushwood. It is painful to think of the disappoint-
ment to which they were doomed.

Besides these events of an historical character, there are scattered
through the Diary a multitude of notices of persons of less social
position than Elizabeth and James, but not by any means of less
interest. Living among lawyers, it was of course that many of the
young student's notes would relate to them. But many of the
lawyers of that day, both those who had earned the honours of their
profession and those who still remained *in statu pupillari*, were
men about whom we can never learn too much. In these notes we
have glimpses of Sir Thomas More, of Bacon, Coke, Lord Keeper
Egerton, of Judges Anderson, Manwood, and Catline, of the merry
old Recorder Fleetwood, of his graver successor Croke, and of the
beggar's friend, Sir Julius Cæsar. Among the younger men we
may notice Sir Benjamin Rudyerd, the future Lord Chief Justice
Bramston, and the man who in the coming stormy times was for
a period more prominent than them all, the statesman Pym. It
will be seen in a note at p. 104, that the publication of this volume
has given an opportunity for the settlement of the question, whether
Pym had what may be termed a regular legal education, which his
biographers have left in doubt. The Middle Temple has clearly the
high honour of reckoning him upon their roll.

Of non-legal persons who are here brought before us with more

or less prominency, we need scarcely allude to the entries relating
to Shakespeare and the performance of his Twelfth Night, which
were first noticed by Mr. Collier, and have been used by every subsequent writer on dramatic subjects. The unfortunate Overbury
comes before us several times, such as we should have expected to
find him, inconsiderate and impetuous. Ben Jonson flits across the
page. Of Marston there is a disagreeable anecdote which has not
been left unnoticed by poetical antiquaries. Sir Thomas Bodley and
Lord Deputy Mountjoy are alluded to. There is an excellent account
of an interview with old Stowe the antiquary, a valuable glimpse of
the Cromwell family during the boyhood of the Protector, and
references, some of them of importance, to Sir Walter Raleigh, to
his foolish friend Lord Cobham, to the wizard Earl of Northumberland, and of course many allusions to the Cecils, both to Sir William,
and to that youngest son to whom, according to the joke which is
here preserved, his father's wisdom descended as if it had been held
by the tenure of Borough-English.

One peculiarity of this Diary is the very large proportion of it
which is given up to notes of sermons. There is something in this
which is characteristic of the time as well as of the writer. It was
a sermon-loving age, and that to a degree which it is scarcely possible for us to understand in our degenerate days. Another thing
which is equally at variance with modern notions is that, when
reading the original manuscript, we pass at once from passages
which we have been obliged to reject as unfit for publication to
notes of pulpit addresses which inculcate a high-toned morality based
upon those sound principles which apply even to the thoughts and
feelings. It is clear that the incongruity in this contrast which
is painful to us was not then perceived. The coarseness of the popular
language on the one hand, and the affection for pulpit addresses,
even among students of the Inns of Court, on the other, were both
parts of what we are accustomed to term the manners of the age,

and, like all things universally accepted, their rights and wrongs were never very minutely criticised. The language we have ob-jected to is of course entirely indefensible. It was the slough of a coarser generation, which our ancestors had not then entirely cast off.

Of many of the sermons as represented in these notes we think highly, but we have printed the whole of them in smaller type, so that they may be distinguished at a glance, and if there be any of our readers to whom they are less acceptable, they may be easily passed over.

Among the preachers who are here commemorated will be found some of the most celebrated divines of the day;—Dr. Lancelot Andrewes, Dr. James Montague, Dr John Buckeridge, Dr. John King, Dr. Parry, and Dr. George Abbot, none of them yet Bishops; Andrew Downes the Grecian; Dr. Thomas Holland, Regius Pro-fessor of Divinity at Oxford; Dr. Giles Thompson, afterwards Dean of Windsor; with two fervid orators, frowned upon by many of their brethren, but most influential with the people,—one of them Mr. Egerton, whose congregation assembled "in a little church or chapel up stairs" in Blackfriars, and the other Mr. Clapham, who was the incumbent of a church at Paul's Wharf.

In notes, for the most part very skilfully taken,[1] of sermons of men so various in their acquirements, and many of them so eminently distinguished, we have examples of the pulpit oratory of the age, with evidences of the nature of the doctrines then generally preva-lent in the Church of England, and of some of the qualities which tended to make the preaching of those doctrines popular.

Nor is the book devoid of notices of many other circum-

[1] So skilfully that one is inclined to suspect that the business of note-taking may have been at that time one of the branches of legal education. A few occasional mistakes of course there are, and when extremely palpable we have sometimes not thought it worth while to notice them.

d

stances which were characteristical of the time. The following are
examples. At p. 22 we find an account of the operation of litho-
tomy, stated to be then first brought into medical practice; at
p. 46 we learn that "a certain kind of compound called
Laudanum" had been recently introduced as the chloroform, and
at p. 132 that the game of shuttlecock was the croquet, of
the day. In another place (p. 110) the fantastical and affectedly
humble salutation to the knee alluded to by dramatists of the period
is said to have been one of the many changes in fashion attributed
to English travellers returned from Italy. At p. 36 there is a
notice of an article apparently of fashionable costume which we
are unable to explain, " Kentish tails." It is said of these things,
whatever they were, that they " are now turned to such spectacles, so
that if a man put them on his nose he shall have all the land he can
see." What connection, if any, there may be between the tails here
mentioned and the old legend of Kentish tails, we are obliged to
leave to the consideration of persons versed in the antiquities of that
county.[1] There are other passages which deal with the fashions

---

[1] We referred the passage to our late dear friend the eminent Kentish antiquary and
founder of the Archæological Society for that county, the Rev. Lambert B. Larking, and
received in reply one of his customary kindly and suggestive letters. Since we wrote to
him, his earthly career has come, alas! to an end. The Camden Council have lost a
distinguished member, and many persons a singularly warm-hearted and unselfish friend.
He was indeed one of those attractive characters who carry into old age the fervour and
generosity of early life. There never lived a man in whose heart of hearts there dwelt a
deeper scorn of everything untruthful, disingenuous, or mean, or who was more distinguished by a total abandonment of all selfish interests. Deeply versed in the history of
his beloved native county, and possessed of large antiquarian collections derived principally from unpublished materials, the information which he had gathered through a course
of many years was at the service of every applicant, and frequently furnished valuable
materials for other writers, whilst an over-anxiety to attain an impossible completeness
prevented his bringing to an end works which would have established his own right to a
high position in the literature of research. His work on the Domesday of Kent we trust
will soon be issued to the subscribers. We doubt not that it will justify our estimate of
the scholarship and diligence in inquiry of our kind and amiable friend.

of the day. It was a time in which ladies' dressing-rooms were
nearly allied to apothecaries' shops, and the art of manufacturing
female beauty seems to have fallen into the hands of probably a
lower and irregular class of medical practitioners. The poets are
full of allusions to this subject. Massinger sums it up in a passage
which we may be excused for quoting:—

> there are ladies
> And great ones, that will hardly grant access,
> On any terms, to their own fathers, as
> They are themselves, nor willingly be seen
> Before they have ask'd counsel of their doctor
> How the ceruse will appear, newly laid-on,
> When they ask blessing.   .   .   .   .
>   .   .   .   Such indeed there are
> That would be still young in despite of time;
> That in the wrinkled winter of their age
> Would force a seeming April of fresh beauty,
> As if it were within the power of art
> To frame a second nature.

The anecdotes jotted down by the young Templar speak for themselves. They of course derive their principal value from the names
to which they are attached. Notices of personal peculiarities are so
singularly evanescent, they live so entirely in the observation and
memory of contemporaries, that it is a biographical gain to have
them recorded in any shape. Apparent trifles, such as the waddling
gait of Sir John Davies, the stately silence of Lord Montjoy at the
dinner table, the description of the popular preacher Clapham—" a
black fellow with a sour look but a good spirit, bold and sometimes
bluntly witty," the fussy particularity of Fleetwood the recorder,
the vanity of old Stowe,—these, and memoranda such as these, impart a life and reality to our conceptions of the men to whom they
relate, which cannot be derived from volumes of mere dates and
facts.

Of the recorded witticisms, the peculiarity which will strike the
reader in this case, as in all others of the same description, is their

singular want of originality. Good things which were current in
the classical period are here re-invented, or warmed up, for the
amusement of the contemporaries of King James. And the same
thing occurs over and over again, from generation to generation.
Mots which descended to the times of Manningham reappeared
in the pages of Joe Miller, are recorded among the clever sayings of
Archbishop Whateley, and in one instance at least may be found
among the pulpit witticisms of Rowland Hill.

The book is one which would bear a large amount of illustrative
annotation. We have endeavoured in most cases to keep down
what we had to say to mere citation of the ordinary standard books
of reference—the tools with which all literary men work. It is well
for them that our literature can boast of instruments so well suited to
their purpose as Dr. Bliss's edition of Wood's Athenæ, Mr. Hardy's
edition of Le Neve's Fasti, and Mr. Foss's Lives of the Judges—the
books to which we have principally referred. May the number of
such works be increased!

Finally, we have the grateful task of returning thanks to two gentlemen who have specially assisted us in issuing this book. To Mr.
John Forster, the author of the Life of Eliot and of many other
valuable historical works, we are indebted for the use of a transcript
of part of the Diary here printed; and to Mr. John Gough Nichols,
like the Editors of most of the volumes printed for the Camden
Society, we owe the great advantage of many most useful sugges-
tions during the progress of the work. The results of their kind-
ness and of the liberality of Mr. Tite will we hope be acceptable to
the Society.

J. B.

MANNINGHAM'S DIARY.

A puritan is a curious corrector of thinges indifferent.[1]

Harl. MS. 5353.
fo. 1.

SONG TO THE QUEENE AT THE MASKE AT COURT, NOV. 2.[2]

Mighty Princes of a fruitfull land,
  In whose richc bosome stored bee
  Wisdome and care, treasures that free
Vs from all feare ; thus with a bounteous hand
You serue the world which yett you doe commaund.
     Most gracious Queene, wee tender back
     Our lyues as tributes due,
    Since all whereof wee all partake
     Wee freely take from you.

Blessed Goddess of our hopes increase,
  Att whose fayre right hand
Attend Justice and Grace,
  Both which commend
True beauties face ;
Thus doe you neuer cease
To make the death of warr the life of peace.
    Victorious Queene, soe shall you liue
     Till Tyme it selfe must dye,
    Since noe Tyme euer can depriue
     You of such memory.

---

[1] This and the subsequent memoranda up to fo. 5 have been apparently jotted down at odd times upon the fly-leaves of the little book in which what is more properly called the Diary was written.

[2] The Queen here mentioned was of course Queen Elizabeth. The writing on this page is in many places so much worn away as to be difficult to decipher.

IN MOTLEYUM.

O cruell death, to murder in thy rage
Our ages flower, in flower of his age. (*Holland.*)

IN SPENSERUM.[1] ⚔

Famous aliue, and dead, here is the ods,
Then God of Poets, nowe Poet of the Gods.

MARCH 29, 1602.

I sawe Dr. Parryes[2] picture with a Bible in his hand, the word
upon it, *Huic credo*, and over his heade an heaven, with a motto,
Hoc spero.

EPIGRAM; Mr. Kedgwyn.

The radiant splendor[3] of Tom Hortons nose
Amates the ruby and puts downe the rose,
Had I a iewell of soe rich an hewe,
I would present it to some monarchs viewe,
Subjects ought not to weare such gemms as those,
Therefore our Prince shall have Tom Horton's nose !

*   *   *   *   *   *   *

EPITAPH IN THE CHAUNCERY[4] AT SANDEY IN BEDFORD[SHIRE.]

Cur caro lætatur dum vermibus esca paratur ?
Terræ terra datur, caro nascitur ut moriatur ;
Terram terra tegat, demon peccata resumat,
Mundus res habeat, spiritus alta petat.

[1] Spenser died Jan. 16, 1598-9.

[2] Dr. Henry Parry was at this time a prebendary of York. He was afterwards successively Dean of Chester, and Bishop of Gloucester, and Worcester, and died 12 Dec.
1616. (Hardy's Le Neve, i. 439; iii. 66, 177, 264.)

[3] The word "lustre" is interlined above "splendor," as another suggested reading
in place of the latter word.

[4] Chancel or chantry?

Why growes our fleshe so proud,
Whiles 'tis but made wormes foode ?
This earth must turne to earth,
To dye flesh tooke it birth,
The earth our earth must hyde,
Our synnes the deuill betyde,
The world our goodes must haue,
And God our soules will saue.

*Certayne devises and empresaes taken by the scucheons in the Gallery*¹ fo. 3.
at Whitehall ; 19 Martij 1601.

The scucheon, twoe windmilles crosse sailed, and all the verge of the scucheon poudred with crosses crosselets, the word *Vndique cruciatus.* Vnder written these verses:

When most I rest behold howe I stand crost,
    When most I moue I toyle for others gayne,
The one declares my labour to be lost,
    The other shewes my quiet is but payne.
Vnhappy then whose destiny are crosses,
    When standinge still and moveing breedes but losses.

The devise manie small tapers neere about a great burning, the word, *Nec tibi minus erit.*

The devise a taper newe blowen out, with a fayre blast from a cloude, the word, *Te flante relucet.*

The scucheon argent with a hand and a pen in it, the word, *Solus amor depinget.*

Two garlandes in a shield, one of lawrell, the other of cypresse, the word, *Manet vna cupressi.*

---

¹ Pepys mentions on two occasions a gallery at Whitehall called the Shield Gallery (Diary, i. 105, 133), and Hentzner enumerates among things worthy of observation in that spacious and memorable palace, " Variety of emblems on paper, cut in the shape of shields, with mottos, used by the nobility at tilts and tournaments, hung up here for a memorial." Journey into England, p. 29, ed. 1757.

A ship in the sea, the word, *Meus error ab alto.*

A man falling from the top of a ladder, the word, *Non quo, sed unde cado.*

A scrole of paper full of cypheres, the word, *Adde vnum.*

A sunne with sweete face in it averted from an armed knight, shaddowed in a cloud all but his handes and knees; which were bended; the word, *Quousque auertes ?*

fo. 3ᵇ. The scucheon, a grayhound coursing, with a word, *In libertate labor ;* and another grayhound tyed to a tree and chafinge that he cannot be loosed to followe the game he sawe; the word, *In servitute dolor.*

A fayre sunne, the word, *Occidens occidens.*

A glorious lady in a cloud in the one syde, and a sunne in the other; beneath a sacrifice of hands, hartes, armes, pennes, &c. the word, *Soli, non soli.*

A kingfisher bird, sitting against the winde, the word, *Constans contrariæ spernit.*

A palme tree laden with armor upon the bowes, the word, *Fero at patior.*

An empty bagpipe, the word, *Si impleueris.*

An angle with the line and hooke, *Semper tibi pendent.*

A viall well strunge, the word, *Adhibe dextram.*

A sable field, the word, *Par nulla figura dolori.*

A partridge with a spaniell before hir, and a hauke over hir; the word, *Quo me vertam.*

The man in the moone with thornes on his backe looking downwarde; the word, *At infra se videt omnia.*

A large diamond well squared, the word, *Dum formas minuis:*

A pyramis standinge, with the mott *Ubi* upon it, and the same fallen, with the word *Ibi* upon it.

A burning glas betwixt the sunne, and a lawne which it had sett on fire; the word, *Nec tamen cales.*

A flame, the word, *Tremet et ardet.*

A torch light in the sunne, the word, *Quis furor.*

A stag having cast his head and standing amazedly, weeping over them; the word over, *Inermis et deformis;* under, *Cur dolent habentes.*

A torche ready to be lighted, the word, *Spero lucem.*

A man attyred in greene, shoting at a byrd in the clowdes; the one arrowe over, the other under; the 3. in his bowe drawne to the heade, with this word upon it, *Spero vltimam.*

A foote treading on a worme, *Leviter ne peream.*

A dyall in the sunne, *In occasu desinit esse.*

A ballance in a hand, *Ponderare est errare.*

A fly in a hors eye, *Sic ultus peream.*

A scucheon argent, *Sic cum forma nulla placet.*

A ship sayling in the sea, *Portus in ignoto est.*

An eagle looking on the sunne, *Reliqua sordent.*

A branche sprung forth of an oake couped, the word, *Planta fuit quercus.*

MARCHE 28, 1602.[1]

At the Temple: sermon, the text, Mark, x. 20.

Notes: All the commandementes must be observed with like respect. It is not sufficient to affect one and leave the rest vnrespect, for that were to make an idoll of that precept. Obedience must be seasoned with love; yf any other respect be predominat in our actions, as feare of punishment, desyre of estimacion &c. they are out of temper.

Christ propoundes these commaundementes of the 2nd table, because, yf a man cannot observe these, he shall never be able to keepe them of the first, for yf a man love not his neighbor whom he hath seene, howe shall he love God whom he hath not seene?

And he that is bound to observe the lesse must keepe the greater commaundement.

The doctrine of justificacion consistes upon these pillars, 1. *Ex merito, si non ex condigno at ex congruo.* 2. And this upon free-will, for noe merrit with[2] a free agent. 3. And this upon a possibilitie of keeping the

---

[1] This was Palm Sunday.　　　　[2] *Sic*, but *qu.* "without."

commaundementes, for *liberum arbitrium* is a power of performing what wee would and should, and *libertas voluntatis* and *liberum arbitrium* are severall.

Noe man can performe anie any action soe well but he shall fayle either in the goodnes of the motion efficient, the meanes, or end.

Justificacion by workes is but old Pharisaisme and newe Papisme; the Papists distinguishe and make *Justiciam legalem* and *evangelicam ;* the 1. in performance of outward required accions; the 2. in the intent supplied [?]

fo. 5^b.

All the sacrifices that God was most delighted with are for the most part sayd to be young, a lambe, &c. and the exhortacion of him which was more the agent and more learned than anie, for he was a King and the wisest that ever was, is, Remember thy Creator in the dayes of thy youth, &c.

There is a generall and a speciall love of Christ wherewith he embraceth men; the 1. is here ment and mentioned, and with that he loves all which doe but endeauour to be morally good; soe doubteles he loved Aristides for his justice, which was a work of God in him, and so being a good, God could not but love it, and him for it.   -

But the speciall is that whereby he makes us heires of eternall lyfe, and adoptes vs for his children.

Beholding him, God regardes the least perfections or rather imperfect affections in us; he will not breake a crazed reede.

AT ST. CLEMENTES;[1] THE PRECHER.[2]

fo. 6.

Note: The breade in the sacrament becoming a nourishment is a medicine to our whole bodye.

The manner of receyving Christes body in the sacrament; as to make a question of it by way of doubting, is dangerous, soe to enquire of it to knowe it is relligious.

Wee receive it [3] *non per consubstantialitatem sed per germanissimam societatem.* (*Chrisostom.*)

[1] St. Clement Danes in the Strand.

[2] The rector at this time was Dr. John Layfield, of Trin. Coll. Cambridge, one of the revisers of the translation of the Bible temp. James I. and one of the first fellows of Chelsea College. Newcourt's Repertorium, i. 572.

[3] In the MS. this word stands "is."

It must be received with five fingers, the first the hand, the 2. the understanding, 3. fayth, 4. application, 5. affection and joy; and this makes it a communion.

"Take and eate," the wordes of the serpent to Eua, the wordes of the brasen serpent to vs; those were beleued and brought in perdicion, these yf beleived are the meanes to saluation.

Out of a booke called THE PICTURE OF A PERFECT COMMON-   ^{fo. 6^b.}
WEALTH.[1]

A wicked King is like a crazed ship, which drownes both it selfe and all that are in it.

Pleasures are like sweet singing birds, which yf a man offer to take they fly awaye.

DR. MOUNFORDES [2] SERMON. (*Ch. Dauers.*)

Of pleasure. *Momentaneum est quod delectat, æternum quod cruciat.*

It is better to eate fishes with Christ, then a messe of pottage with Esau.

Nil turpius quam plus ingerrere quam possis digerere.

The glutton eates like a dogge, and lives like a hogg, having his soule as salt onely to keepe his body from stinkinge.

He that filleth his body empticth his soule.

Id pro Deo colitur quod præ omnibus diligitur.

Vtinam, sayth Augustine, *tam finiatur quam definitur ebrietas.*

Bacchus painted yonge, because he makes men like children, vnable to goe or speake, naked because discouers all.

It is noe better excuse for a drunkard to say that it was his owne that he spent, then yf one should say he would cut his owne throate, for the knife that should doe it is his owne.

Drunkennes is the divells birding synne; the drunkard like the stale that allures other to be taken like it selfe.

---

[1] Written by Thomas Floyd; published Lond. 1600, 12mo.

[2] Dr. Thomas Mountford was a prebendary of Westminster from 1585 to 1631-2. (Hardy's Le Neve, iii. 350.)

Matt. 12.

Envie and mallice will barke though it be so mussclled that it cannot bite.

It is almost divine perfection to resist carnall affection.

When wee censure other men wee should imitate that good imitator of nature Apelles, whoe being to drawe a face of an great person[1] which wanted an eye, drewe that syde only which was perfect.

The malicious man is like the vultur, which passeth ouer manie sweete gardens and never rests but vpon some carrion or garbage, soe he neuer takes notice of anie thing but vices.

Libellers are the divels herauldes.

Invidus alienum bonum suum facit peccando malum.

Envy, though in all other respectes it be a thing most execrable, yet in this it is in some sort commendable, that it is a vexacion to it selfe. It is like gunpowder, which consumes itselfe before it burnes the house. Or the fly *pyrausta*, which would put out the candle, but burns itselfe.

Honor is like a buble, which is raysed with one winde and broken with an other.

MR. DOWNES.[2]

The love of the world is the divels eldest sonne.

Honour, riches, and pleasure are the worldly mans trynitie, wherewith he committs spirituall idolatry.

Thankefullnes is like the reflex of the sunne beame from a bright bodie.

After a full tyde of prosperitie cometh a lowe ebbe of adversitie. After a day of pleasure a night of sorrowe.

Honour is like a spiders webbe, long in doinge, but soone vndone, blowne downe with every blast. It is like a craggy steepe rocke, which a man is longe getting vpon, and being vp, yf his foote but slip, he breakes his necke. Soe the Jewes dealt with Christ ; one day they would have him a king, an other day none ; one day cryed Hosanna to him, an other nothing but crucifie him.

---

[1] Originally written " Emperour " and afterwards " great person." When the word " Emperour " was altered, the writer omitted to correct the preceding article.

[2] The celebrated Andrew Downes, appointed Regius Professor of Greek at Cambridge in 1595. (Hardy's Le Neve, iii. 660.)

The world is like an host; when a man hath spent all, body, goodes, and soule with it, it will not vouchsafe to knowe him.

Laban chose rather to loose his daughters than his idols, and the riche man had rather forsake his soule then his riches.

If a citizen of Rome made him selfe a citizen of anie other place, he lost his priviledge at Rome ; yf a man wilbe a citizen of this world, he cannot be a citizen of heaven.

Ambitious men are like little children which take great paynes in runninge vp and downe to catch butterflyes, which are nothing but painted winges, and either perishe in takinge or fly away from them.

Covetous man like a child, which cryes more for the losse of a trifle then his inheritance; he laments more for losse of wealth then soule.

A covetous man proud of his riches is like a theife that is proud of his halter.

MR. PHILLIPS.

The proverbe is that building is a theife, because it makes us lay out more money then wee thought on; but pride is a theife and a whore too, for it robbes the maister of his wealth, and the mistress of her honesty.

The drunkard makes his belly noe better then a bucking tubb, a vessell fo. 8. to poure into, and put out at.

Bona opera habent mercedem, non ratione facti, sed ratione pacti.

Non est refugium a Deo irato, nisi ad Deum placatum.

Synn is Adams legacy bequeathed to all his posteritie : nothing more common then to committ synn, and being committed to conceale it.

A concealed synn is *tanquam serpens in sinu, gladius in corde, venenum in stommacho ;* it is like a soare of the body, the closer it is kept the more it festers.

Scelera quandoque possunt esse secreta, nunquam secura.

Confession must be *festina, vera, et amara.*

Confession of synne onely at the hour of death, is like a theifes confession at the gallowes, or a traytors at the racke, when they cannot choose.

Sine confessione justus est ingratus, et peccator mortuus.

The mercy of God is never to be despayred of, but still to be expected, even *inter pontem et fontem, jugulum et gladium.*

Dissembled righteousnes is like smoake, which seemes to mount up to heaven, but never comes neare it.

Prayse is a kinde of paynt which makes every thing seeme better then it is. (*Cha. Dauers.*)

To prayse an unworthy man is as bad as to paint the face of an old woman. (*Idem.*)

Sorrowe is the punishment and remedy for synn ; *sic Deus quod pœnam dedit, medicinam fecit.* (*Augustine.*)

fo. 8ᵇ.   ## MR. MUNOES[1] OF PETERHOUSE IN CAMBRIDGE.

Primum querite regnum Dei, et omnia adjicientur vobis. Tullies brother, in a sort reprehending or discouraging his suit for the consulship, tells him that he must remember that he is *novus, consulatum petit,* and *Romæ est ;* the Devill, perhaps least any should attempt to put this precept in practise, will terrifie us by shewinge vs our weakenes, and that greatnes. *Terræ filius es ; regnum quæris? Cœlum est, &c.*

Sit modus amoris sine modo.

Beatus est, Domine, qui te amat propter te, amicum in te, et inimicum propter te.

Quere 3. (1.) *Quere Deum et non aliud tanquam illum.* (2.) *non aliud præter illum.* (3.) *non aliud post illum.*

Diuitiæ non sunt bonæ, quæ te faciant bonum, sed unde tu facias bonum.

Beda interpreted those letters, S. P. Q. R. written upon a gate in Rome, *Stultus Populus Quærit Romam,* intimating they were but fooles that went thither for true relligion.

Yf Christ had thought well of wealth he would not have bin soe poore himselfe. He was *pauper in ingressu,* borne in a manger; *in progressu,* not a hole to hide his head in; *in egressu,* not a sheet of his owne to shroude him in.

The covetous persons like the seven leane kine that eate up the seven fatt, and yet remaine as ill favoured as before. .

---

[1] Monoux or Munoux ?

Yf thou carest not to liue in such a house as hell is, yett feare to dwell with such a companion as the Divel is.

SERCHEFEILD OF ST. JOHNS IN OXFORD.[1]   fo. 9.

Cursus celerimus, sæpe pessimus.
Sit opus in publico, intentio in occulto.
A dissembled Christian, like an intemperate patient, which can gladly heare his physicion discourse of his dyet and remedy, but will not endure to obserue them.
Minus prospere, qui nimis propere.

MR. SCOTT, TRINIT. CANT'BR.

Dum sumus in corpore peregrinamur a Domino.
Non contemnenda sunt parva, sine quibus non consistunt magna.
The soules of the just men are like Noahs doue sent out of the arke; could finde noe resting place upon the earth.

He that hath put on rich apparrail will be carefull he stayne it not; he that hath put on Christ as a garment must take heede he soile not himself with vices.

  *   *   *   *   *

An high calling is noe priviledge for an impious action.

All our new corne comes out of old feilds, and all our newe learning is gathered out of old bookes. (*Chaucer.*)

Words spoken without consideracion are like a messenger without an errand.

Our owne righteousnes at the best is but like a beggars cloke, the substance old and rotten, and the best but patches.

[1] Dr. Rowland Searchfield, Bishop of Bristol from 1619 to 1622. (Wood's Athenæ, ii. 801.)

AT BRADBORNE WITH MY COSEN THIS CHRISMAS. 1601.

My cosen[1] told me that Mr. Richers would give his cosen Cartwright 8,000l. for his leas of the abbey of towne Mallinges, the Reversion whereof the L. Cobham hath purchased of hir Majestie.

An old child sucks hard; i.[e.] children when they growe to age proue chargeable.

Peter Courthope said it would be more beneficiall yf our woll and cloth were not to be transported but in colours; but my cosen[2] said we may as well make it into clokes and garmentes, as dye it in colours before we carry it ouer; for both variable, and as much change in colour as fashion.

JANUARY.

To furnishe a shipp requireth much trouble,
But to furnishe a woman the charges are double.

(*My cosens wife said.*)

The priviledge of enfranchising anie for London is graunted to every alderman at his first creation for one: to every sherif for 2: to every maior for 4. (*Cosen.*)

And almost any man for some 40l. may buy his freedome, and these are called free by redemption.

If a man prentice in London marry, he shall be forced to serve of his time, and yet loose his freedome. But yf a woman prentice marry, shee shall onely forfayte hir libertie, but shall not be forced to serve. (*Cosen.*)

---

[1] The cousin alluded to, and frequently vouched as an authority by the Diarist, was Richard Manningham, esq. of Bradbourne in East Malling, Kent. He survived his wife, who is mentioned in this page, and died 25th April 1611, æt. 72.

[2] Cousin Richard Manningham had been a successful merchant in London. Hence the importance evidently attached to his remarks on subjects connected with commerce and foreign countries.

To be warden of the Companie of Mercers is some 80*l*. charge; to be one of the livery, a charge but a credit. A bachelor is charged at the Maiors feast some 100 markes.

The Flushingers wanting money, since hir Majesties tyme, and while they were our friends, seised certayne merchant ships [and] forced them to give 40,000*l*. The merchants complayned but could not be releived. Oftymes the Princes dutys are defrayed with the subjectes goods. fo. 10. Jan. 1601.

Sir Moyle Finche of Kent married Sir Frauncis Hastinges daughter and heir,[1] worth to him 3,000*l*. per annum. All his livinge in Lincolnshire and Kent, &c. worth 4,000*l*. per annum. (*Dene Chapman.*)

8. Dyned at Mr. Gellibrands, a physician, at Maidstone.

11. Mr. Fr. Vane, a yong gent. of great hope and forwardnes, verry well affected in the country already, in soe much that the last parliament the country gave him the place of knight before S^r. H.(?) Nevell; his possibilitie of living by his wife verry much, shee beinge daughter and co-heire to S^r. Antony Mildmay; and thought hir mother will give hir all hir inheritance alsoe; the father worth 3,000*l*. per annum, the mother's 1,200*l*.[2] (*Mr. Tutsham.*)

The Duke of Albues [Alva's] negligence in not fortifying Flush-

---

[1] This marriage is not mentioned by Dugdale (Bar. ii. 445) nor in Collins (iii. 382, ed. Brydges). Both of them mention only one marriage of Sir Moyle, which was the source of all the importance of his family, namely, with Elizabeth sole daughter and heir of Sir Thomas Heneage. After Sir Moyle's death this lady was created Countess of Winchelsea.

[2] These expectations of the growing importance of Mr. Francis Vane were not altogether disappointed. At the coronation of James I. he was made K.B. and on 19th December 1624 was created Baron Burghersh and Earl of Westmoreland. He died in 1628. The Sir Anthony Mildmay here alluded to was of the Mildmays of Apethorp, co. Northampton.

inge before other places in the Netherlands was the cause he lost the country, for, when he thought to have come and fortified, the towne suddenly resisted his Spanish souldiers, and forced them to returne. (*Cosen.*)

18. I rode with my cosen's wife to Maidstone; dyned at Gellibrands.

As we were viewinge a scull in his studye, he shewed the seame in the middle over the heade, and said that was the place which the midwife useth shutt in women children before the wit can enter, and that is a reason that women be such fooles ever after.

My cosen shee said that the Gellibrands two wives[1] lived like a couple of whelpes togither, meaninge sporting, but I sayd like[2] a payre of turtles, or a couple of connies,[3] sweetely and lovingly.

* * * *

Mr. Alane, a minister, was very sicke. Gellibrand gave him a glyster, and lett him bloud the same day, for a feuer; his reason was, that not to have lett him bloud had bin verry dangerous; but to lett bloud is doubtfull, it may doe good as well as harme.

* * * *

My cosen shee told me, that when shee was first married to hir husband Marche, as shee rode behinde him, shee slipt downe, and he left hir behinde, never lookt back to take hir up; soe shee went soe long a foote that shee tooke it soe unkindly that shee thought neuer to have come againe to him, but to haue sought a service in some vnknowne place; but he tooke hir at last.

Wee were at Mrs. Cavils, when she practised some wit upon my cosen.[4] Cosen she called double anemonics double enimies.

---

[1] It appears in an omitted passage that, besides the physician Gellibrand, there was another of the same family, who is mentioned as Th. Gellibrand.

[2] Live, MS.   [3] *i. e.* rabbits.

[4] My cosen, shee, MS.

Mrs. Cavill desired some rootes, and she referd hir to hir man Thomas Smith.

My cose she speaking lavishly in commendacions of one Lovell ^{fo. 11.} of Cranebrooke (a good honest poore silly puritane,) " O," said ^{Jan. 1601.} shee, " he goes to the ground when he talkes in Divinitie with a preacher." "True," said I, "verry likely a man shall goe to the ground when he will either venture to take vpon him a matter that is to waightie for him, or meddle with such as are more then his matche." "I put him downe yfaith," said one, " when he had out talked a wiser then himselfe." "Just," said I, " as a drumme putes downe sweete still musicke, not as better, but mor soundinge."

22. AT LONDON.—*In a booke of Newes from Ostend.*
Touchinge the parly which Sir Fr. Vere held with the Archduke there, till he had reenforced himself, Sir Franc. said that the banes must be thrice askt, and yf at the last tyme anie lawefull cause can be showen, the marriage may be hindred. The Duke answered, he knewe that was true, yet, he said, it was but a whore that offered hir selfe.

Divers merchants arrested by Leake for shipping ouer cloth abouc the rate of their licence. (*Theroles* [?] *nar.*)

The Companie of Peweterers much greived at a licence graunted to one Atmore to cast tynne, and therefore called him perjured knaue; whereupon he complayned to the Counsell, and some of them were clapt vp for it. " I will be even with him for it yfaith," said one that thought he had bin disgraced by his credit; " Then you will pay him surely," quoth I.

> Nature doth check the first offence with loathing, ^{fo. 11^b.}
> But vse of synn doth make it seeme as nothing. ^{Jan. 1601.}

The spending of the afternoones on Sundayes either idly or about temporall affayres, is like clipping the Q. coyne; this treason to the Prince, that prophanacion, and robbing God of his owne.—(*Archdall.*)

*　　*　　*　　*

Hide to Tanfeild ;[1] "It is but a matter of forme you stand so much upon." "But it is such a forme," said Tanfeild, "as you may chaunce to breake your shins at, unless you be the nimbler."

· Certaine in the country this last Christmas chose a jury to finde the churle of their parishe, and, when they came to give their ver-dick, they named one whose frende, being present, began to be verry collerick with the boys for abusing him. "Hold you content, gaffer," said one of them, "if your boy had not bin one of the jury you had bin found to have bin the churle." The gaine of vntimely reprehension and the verry course of common Inquests, all led by some frend.

The L. Paget upon a tyme thinkinge to have goded Sir Tho. White (an alderman of London) in a great assembly, askt him, what he thought of that clothe, shewing him a garment in present.

fo. 12. "Truly, my Lord," said he, "it seemes to be a verry good cloth, but I remember when I was a yong beginner I sold your father a far better to make him a gowne, when he was Sergeant to the L. Maior ; truly he was a very honest sergeant!"[2] None so ready to carpe at other mens mean beginnings as such as were them-selves noe better. (*Reeves.*)

Jan. 26.

Tarlton[3] called Burley house gate in the Strand towardes the

---

[1] The "Hide" here mentioned was probably the future Sir Lawrence, elder brother of Sir Nicholas the future Lord Chief Justice, and uncle to Lord Chancellor Clarendon. (Foss's Judges, vi. 335.) Tanfield was the future Lord Chief Baron, whose only daughter was mother to Lucius Lord Falkland. (Ibid. 365.)

[2] Dugdale remarks that the first Paget who "arrived to the dignity of Peerage" was son to "—— Paget, one of the Serjeants at Mace in the City of London." (Bar. ii. 390.) Sir Thomas White was of course the founder of St. John's college, Oxford.

[3] Richard Tarlton, the celebrated low comedian and Joe Miller of his day.

Savoy, the Lord Treasurers Almes gate, because it was seldom or never opened. (*Ch. Dauers.*)

Repentaunce is like a drawebridge, which is layd downe for all to passe over in the day tyme, but drawne up at night: soe all our life wee have tyme to repent, but at death it is to late. (*Ch. Dauers recit.*)

It was ordered by our benchers, that wee should eate noe breade but of 2 dayes old. Mr. Curle said it was a binding lawe, for stale breade is a great binder; but the order held not 3 dayes, and soe it bound not.

EPITAPHE OF JOHN FOOTE.

Reader look to' it ! Here lyes John Foote,
He was a Minister, borne at Westminster.

ALIUD OF MR. CHILD.

If I be not beguild,
Here lies Mr. Child.
(*Ouerbury recit.*) [1]

I will be soe bolde as to give the Assise the lye:
(*Ch. Dauers in argument.*)

" I came rawe into the world, but I would not goe out rosted," said one that ment to be noe martyre. (*Curle nar.*)

* * * *

This last Christmas the Conny-catchers would call themselves Country-gentlemen at dyce.

fo. 12 b.
Jan. 1601.

When a gentlewoman told Mr. Lancastre he had not bin soe good as his word, because he promised shee should be gossip to his first child (glaunceing at his bastard on his landres), " Tut," said he, " you shall be mother to my next, if you will."

---

[1] We have retained these trifling entries solely on account of the name appended to them. The unfortunate Sir Thomas Overbury, who was son of a gentleman of Gloucestershire, having taken his B.A. degree at Queen's College, Oxford, removed in 1598 to the Middle Temple.

ANAGRAM.

Margaret Westfalinge.

My greatest welfaring.[1]

(*Streynsham nar.*)

Davis.

Advis.   Judas.

(*Martin.*)

FEBR. 1601.

Feb. 2. At our feast wee had a play called "Twelue Night, or What
you Will," much like the Commedy of Errores, or Menechmi in Plau-
tus, but most like and neere to that in Italian called *Inganni.*[2] A
good practise in it to make the Steward beleeve his Lady widdowe
was in love with him, by counterfeyting a letter as from his Lady
in generall termes, telling him what shee liked best in him, and pre-
scribing his gesture in smiling, his apparaile, &c., and then when he
came to practise making him beleeue they tooke him to be mad.

12.   *Quæ mala cum multis patimur læviora putantur.*

11.   Cosen Norton was arrested in London.

fo. 13.   He put up a supplicacion to Sir Robt. Cecile presented by his
Febr. 1601. wife, whome he tooke notice of the next day, which remembring
[was?] with out being remembred what he had done in it. The
effect of this petition was, that, whereas Copping had their goods

---

[1] Herbert Westfaling, Bishop of Hereford (1585—1602) had a daughter Margaret who
may have been the lady here alluded to, although at this time married to Dr. Richard
Eedes, Dean of Worcester. (Wood's Athenæ, i. 720, 750.) Like many of these trifles, it
will be observed that the anagrammatic reading is incomplete.

[2] It seems from remarks of Mr. Hunter, in his Illustrations of Shakspeare, i. 391, that
the Italian play here alluded to was not one of those termed the *Inganni*, of which there
are several, but the *Ingannati*, which, like the Taming of the Shrew, is a play preceded by
a dramatic prologue or induction, entitled *Comedia del Sacrificio di gli Intronati.* There
is no separate title-page to the *Ingannati*, but there are several editions of the *Sacrificio
di gli Intronati*, in which the *Ingannati* is introduced, printed at Venice in 1537, 1550,
and several subsequent years.

forth of Mr. Cranmers hand (whoe had dealt but to honestly for
such vnthankefull persons), and they should have a certaine summe
yearely, they could neither gett payment, nor haue him account;
he said twenty pounds were enough to keepe the Lunatike their
mother, when Cranmer had the goodes; nowe he deductes 50*l.* for
hir, and yett keepes hir far more basely. And therefor humbly
desyre Copping might be brought to some order. Norton tels me
this Copping is a notable riche practiser, &c.

Cosen Norton told me that one Mr. Cokayne of Hertfordshire gott
his brother H. Norton by a wile to his house, and their married him
upon a pushe to a kinswoman of his, and made a serveingman serve
the purpose insted of a preist.

Bounty is wronged, interpreted as duty.   Feb. 14.

My Cosen Garnons told me that the old Earle of Sussex, [1] being in
seruice in the North, was intangled by his Marshall, but extricated
by the Earle of Leycester, whose overthrowe afterward he covertly
practised. *Quædam beneficia odimus; vitam nulli debemus libenter.*

· The office of the Lord Keeper better worth then 3000*l.* per annum, of the Admirall more, of the Secretary little lesse. (*Idem.*)

My Cosen Garnons told me that the Court of Wardes will send   fo. 13ᵇ.
a prohibicion to anie other Court to cease from proceeding in anie Febr. 1601.
suite, whereof themselues may have colour to hold plea in that
Court. Soe prædominat a Court is that nowe become.

Went to my Cosen in Kent.   18.

I was at Malling with Mr. Richers.   19.

The Bishop of London [2] is Dr. Parrys crosse frend. (*Mr.
Richers.*)

---

[1] Thomas Ratcliffe, third Earl of Sussex (1556—1583.) The reader of Kenilworth will
need no further illustration than a reference to those attractive pages.

[2] Bishop, afterwards Archbishop, Bancroft.

In discourse of Mr. Sedley,[1] he told me, that his lady said he is gone over sea for debt, which Mr. Richers thinks was caused by his lavishe almes; for Mr. Sedley would not sticke himselfe to say, yf any gentleman spent not aboue 500*l.* a yeare, he gaue as muche to the poure; and as he was prodigall in giuinge, so was he indiscreet in bestowinge, appointinge vile fellowes to be the distributors of it: he is now at Padua, without anie man attendant. He went into Italy to learne discourse, he was nothing but talke before. I maruaile what he will be when he returnes, said he. Reade muche but not judicious. (*Idem.*) Mrs. Frauncis Richers said he was a gentle gentleman. F. is open in talke. Plotters for him.

Miller, a rich yeoman about Rotham,[2] when he came to entreate he might be abated in the assessment for subsidies, threwe in a note that he was worth but 550*l.* land fee simple : one of Mr. Sedley's almesmen.

fo. 14.

Febr. 1601.

pag. prox.

This day Mr. Cartwright had bin with my cosen to knowe whether he denied to hold anie land of him. My cosen acknowledged that he held divers parcells of him, but doth not certainely knowe howe it is all bounded. My cosen told me it was concealed land, and recovered by Mr. Cartwright's father against Mr. Catlin, of whom my cosen bought Bradborne.

Sir Robert Sydney hath bought Otford House, and sells it againe by parcells.

Mr. Cartwrightes father and Mr. Richeres mother were brother and sister, soe they first cosens.

Mr. Jo. Sedley[3] hath built a house in Aylesford which cost him aboue 4000*l.*; hath not belonging to it aboue 14 acres of ground.

---

[1] Probably Mr. William Sedley of the Friars in Aylesford, afterwards the first Baronet of this family. His lady, here alluded to, was Elizabeth, daughter and heir of Stephen Darell of Spelmonden, and widow of Henry Lord Abergavenny, ob. 1587. Hasted, ii. 170, ed. 1782.

[2] Wrotham ?   [3] Qu. John afterwards the second Baronet ?

Perhaps he purposed to haue bought the Lordship, which indeede was afterward offered vnto him, but he soe delayed the matter, that particuler men haue it nowe. It is thought the Lord Buckhurst would buy the house, &c. (*Cos.*)

Yf a man in the Lowe Countryes come to challenge a man out **Feb. 20.** of his house, and because he comes not forth throwes stones at his windowes, this [is] a crime capitall, because an assault in [on ?] his house, which is his castle. (*Cosen told me.*)

Out of a book intituled " Quodlibets "[1] written by a secular priest called Watson, against the Jesuites, fol. 151 & 152. His special arguments for a tolleracion in relligion. 1. That yf tolleracion were induced, then there should be no collor to publishe bookes howe tyrannical the persecution of Catholikes is. 2. Then England should not be called the nursery of faction. 3. Then the Spaniard should have noe Prince to band on his side.[2] 6. The subjects would not be so fitt to be allured to rebellion. 7. The safety of hir Majesties person is mutche procured. All slight.

One Kent, my cosen's brother by his mothers side, living in Lincolneshire, bought a jewell, part of a price [prize?] that was brought in to that country. The Earle of Lyncolne[3] hearing of it, sent for Kent, and desyred him to bestowe it on him, but when Kent would not part from it for thankes, the Earle gaue him a bill of his hand

---

[1] " A Decacordon of Ten Quodlibeticall Questions concerning Religion and State : wherein the author, framing himself a Quilibet to every Quodlibet, decides an hundred crosse Interrogatorie doubts, about the generall contentions betwixt the Seminarie priests and Jesuites at this present." 4to. n. p. 1602.

[2] There are in Watson's book other arguments numbered 4 and 5, but probably the Diarist did not think them worthy of note. Watson's remarks are not so much arguments in favour of toleration abstractedly considered, as reasons why it would not answer the purpose of Father Parsons and the Jesuits to support its introduction into England.

[3] Henry Clinton, the second Earl of Lincoln of that family, succeeded to the title in 1585, as heir to his father the Lord High Admiral, and held it till his death in 1616.

for the payment of 80*l.* at a certaine day. At the day, came and demaunded it, the Earl would see his bill, and when he had it he put it in his pocket, and fell in talke with some gent. then present; but when Kent continued still in the roome, expectinge either his bill or his monie, the Earl gave him hard wordes and sent him away without either. (*Durum.*)

Feb. 19.

*

Mr. Cartwright demaundes some three acres of land of my cosen, which he saith one John Sutor of Bradborne gave vnto the Abby of Towne Mallinge, by the name of Sutors Croft, lying betwixt his house and the churche. My cosen denies it.

My Cosen shee told him that Joane Bachellor vpon Thursday last had sent hir some fishe, which she sent back againe. Whereupon he said shee was of an ill nature that could not forgive. And this shee tooke in such snuffe that she could not afford him a good look all that day, but blubberd, &c.

fo. 15.
Febr. 1601.

This day there came certaine bags of pepper to New Hide to be conveyed to one Mr. Clarke of Ford, but they were seised by the Searcher of Rochester as goods not customed, &c.

S*r.* Jaruis Clifton [1] beinge at a bare baytinge in Nottinghamshire: when the beare brake loose and followed his sonne vp a stayres towards a gallery where himself was, he opposed himselfe with his rapier against the fury of the beast, to saue his sonne. This same his beloued sonne not long after dyed, and his death was opened vnto him very discreetely by a gent. that fayned sorrowe as the case had bin his owne, till S*r.* Jaruis gave him wordes of comfort, which after he applyed to S*r.* Jaruis himselfe. (*My cosen.*)

One Burneham of London, whoe was the Watergate officer at Flushinge, being troubled with the stone, soe much that it was a

---

[1] Sir Gervase Clifton, a man of great wealth and power in Nottinghamshire, was created a peer in 1608. In 1618 he died by an act of the same hand which had so gallantly defended his son from the bear. His title of Lord Clifton is now united to that of Earl of Darnley.

hindraunce vnto him in the execution of his office, ventured a dangerous cure, and was cutt for it, but dyed of it. This cure by cutting is a newe invention, a kinde of practise not knowne to former ages. There is a scame *   *   *   which the surgeons searche with a crooked instrument concaued at the one ende called a catheter, wherinto they make incision, and then grope for the stone with an other toole which they call a duckes bill: yf the stone be greater then may be drawne forth at the hole made by the seame, the partie dyes for it. (*My cosen.*)

fo. 16.

Febr. 1601.

A certaine goldsmith in Cheape was indebted to my cosen above 100*l*. and after executed for clipping gold. Sir Richard Martin [1] seised the goodes for the Queen. After hir Majestie gave commaund by word of mouth, that all the debtes should be paid, but, because there was noe warrant under hir Majesties hand, Sr.Richard refused to pay, yet he deliuered certaine of the goodes to my cosen, to be sold by him, which he made 30*l*. of and retained it. All the satisfaccion he could haue.

Vita cœlibis bis cœlestis, considering the crosses of marriage, and the aduise of the Apostle.

AT ROCHESTER, AT THE ASSISES.

Feb. 24.

Mr. Thomas Scott of Scottes Hall,[2] in Kent, is Sherife of Kent.

One Tristram Lyde, a surgeon, admitted to practise by the archbishops letters, was arraigned for killing divers women by annoyntinge them with quicksylver, &c. Euidence giuen that he would haue caused the women to haue stript themselues naked in his presence, and himselfe would haue annoynted them; that he tooke upon him the cure, and departed because they would not give him more then their first agreement. He pleaded theire diseases were such as required that kinde of medicine, that it was there owne negligence by

---

[1] Warden of the Mint.
[2] In the parish of Smeeth. The Scotts of Scotts Hall were originally seated at Braf-bourne.

takinge cold, by going abroade sooner then he prescribed, soe he was acquited.

Sergeant Daniel[1] sitting there as judge sayd he knewe that there might be a purgacion by a fume, and that to cure by cutting a gutt was a dangerous venture, and a rare skill, for he could neuer heare of anie had that cunning but onely one man, and that was learned in Turkie.

If a man kill an other (as they say) in hott bloud, excepte there appear some cause to heate his bloud, the jury must finde it murder. (*Per Sergeant Danyell.*)

There was one gave another rude words, whereupon a third standing by said to him to whome they were spoken, "Will you endure such an injury? Fayth, putt vp them and put vp any thing." Hereupon the party present fetcht his weapon, mett with the other that gaue him those wordes, and [in] the presence of the setter on fought with him, and slewe him, the other standinge by and doinge noe more. Yet they were both condemned at this assises, and after executed.

There was one had his booke given him at the prisoners barr, where the ordinary useth to heare and certifie there readinge. And one Mr. Gylburne start up sayinge, "He will reade as well as my horse;" which wordes Sergeant Daniel, havinge before allowed the cleargy, tooke verry ill, telling him playnely that he was too hasty: and yet caused the prisoner to be brought nearer that Gylburne might hear him reade, and he reade perfectly.

In the Cathedrall Churche at Rochester.

Monuments. Of Jo. Somer of Newland, clerke of the Privy Signet, and Martin (*sic*) his wife, daughter to Ed. Ridge, late widdowe of Th. Colepepper. They had 6 sonnes, but all deade, and 2 daughters: whereof the one called Frances was married to James Cromer, by whom one daughter called Frances. *Versus.*

Sunt nisi præmissi quos periisse putas.

---

[1] Judge in the Court of Common Pleas, 1604—1610.

In Naui Ecclesiæ.

Thomas Willowbee, Decanus 3', *obiit anno* 25 *Reg. Elizab.*, 76 *ætatis suæ, et* 10° *decanatûs.*

Gualterus Phillips, nouissimus prior et primus decanus, obijt 23° *Nouemb.* 1570, *ætatis* 70, *decanatûs* 30°.

At Glastenbury there are certaine bushes which beare May flowers at Christmas and in January, and there is a walnut tree which hath no leaues before Barnabies day in June, and then it begins to bud, and after becomes as forward as any other.

May 2, 1602.
fol. 17ᵇ.

(*Mr. Towse narravit.*)

I heard that the old Earle of Hartford [1] maried Alderman Parnels [Pranell's] sonnes widdow; shee was the daughter of Viscount Bindon.

ATT THE TEMPLE CHURCHE.

May 9, 1602.
fo. 18.

Dr. Montague,[2] his text Joh. iii. 14: " As Moses lift up the Serpent in the Wildernes so must the Sonne of Man be lift up."

Speaches are either historicall of a thing past, propheticall of a thing to come, legall of a thing to be done, or figurative when one thing is said and an other ment. Figures there are in scripture, two almost peculiar, typicall and sacramentall, the one shewing one thing by an other, the other declaring what is conferred by another.

Moses had speciall commaundment to erect this Serpent, and yet God did not dispense with the 2nd Commaundment, for this Serpent was not made to be worshipped, but to be looked upon.

---

[1] Edward, son of the Protector Somerset, Earl of Hertford from 1559 to 1619, the same who married Lady Catherine Grey. The lady here alluded to, Frances daughter of Thomas first Viscount Howard of Bindon, became ultimately the celebrated Duchess of Richmond and Lennox of the reigns of James I. and Charles I.

[2] Dr. James Montague, first master of Sidney Sussex College, editor of King James's Works, and subsequently Bishop successively of Bath and Wells and of Winchester.

God cannot dispense with anie commandment of the first table but he should cease to be God, as the first, Thou shalt have none other [1] Gods but me; admit a pluralitie, and himselfe should be none, &c. but with the 2nd table he often dispenseth, for those concerne man immediately.

The text is hystoricall, Numb. xxi. 9, and typicall. Christ resembled by the brasen Serpent, Syn by the stinging.

May 9, 1602.
fo. 18^b Moses while he was in the Wildernes had onely the place of a mediator not a iudge, and therefore we read that whensoeuer the people murmured, God punished them. But when Moses left his station, and would at any tyme become a iudge ouer them, God neuer punished the people that murmured, but Moses that forgot his place. Christ, vntill the latter day, hath the place of an aduocate, but then he shalbe a iudge of the quicke and dead.

Wee reade of three exaltacions of our Saviour, one upon the crosse to purchase our pardon; 2, from the graue for the publicacion thereof; 3, to heauen for the application of his resurrection ; and all these were necessarilie to be performed by him, for the consummacion of our salvacion.

The Serpent was not lifted up in the Wildernes before the people were stung by the serpents, and Christ is not to be propounded on the Crosse as a comfort untill the sting of Synn be felt throughly.

The Scripture telleth us that of all beasts the Serpent is the most subtill, and his subtilty is obserued in three points: first, when those nations in Syria and other hott countries found themsclues often endangered by the stinging of venomous beasts, amongst other remedies they invented charming, which the serpent perceuinge, to auoyd their cunning and effect his malice, he would stop both his eares, the one by laying it close to the earth, the other by stopping it with his tayle. Soe fareth the synner ; lett the preacher speake never soe heauenly, yet will he close one eare with worldly thoughts, and the other with fleshly imaginacions.

May 9, 1602.
fo. 19. The second property of his subtilty is in defending his heade, where his lyfe lyes, it will soe winde it selfe about that part, that [it] is a matter of greate difficulty to cutt of a serpentes heade. In every man there is some radicall and capitall synn, which is predominant, and this the devil endeavours by all slightes to preserve. The third point of the serpents subtilty is ac-

---

¹ others, in MS.

counted the attractiue power which remayneth in the heade deuided from the body, for it is proved by experience that, yf a serpent be cutt in many peeces, yf his heade remaine aliue, yet that part will gather the rest togither againe; soe leave the head synn alive, and it will gather a whole body againe.

As Christ is the heade of the Churche he never suffered nor dyed.

The brasen Serpent was made like the live and true serpents in all thinges, the sting onely excepted; Christ was made like man in all things sauing synn.

All which beheld the brasen Serpent were cured; all that beleeve in Christ are saved.

Remedies are either naturall, by virtue of some inherent qualitie in the medicine applied; or by diuine influence and institution, when some thing is effected either beyond or contrary to the force and nature of that which is used. And this is miraculous; soe was the curing of the blind by laying spittle and clay upon the eyes of the blinde. Soe the cure of the lame by washing in the poole of Bethesdas, and soe the healing of the Israelites by beholdinge the brasen Serpent.

Fayth properly in things beyond or contrary to reason.

As by the institucion of marriage the heate of the flesh is abated, soe by our mysticall connection with Christ the heate of syn is allayed.

May 9, 1602.
fo. 19^b.

MAY 13. AT THE TEMPLE CHURCHE.

One Moore of Baliol Colledge in Oxford; his text Amos iii. 6 : "Shall there be evil in the city and the Lord hath not done it?" *Malum culpe et malum pœne;* of the latter onely God is the author. God may be said to be the author of synn permissive, and an actor in synn, though not the author of the synne, for ther is noe action but he is the first cause of it: and yet he is noe partner or cause of the il in the action, noe more then he which rideth vpon a lame iade, can be said to be the cause of his limpinge, though he be the cause of his paceinge, nor a cunning musician the cause of discordes when he playeth on a lute that is out of tune. There is a two-fold power in every thing, and both derived from God; the one of creacion, whereby every thing worketh according to nature, as the fyre to burne, &c.; and the other of preservacion, whereby that force is continued, and if the

May 13, 1602.
fo. 20.

second be withdrawne the first perisheth, for God is not a mere efficient
externall, as the taylour of the garmente, or a carpenter of the house,
whose effects may continue though their labour continue not, but he
is an inherent continuall assistant cause, soe that yf he withdrawe his
power of preseruing the power of creacion is idle, soe the fire in furnace
could not burne the children, &c.

DE ASCENSIONE DOMINI.

Non omnis questio est doctrinæ inquisitio,
Sed quædam etiam est ignorantiæ professio.

.Cicatrices Dominus seruauit post resurrectionem et in judicio
seruaturus est, vt fidem resurrectionis astruat: 2. Vt pro omnibus
supplicando ea patri representet: 3. Vt boni quam misericorditer
sint redempti videant. 4. Vt reprobi quam iuste sint damnati re-
cognoscant. 5. Vt perpetuæ victoriæ seu [suæ ?] triumphum deferat.

(Beda.)

May 16, 1602.
fo. 20b.
May 16, 1602.   AT PAULES CROSSE.

One Sanders made a Sermon, his text 1 Timoth. vi. 17: " Charge
them that are riche in this world that they be not high mynded; and
that they trust not in vncertayne riches; but in the liuing God, which
giueth us abundantly all things to enioye."

Charge them that they lift up their soules to God in heavenly meditacion, not against God by worldly presumption.

Charge the riche, therefore there were diversitie of condicion and estates
of men in the primitiue Churche, not all thinges common in possession, as
the Anabaptists would haue it.

When there came one to Pope Benedict to entreat him to make more
Cardinals, he demaunded first yf he could denise how he might make
more worldes: for this was to litle for the Cardinals which were already.
Such ambitious couetousnes the Pope noted in those holie ones.

Good meate is often tymes corrupted by a bad stommache, and good doctrine of small effect with bad hearers. Yett the minister must not be discouraged : but proceed in his calling, that yf synn cannot be avoyded yet it may become ynexcusable.

Ephesus, whereof Tymothie was Bishop, was the confluence of honour and wealth, like our London.

The surgeon is not to be blamed that findes and shewes the corrupt and rotten parts of the body, but the body which is soe corrupt as to breed them ; soe the preacher not to be disliked for reprehending our synnes, but our selves for committing things worthy reprehension.

Good things though common are not to be contemned for their commonness, noe more then the sunne, the light, the ayre, &c.

May, 1602.
fo. 21.

The vsuror sometymes looseth both his principall and interest, the husbandman his labour and his seede, the merchant aduentures lyfe and goods ; but the profession of the preacher is subiect to greater then all these, for he may loose both his owne and the peoples soules.

It is one of the most heauie judgments that God useth to threaten to anie nation with whom he is displeased, that he will remoue their candlesticke and send a famine of the word amongst them.

God made some riche, and some poore, that twoe excellent virtues might flourishe in the world, charitie in the riche, and patience in the poore. Pride is the sting of riches. *Tolle superbiam, et diuitiæ non nocebunt.*

A man may speake of his owne riches, soe it be without arrogancy, for it is a good thinge to speake of the loving kindenes of the Lord.

Magistrates and rich men must not be like the filling stones in a building, but arche and corner stones, which support others.

When persons of meane worth thrust themselves into places beyond their condicion and hability, it is all one as yf the rough mortar and pebles should appeare in the roomes of the squared stones in a fayre building.

Themistocles said there was no musicke so sweete vnto him as to heare his owne prayses.

In the primitiue-Churche the riche men were soe proud that they refused to receive the Sacrament with the poore.

The examples of the incertaintie of riches by often and suddain casualtyes should be like Lott's wife to the beholders, to remember and avoid the like. The multitude followe the riche men, as a swarme of bees followe a man that carries the hiue of honie combes, rather for the love of the honie then his person, more for the love of his money then his manhood.

AT WESTMINSTER.

Dr. Androes, Deane of that Churche,[1] made a Sermon, his text John xvi. 7 : "Yet I tell you the truth, It is expedient for you that I goe away, for if I goe ńot away the Comforter will not come vnto you, but if I depart I will send him vnto you."

These wordes have reference to the feast which is celebrated this day : whereupon St. Augustine said, *In verbo fuit promissio missionis, et in festo missio promissionis* : for soe it is in the second of the Acts. " When the day of Pentecost was come they were all filled with the Holy Ghost."

These words were spoken to the disciples when their hearts were full of sorrowe that Christ must part from them, and therefore had need of comfort, for they had cause of sorrowe, for yf a man would not willingly be forsaken of any, as Paule complayneth 2 Tim. iv. 10, that Demas had forsaken him, would it not greiue the disciples to [be] forsaken by such a frend as Christ had bin vnto them, whoe in one place speaking vnto them asketh this question, Which of you hath wanted any thing since you followed me ? And in an other place he compareth them while he continues with them to the children of the bridechamber.

Besides the tyme of his departure might aggravate their sorrowes, for it was then when he foretold soe many persecutions should come upon
them. And therefore here he ministers words of comfort, telling them that is expedient, and expedient for them, that he should leaue them, for thereby they should receive a benefit, and that of soe high a nature as they were better to want him then it. And further for their comfort he added, that, though he would forsake them, yet he would not leaue

---

[1] Dr. Lancelot Andrewes was Dean from 1601 to 1605, when appointed Bishop of Chichester. He was afterwards translated, first to Ely, and afterwards to Winchester. This sermon was preached on Whitsunday.

them like orphanes destitute of all frends, but would send them a Comforter.

And here he made his prayer, which being ended with the Lordes
prayer, he proceeded with his text: and first noted that Christ rendred a
reason of his departure, though it be not requisite alwayes that gouernors
should render a reason to their subiects of all their commaundments, for in
the 1 Sam. the Kinge gives noe other reason but it was his pleasure.
2. It is a mylde reason, not harshe like that in Marke ix. cap. 19 v. "O,
ye faythles generacion, howe long shall I bee with you, how long nowe
shall I suffer you?" but here he deliueres it meekely, and moues them
with expediency, and that not for himselfe, *non nobis, sed vobis expedit.*
And therefore because it is expedient it ought not to greive them, in soe
much as the profit they shall gayne will countervayle the pleasure which
they must forgoe by his departure.

And yet it might seeme strange that they should gayne by loosing him;
it is reade, *Dissolve cælum et veni ad nos, Domine,* and againe, *Veni ad nos,
et mane nobiscum.* But to goe from them what desyre could they haue?
Here may arise three difficulties. 1. The disciples might have rejoyned,
and sayde, What neede, what care wee for any other Comforter? soe long
as you are with us, wee desyre noe other. 2. Why might not the Holy
Ghost have come, and yet Christ tarried with them; could they not be
togither? 3. Howe can it be expedient for anie to loose Christ? what
comfort can there be in those wordes which tell them Christ will forsake them?

23 May, 1602.
fo. 22ᵇ.

1. Our happiness is to be reunited to God, from whom we were fallen
by our first fathers synn; for as it is the perfection of a branche that is
broken of to be ingrafted againe that it may growe with the body, soe is
it the felicitie of man to be vnited to his Creator. And in this vnion, as
well as God must be partaker of man, soe must man be made partaker of
God, otherwise there can arise noe vnion: the former was effected by
Christ's incarnacion, and the second is perfected by the inspiration of the
Holy Ghost, whoe is as it were the connexion and loue knot of the deitie.
Christ hath as it were made his testament, and the Holie Ghost is the
executor, 1 Cor. xii. Christ is the word: and the Holy Ghost is the
seale of it, 2 Corin. i. 22. "Christ hath purchased redemption for us:"
and the Holy Ghost must give us seisin, Eph. i. 14. And in conclusion Paule sayth, viii. Rom. 9, "He that hath not the Spirit of Christ is

not his :" and therefore was it expedient and necessary that the Holy
Ghost should come ; for, as Christ was *complementum legis*, soe is the
Holy Ghost *complementum Evangelii.*

23 May, 1602.
fo. 23.

2. They may stand togither, they may beare one an others presence,
for the manhood of Christ was conceiued by the Holy Ghost, and the
Euangelist sayth, *Vidi Spiritum descendentem et manentem super eum.*
But yet it was expedient they should not be togither vpon the earth ;
expedient, as Augustine noteth, *non necessitatis pondere, sed divini
consilii ordine,* and two reasons are given for [it] in the part of the Holy
Ghost. 1. Yf. the Holy Ghost should have come downe while Christ
was upon the earth, whatsoever the Holy Ghost should have done in
his person would have bin ascribed to Christ. 2. He would have appeared
to have bin sent from the Father alone. And soe it would not have
bin so apparant that he proceeded from the Father and the Sonne bothe.

3. Expedient it was that Christ should depart from them, howe good
soeuer his presence was vnto them. Wee knowe that bread is the strength
of mans hart, yet sometymes it may be expedient to fast : our bloud is
the treasury of our lyfe, yet sometymes it is expedient to loose it ; our
eyesight is deare and precious vnto us, yet sometymes it is expedient to sitt
in a darke roome. And here it is expedient that Christ should withdrawe
his presence, not corporal onely, but his invisible presence of grace alsoe.
1. It is expedient that children which growe fond of their parentes should
be weaned. The Apostles were to full of carnall and terrene cogitacions
even after his resurrection ; they asked him, Wilt thou restore the Kingdome to Israell ? therefore nowe it was highe tyme they should put of
childishnes and be taught, as Paule sayth that henceforth they knowe him
no more in the fleshe ; and this must be effect[ed] by withdrawing his cor-
porall presence, which they began to dote upon ; and for the taking away
the presence of his grace, that was expedient alsoe. 1. Least being to full
they should begin to loath it, as the Children of Israel did manna in the
wildernes. And upon this reason did the prophet threaten a famine of
the word when the people, being full, contemned it. 2. That they should not
growe proud with abundaunce; the Psalmist sayth, "Yf I say I cannot be
removed," and "It is good that I was in trouble, for before I went wronge."
Peter was soe sure and confident upon himselfe, that yf. all the world
should haue forsaken Christ, he would not, and therefore because he

23 May, 1602.
fo. 23ᵇ.

stoode soe much vpon himselfe it was expedient that suche a swollen
bladder should be prickt, as he was till he denied and forswore his master;
And even this withdrawing of grace was a kind of grace, that seing his
owne weaknes he might possesse his soule in humility, with[out] which
there is noe grace to be expected.   And therefore, *expedit superbo vt
in peccatum incidat.*   And to this purpose are these wordes of Paule
that the messengers of Sathan, *i. e.* temptacions, were sent to punish
him, least he should growe proud.

Christ is our advocate in defending vs when the Divel accuseth vs
falsely; he is our intercessor and mediator by pleading a pardon for vs
when Sathen layes his greatest and truest accusacions against us; he is
our high priest to offer sacrifice for vs.

Christ left them not as orphanes, but sent another vnto them whoe was
equall with himselfe, otherwise they should have loss by the change.

The Holy Ghost hath diuers offices and soe diuers effects : he enlightens   23 May, 1602.
the understandinge, and soe is called the Spirit of truth : he certifies the   fo. 24.
will, and soe is named the Spirit of Holines : he delivers from the
bondage of Sathan, and soe is the Spirit of comfort, which is the cheife
and very consummacion of all.   The Holy Ghost is not given to all in
the same measure, nor the same manner.   When Christ breathed vpon
his disciples they received the Holy Ghost; and, when the Holy Ghost
came like fyrey tongues, they were filled with him : breath was warme,
but fyre is hotter : there was heate in both, but not equally. Elias prayed
that the Spirit of [Elijah] might be doubled upon him.

The gifts of the Holy Ghost are obteyned and perfected divers wayes ;
vnderstanding and fayth by the word which is the truthe ; holynes of lyfe,
by prayer, meditacion, and good workes; consolacion by receiving the
sacraments.

A lewde fellowe coming before Sir W. Rawley to be examined con-   7 Junij, 1602.
cerninge some wrecke which he had gotten into his handes, and being   fo. 24b.
demaunded whether he would sweare to such articles as they would
propound, answerd that he would sweare to anie thinge they would
aske him, and then being admonished he should not be soe rashe in
soe serious a matter as concerned his soule soe nearely, " Fayth,"

said he, " I had rather trust God with my soule, then you with my goods." (*Ch. Da.*)

*   *   *   *   *

AT PAULE'S CROSSE.

Mr. Barker; his text Luke ix. and the last verse, " Noe man that putteth his hand to the plough and looketh back is apt to the Kingdome of God.   -

The fyre from Heaven which consumed the sacrifices in the old lawe was preserved by continuall addicion of fuell, soe the heauenly virtue of Chrystian charitie being kindled in the hart of man, must be preserved by continuall meditacions on the word of God. Yf any should aske why it was commaunded in Leviticus that the people should offer *primitias* and in Exodus that they should alsoe give *decimas*, I should make no other answer, but that wee should not onely remember our Creator in the days of our youth, but alsoe serue him in holines and rightcousnes all the dayes of our lyfe.

Aliud est incepisse, aliud perfecisse.

Some in their liues, like the image in Nebuchadnethers dreame, Dan. ii., goodly beginninges, but earthie endings.

The Diuel laboureth most against our perseveraunce because that virtue onely hath a promise of coronacion.

There be but seven steps in the ladder that leades downe to hell, and the lowest, saving desperacion, is a custom of synning.

These combined discommodities ensue the custome of synning; *fit*

diabolus ad oppugnandum audacior, anima ad peccandum promptior, Deus ad condonandum difficilior. This virtue of Christian magnanimity or perseveraunce consisteth in *patiendo et faciendo* : in *patiendo*, 2°, in *ferendo et perferendo ; faciendo*, by continuance in preaching fayth, and in good lyfe.

Christ compared Christian profession to a plough. And why, 1. to soe base a thing, 2. to soe laborious a thing, 3. to that onely? 1. That none howe base soever by condicion or profession should despayre of attayning Heaven ; and meane thinges may be compared with the greatest. Christ sayth the Kingdom of Heaven is like a litle leaven, and to a smaller thing then that, it is like a grayne of mustard seede; and here to a plough, that none might despayre. Simon a tanner, Peter a fisher, Paul a tent-maker, Joseph a carpenter.

Some great ones, Theophilus. Some ladyes, in the Acts. Some customers, and some from the beggars, as Lazarus. And yet, that rich men might not contemne it for the baseness, he compares it to a riche jewell, a precious stone, &c.

2. The place of the preacher is a calling of great paynes and trauaile. He selected and spake of the Archbishop of Canterbury as the sunne amongst the ministers, and the old Deane of Paules [1] compared to the moone. And Dr. Overall, the newe deane, to the newe moone, gravity and learning and life; the ministers to starrs.

Junij 9, 1602.
fo. 26.

MARTI. lib. 10, Epig. 47. [2]

I take noe care to gett, my wealth was left me,
I reape the harvest of what'ere I sowe,
I stur not muche abroade, home best befits me,
I ne're received wronge, nor none I owe.
I travaile not in publique busines,
Nor ought's within my charge but myne owne soule,
My body's healthfull, fitt for exercise,
Myselfe enioys myselfe without controule.
I have a harmeles thought, an æqual friend,
My clothes are easy, and my face wants art,
I greive not when I rest, nor doe I spend
More tyme in sleepe then nature can impart.
I cast the worlde behinde, Heauen is my guide,
I would be what I am, and nought beside;
But above all, [and] which is all and summe,
I neither wishe nor feare the day to come.

TH. SM.

[1] Dr. Alexander Nowell, died 13th Feb. 1601-2; Dr. John Overall was elected 29th May 1602. (Hardy's Le Neve, ii. 315.)

[2] This epigram was a great favourite with our forefathers, and consequently there are many tranlations of it. Mr. Collier, in his Bibliographical Account of Early English Literature (i. 223), gives two examples, one by D. T. an author whose name is not yet discovered, and the other by Ben Jonson, printed from his own MS. at Dulwich. We have not been able to identify TH. SM. with any certainty.

June, 1602.
fo. 26ᵇ.

Arbella Stuarta: tu rara es et bella.
Henricus Burbonius: rex bonus orbi.

12. Common preachers worse then common swearers, for these doe abuse but Gods name, but they abuse Gods worde. (*Curle.*)

15. Upon a tyme when the late Lord Treasurer, Sir William Cecile, came before Justice Dyer [1] in the Common Place with his rapier by his side, the Justice told him that he must lay aside his long penknife yf he would come into that Court; this speache was free, and the sharper, because Sir William was then Secretary. (*Bradman.*)

There is nowe a table placed for the barresters crosse over the hall by the cuppord, which one called St. Albanes, because he said it was in the waye to Duns-table.

* * * * *

16. "Roome! Roome!" said one, "Here comes a woman with a cupbord on hir head;" of one that had sold hir cupboard to buy a taffaty hat. (*Franklin.*)

16 June, 1602.
fo. 27.

Kentish tayles are nowe turned to such spectacles, soe that yf a man put them on his nose he shall haue all the land he can see. ' (*Idem.*)

22. Sergeant Heale, since he became the Queens Sergeant, came to the Lord Keeper,[2] desyring that he would heareafter give him more gratious hearinge; otherwise, his clients already beginning to fall from him, he would nowe betake himself to his ease in the country, and leave this troublesome kinde of lyfe. The Lord Keeper made him noe other answere but said, yf that were his reso-

---

[1] Sir James Dyer, Chief Justice of the Common Pleas from 1559 to 1582. He was of the Middle Temple, the Inn of Court to which our Diarist belonged. (Foss's Judges, v. 480.)

[2] Egerton, Lord Keeper from 1594 to 1603. Sergeant Hele was one of the legal butts of the time. (See Foss's Judges, vi. 141; Egerton Papers, pp. 315, 391 399.)

lucion he doubted [1] not but the blessing of Issakar would light upon him. (*Mr. Bennet narr.*) *Vide* Gen. xlix. 14: "Issachar shall be a stronge asse couching downe betweene two burdens; and he shall see that rest is good; and that the land is pleasaunt, and he shall bowe his shoulders to beare, and he shalbe subiect unto tribute."

AT PAULES, ONE OF BALIOL COLLEDGE IN OXFORD.

June 20, 1602.
fo. 27ᵇ.

His text iii. Jonah, 4 et 5. "Yet forty dayes and Niniuy shall be destroyed. 5. So the people of Nineuch beleeued God," &c. He diuided his text into Jonahs sermon to the people of Nineueh, and the peoples repentaunce at the sermon; the former consists of mercy, "yett fourty dayes," and justice, "and Nineuch shall be destroyed;" Gods patience and his iudgment. He might have sayd, as the prophet David sayd, "My song shall be of mercy and iudgment."

Four things in the effect of the Sermon; fayth in beleuing God, and that was not fruitles. 2. fasting, and that was not frivolous. 3. their attyre, that was not costly, but sack cloth. 4. their number, that was not small, from the greatest to the lowest. As Noah's doue came from the floud with an oliue braunch in the mouth, soe this heauenly dove (for soe Jonah signifieth) came from the waters of the sea with a sermon of mercy in his cry, "Yett fourty dayes."

God is pitifull; it was Christ's commaundement to his Apostles that they should say "Peace be vnto you" when they entred into anie house.

Noted by Jonahs crying in the middest of such a city, that the preachers must not be timerous to tell anie of their faults, nor feare the person of anie man. Yet he reprehended those which are to sharpe reprehenders without circumstaunce. Such as Bernard calleth *non correptores, sed corrosores,* such may be termed *bilis et salsugo,* like the people of India which are said to barke instead of speakinge ; *canis et tuba vitiorum.* But, as he misliked those sharpe biters, soe must he needes speake against such preachers as flatter greate men, and sowe cushions under their elbowes. They are like Heliotropium, which turnes the flower with the sunne, though a cloud be interposed, soe they follow greatnes though

20 June, 1602.
fo. 28.

[1] doubt it, MS.

clouded with synn; like the riuer Jordan, turnes and windes euery way; speake nothing but silken wordes; at last the[y] become *serui multitudinis*, say anie thing to please the people.

Nineveh, as St. Augustine in his booke *De Civitate Dei*, signifieth not the citie but the synns of the people; and soe the prophecy verryfied, for that synn was destroyed by their repentaunce within 40 dayes. But he rather inclined to expound it by way of an implyed condicion, that they should be overthrowen vnles they repented; soe was that prophecy of Isah vnderstoode to Hezekiah, Isaiah xxxviii. " Thou shalt dy and not live."

God is slowe in punishing, yet *tarditas pœnæ gravitate pensatur.*

Gratious and righteous is the Lord in sparing and punishing.

The synne of Ninevch was Idolatry.

20 Juno, 1601.[1]
fo. 28b.

DR. BUCKRIDGE,[2] AT THE TEMPLE CHURCHE.

Compared the lawe of nature to the night, reason to the starres, the written lawe to the morning or dawning of the day, and the lawe of grace to the sunnshine of the day; the first to the blade, the second to the care, the third to the seede of corne.

Synn must be like an hedge of thornes sett about, not within, our garden to keepe us in goodnes. In tymes past men were afeard[3] to committ synn, but ready to make confession; nowe the world is changed, for nowe every one dares comitt anie synne, but is ashamed to make confession.

25 June, 1602.
fo. 29.

Mr. Foster of Lyncolnes Inn told these jeastes of Sir Thomas Moore as we went to Westminster. One which had bin a familiar acquaintaunce of Sir Th. Moores in his meaner fortunes, came to visit him when he was in the height of his prosperitie. Sir Th. amongst other parts of entertaynement shewed him a gallery which he had furnished with good variety of excellent pictures, and desyred

---

[1] There is a chronological confusion, either of the writer or the bookbinder, in this and subsequent entries. Having in vain endeavoured to unravel it, we have thought it better to follow the manuscript as it stands.

[2] Subsequently President of St. John's, Oxford, and occupant in succession of several episcopal sees. He died Bishop of Ely in 1631.

[3] " ashamed " is interlined in the MS. above " afeard."

his frendes iudgment which he liked best; but he making difficulty to prefer anie Sir Tho. shewed him the picture of a deathes head with the word *Memento morieris,* which he commended as most excellent for the deuise and conceit. The gent. being desyrous to knowe what he conceiued extraordinary in soe common a sentence, he told him, " Sir, you remember sometymes you borrowed some monie of me, but I cannot remember that you have remembred to repaye it: it is not much, and though I be chauncellor I have vse for as little, and nowe me thinkes this picture speakes vnto you *Memento Mori æris,* remember to pay Moore his money."

After he was deprived of his place and dignity, whereas his gentlemen were wont after he was gone forth of church to signifie to their lady that his lordship was gone before, himselfe upon a Sunday came from his seate when prayer was ended, opened his ladyes pue dore, saying, " Madame, his lordship is gone before " (alluding to the losse of his place); and then, " Come wife, nowe wee may goe togither and talke."

*　　*　　*　　*　　*

Mr. Watts and Mr. Danvers had fiery wordes.

13 March, 1601.
fo. 29ᵇ.

Commonly those which speake most against Tullie are like a dog which comming into a roome where he espies a shoulder of mutton lying upon some high'place, falls to barking at it, because he cannot reache it. (*Watts.*)

Vpon a tyme when Burbidge played Richard III. there was a citizen grone soe farr in liking with him, that before shee went from the play shee appointed him to come that night vnto hir by the name of Richard the Third. Shakespeare ouerhearing their conclusion went before, was intertained and at his game ere Burbidge came. Then message being brought that Richard the Third was at the dore, Shakespeare caused returne to be made that William the Conqueror was before Richard the Third. Shakespeare's name William. (*Mr. Touse?*)

14. Mr. Fleetewood the Recorder[1] sitting in judgment when a prisoner was to have his clergy and could not read, he saued him with this ieast, "What, will not that obstinat knave reade indeede? Goe take him away and whip him." (*Mr. Bramstone.*[2])

He imprisoned one for saying he had supt as well as the Lord Maior, when he had nothing but bread and cheese.

fo. 30.
2 Marche,
1601.

This day there was a great Court of Merchant Adventurers; two were sent from the Counsell to sitt and see their proceedinges at their Courtes, and to make relacion. At this Court two questions were moved. 1. Whether their Companie were able to vent all the clothes made in England yf they might choose their place in the Lowe Countries, and be ayded by hir Majestie for the execution of their orders? Resolved that they are able. 2. Whether they can continue a Companie to trade yf the Earle of Cumberlandes licence take effect, whereby he hath liberty to ship over what cloth he pleaseth, contrary to hir Majesties patents and graunts to the merchaunts? Resolved by handes that they cannot. (*Mr. Hull nar.*)

Their Courts consist of one Gouernor, one Deputy, a Secretary, and these sitt at a table raysed a little, and 24 Assistants sitt about; the autority of these continues but six moneths; these speake, heare, and iudge of other mens speaches in Court. The greater part of the present at any Court carries the iudgment. (*Idem.*)

fo. 30[b].
3 May, 1602.

Mr. Touse told that in the last cirquit into Yorkeshire the Vice President of Yorke would have had the upper hand of Justice Yeluerton, but he would not yeld. (*Mr. Touse.*)

---

[1] Fleetwood, like the Diarist, was of the Middle Temple. Many of his curious letters were published by Sir Henry Ellis (Orig. Letters, 1st Ser. vol. ii.)

[2] The Lord Chief Justice from 1635 to 1642, whose Autobiography was published by the Camden Society.

Long since, when Justice Manwood [1] roode Somersetshire circuit with Lorde Anderson, there happened a great quarrell between the Lord Sturton and Sir Jo. Clifton, in which affray the Lord Anderson himselfe, onely with his cap in his hand, tooke a sword from a very lustie tall fellowe. Of such a courage is Anderson. (*Idem.*)

My chamberfellow [2] told me of Mr. Long's opposition against him, and howe he had ouermatcht him; told me of his owne preferment to Sir Robert Cecile by the Lord Cheif Baron Periams and Lord Cheif Justice Pophams meanes, almost without his owne suite. By Sir Roberts fauour he obtayned the cancelling of an obligacion wherein his father [3] stoode bound to Auditor Tucke not to vse that office or receive the profits for a certaine tyme.

Those which presume upon repentaunce at the last gaspe by [the] theeves example on the crosse, doe as yf a man should spurr his horse till he speake because wee reade that Balams asse did soe when his maister beate him.   4.

This day Serjeant Harris was retayned for the plaintife, and he argued for the defendant; soe negligent that he knowes not for whom he speakes.

Soe many accions of *Quare impedit* in the Common Place, that it were well a *Quare impedit* were brought against the *Quare impedit* for hindering other accions.

---

[1] Sir Roger Manwood was a Justice of the Common Pleas 1572 to 1578, and Lord Chief Baron from 1578 to 1593. Sir Edmund Anderson was Lord Chief Justice of the Common Pleas from 1582 to 1603. (Foss's Judges, v. 516 ; vi. 51.)

[2] Edward Curle, who is so frequently mentioned in other parts of the Diary. At this time he was keeping his terms in the Middle Temple preparatory to being called to the bar. He had been admitted of the Inn, *specialiter*, on the 29th Nov. 1594. The Diarist subsequently married Curle's sister Anne.

[3] William Curle of Hatfield, one of the Auditors of the Court of Wards.

One that would needes be married in all the [*sic*] hast, though he
were soe verry a beggar that the preist told him he would not marry
him because he had not money sufficient to pay him his duty for
that service, " Why then," said he, " I pray you, Sir, marry me as
far as that will goe. Nowe I am here I must needes have something
ere I goe."

＊   ＊   ＊   ＊

A Puritan scholemaister that taught litle children in their horne
bookes, would not have them say " Christ crosse A. &c." but
" Black spott A." Another being to invit his frend, desyred him
come and take part of a Nativity pie at Christ tyde with him.

When a Puritan that had lost his purse made great moane as desyrous to haue it againe, another minister (meaning to try his spirit)
gaue forth that he was able to helpe him to it by figur-casting; whereupon the Puritan resorted vnto him; and the day appointed for the
purpose, the other told him that when he caste a paper into the
chaffing dishe of coales which he placed before them, he should
looke in the glasse to see the visage of him that had it; but the flame
being too short for him to aduise well what face it was, he earnestly
entreated to see it againe. " Oh," said the other, " I perceue well
the cause why you could not discerne it was that you trust to much
in God." " Whoe, I," said the Puritan, " I trust noe more in God
then the post doth. Lett me see it once againe." Such hyppocrytes
are those professors. (*Ch. Dauers.*)

Mr. Fleetwood, after he was gone from supper, remembred a
case to the purpose he was talking of before he went, and came
againe to tell vs of it, which Mr. Bramston said was as yf a reueller,
when he had made a legg at the end of his galliard, should come
againe to shewe a tricke which he had forgotten.

This day there was a strange confused pressing of souldiers, carrying soe to the ships, that they were thrust togither under hatches like calues in a stall.

When hir Majestie had giuen order that Spenser should haue a reward for his poems, but Spenser could haue nothing, he presented hir with these verses:

> It pleased your Grace vpon a tyme
> To graunt me reason for my ryme,
> But from that tyme vntill this season
> I heard of neither ryme nor reason.
>
> *(Touse.)*

A gentleman whose father rose by the lawe, sitting at the benche while a lawyer was arguying in a case against the gentleman, touching land which his father purchased, the gentleman, more collerick then wise, sayd the lawyer would prate and lye, and speake anie thing for his fee: "Well," said the lawyer, "yf your father had not spoken for a fee, I should haue noe cause to speake in this cause to day." The posterity of lawyers hath more flourished then that either of the clergy or citisens.

Notes out of a copie of a letter written by way of dedicacion of CHARLES THE FIFTH HIS INSTRUCTIONS TO HIS SONNE PHILLIP : TRANSLATED OUT OF SPANISHE, *and sent to hir Majestie* BY LORD H. HOWARD.[1]

Hir Majesties affections are not carued out of flint, but wrought out of virgin wax, and hir royall hart hath ever suted him in mercy, whom hir state doth represent in Maiesty.

If anie sentence were mistaken by equivocacion of wordes, or ambiguity in sence, I onely blame the stintles rage of destinie, which ever carryeth the best shaftes of my unluky quiuer to such endes as are most distant from the white I aymed at.

[1] Created Earl of Northampton in 1604-5, died 1614.

Since I began, each fruit hath answered his blossom, each grayne his seede, all eventes there hopes; my selfe onely, more vnfortunate then all the rest, have sowne with teares, but can reape with noe renolucion.

I have presumed once againe (least the ground of my deuocion, by lying to long fallowe, might seeme either waxen wyld or ouergrowne with weedes,) to breake the barren soyle of myne vnfruitfull brayne, that prosperous successe may rather want at all tymes to myne endeuors, then endeuor to my loyall determinacion.

You are that sunne to me, whose going downe leaues nothing but a night of care.

The divel, like those painters which are skilfull in the art of perspectiue, taketh pleasure, by false colours and deceitfull shaddowes, to make those things seeme farthest of which are nerest hand (as death), and to abuse our nature with vayne hopes.

fo. 32^b.
August, 1602. As the glasse of tyme is turned euery hour vpside downe, soe is the course of our vncertaine lyfe; as that part which before was full is emptied, and that other which was emptied is replenished, soe fareth this world interchangeably.

As the highest region of the ayre is cleare and without stormes, soe hir minde free from all distemperes of affection.

Those that liue not in the safe arke of your gracious conceit, &c.

The sea can brooke noe carcasses, nor hir Majesties thoughts admit of castaways.

The fig-tree never bare fruit after it was blasted by the breath of Christ; noe plant can prosper that never feeles the comfort of the same; soe, &c.

In this the difference, Adam dyed because he eat of it (i. e. the tree of lyfe), but I shall dye before I looke on it.

Manie find frends to couer faults; my cloke is innocency. An eye may be cleare enough yet not discerne without your light; a course may be direct yet endles without your clewe. My dealings may be free from base alloy, but yet not currant amongst honourable persons without the liuely print of your cherefull countenaunce. What dangerous diseases breed in bodyes naturall by putrefaction springing out of the sunnes eclipse, the same, or rather greater by proportion, must growe in well affected myndes fo. 33.
August, 1602. by the darke vayle of your discouragement.

Patience like a pill by continuall vse looseth his virtue.

I wonder at your matchles worth as they that are borne vnder the North Pole doe at the sunne, whose comfort they feele not at all, or without anie great effect.

Praye that since there is but one period and bounder, one high water marke both of your happie life and our countryes good, the same may be inlarged aboue ordinary termines, defended by all extraordinary meanes, and augmented with all speciall fauour which either death possesseth or heauen promiseth. That euer in the zodiack, our princely virgin may assend with assistance of all happie planets.

Such is my beliefe in your administracion of right, as with the faythfull daughter of Darius, while I liue I will deeme *me captum esse quamdiu Regina vixerit.*

The world is gouerned by plancts, not fixed starrs.

fo. 33ᵇ.
8 August, 1602.

One Mr. Palmes told at supper that one Mr. Sapcotts, a Northamptonshire gentleman, married his owne bastard; had neuer anie issue by hir. After his death shee was with child, would not discouer the father. Sapcotts left hir worth some 400*l.* yearely, yet none will marry hir.

October 1602.

Mr. Kempe in the King's Bench reported that in tymes past the counsellors wore gownes faced with satten, and some with yellowe cotten, and the benchers with jennet furre; nowe they are come to that pride and fa[n]tasticknes, that every one must[1] have a veluet face, and some soe tricked with lace that Justice Wray[2] in his tyme spake to such an odd counsellor in this manner: *Quomodo intrasti, domine, non habens vestem nuptialem?* Get you from the barre, or I will put you from the barr for your folish pride. (*Ch. Da: nar.*)

9.

Every man semes to seruc himselfe.

October, 25.

As the fox and the asse were travayling by the way, they overtooke a mule, a strange beast as they thought, and began to be verry

---

[1] much *in MS.*

[2] Sir Christopher Wray was a puisne Judge of the Queen's Bench from 1572 to 1574, and Lord Chief Justice of that court from that time to 1592. (Foss's Judges, v. 546.)

inquisitive, like a couple of constables, to know whence he came and what his name might be. The mule told them his name was written in his foote, and there they might reade it yf they would; the foxe dissembling sayd he was not bookish, and askt the asse what he could doe. He like an asse, without feare or witt, went about to shewe his schollership; but, while he was taking up the foote to reade what was told him, the mule tooke him such [a] blowe with his foote that the asse paid for his cuning [?]. Such are meere schollers. (*Ed. Curle.*)

fo. 34.　　*Maiores in sacris litteris progressus præmia maiora postulant; et plures in vita necessitates plura vitæ necessaria subsidia requirunt:* these causes of a plurality in a dispensacion.

Dr. Parryes Ale for the Spring.

℞. Of the juyce of scouruy-grasse one pint; of the iuyce of watercresses, as much; of the iuyce of succory, half a pint; of the iuyce of fumitory, half a pint : proportion to one gallon of ale: they must be all tunned vp togither.

There is a certaine kinde of compound called *Laudanum*, which may be had at Dr. Turner's, appothecary, in Bishopgate Streate; the virtue of it is very soueraigne to mitigate anie payne; it will for a tyme lay a man in a sweete trans, as Dr. Parry told me he tryed in a feuer, and his sister Mrs. Turner in hir childbirth.

The Lord Zouche, a verry learned and wise nobleman, was made Lord President of the Marches of Wales after the death of the old Earle of Pembroke.[1]

---

[1] Henry Herbert, second Earl of Pembroke of that family, died 19 Jan. 1600-1. His successor in the Presidency of Wales here alluded to was Edward the last Lord Zouche of Haryngworth, before the abeyance was determined in 1815.

My cosen told me that the custome of burning women with their husbandes in Goa began vpon this occasion; the women of that country being skilfull in poysoninge, and exceedingly giuen to the synn of lechery, could noe sooner like an other, but presently their husband would dye, that they might marry him whom they best liked: whereuppòn it came to [1] passe that one woman burried manie husbands, and soe the King lost many subiects. And therefore to preuent this mischiefe the King ordeined, that, whensoeuer the husband died, the wife should be burned with him, in great solemnitie of musike and assembly of frendes, esteeming by this meanes to moue the wiues to make much of their husbands, yf not for the loue of their companie, yet for loue of their owne liues, since their safety consisted in their preseruacion.

fo. 34^b.

EPITAPHES IN THE TEMPLE CHURCHE.

Hic jacet corpus H. Bellingham, Westmerlandiensis, generosi, et nuper Socij Medii Templi, cuius relligionis synceritas, vitæ probitas, morumque integritas, eum maxime commendabant: obijt 10 Decembr. 1586, ætatis suæ 22°.

On the South side on a pillar.

D : O : M

Rogerio Bisshopio, illustris interioris Templi Societatis quondam studioso, in florentis ætatis limine morte immatura prærepto, qui ob fælicissimam indolem, moresque suauissimos, magnum sui apud omnes desiderium relinquens, corpus humo, amorem amicis, cælo animum dicavit.

Monumentum hoc amoris et mœroris perpetuum testem charissimi posuere parentes.

Obijt 7° Sept. 1597: ætatis suæ 23.

fo. 35.

EPITAPHE IN THE CHURCHE AT HYTHE IN KENT.

Whiles he did live which here doth lye
Three suites [he] gott of the Crowne,
The Mortmaine, fayre, and Mayralty,
For Heith this auncient Towne;

[1] it, in MS.

And was himselfe the Baylif last,
And Mayor first by name;
Though he be gon, tyme is not past
To prayse God for the same.

(Of John Bridgman; obijt 1591.)

fo. 35ᵇ.
May.

W. Wats, Antagonista. Summum jus non est summa injuria jure posi-
tivo, sed equitate.

*   *   *   *

14.

Mr. Curle, my chamber-fellowe, was called alone by parliament to the barr.

*   *   *   *

29.

Those which goe to churche onely to heare musicke, goe thither more for *fa* then *soule.* (*B. Reid.*)

One said, yong Mr. Leake was verry rich, and fatt, "True," said B. Reid, "pursy men are fatt for the most part."

"He takes the stronger part still," of one that would be sure to drinke stronge beare yf he could come to it.

fo. 36ᵇ.
April, 1602.

A medicine for the windines in the stomach.

℞. A quarter of a pint of lavanda spike water, half as much balme water, a fewe cloues, and a little long pepper beaten together ; drinke this at twise. (*Mrs. Cordell's exper.*)

For the haymeroyds.

℞. Two ounces of shoemacke brayed, and put it to halfe a pint of red rose water; warme them over the fyre, and bath the place with it. (*My Cosen exper.*)

The covetous man rides in a coache which runnes upon 4 wheeles. The 1. Pusillanimity. 2. Inhumanity. 3. Contempt of God. 4. Forgetfulnes of death. (*Dr. Chamberlayne.*) It is drawne with two horses. 1. *Rapacitas.* 2. *Tenacitas.* The divel the coachman, and he hath two whippes. 1. *Libido acquirendi.* 2. *Metus amittendi.*

This day there was a race at Sapley neere Huntingdon, invented 6. by the gentlemen of that country: at this Mr. Oliuer Cromwell's[1] horse won the syluer bell : and Mr. Cromwell had the glory of the day. Mr. Hynd came behinde.

While I was at Hemmingford Dr. Chamberlayne told me that Dr. fo. 37. Bilson was made Bishop of Winchester[2] by the meanes of the Earl Aprill, 1602. of Essex. Nowe the Bishop, being visitor of Trinity Colledge in Oxeford by his place, promised to the Lady Walsingham,[3] that he would make him that nowe is President after Dr. Yeilder's[4] decease, and for this purpose expelled such fellowes as he thought would be opposite, and placed such in their roomes as he knewe would be sure vnto him. By this meanes Dr. Chamberlaine was defeated of his right, being an Oxefordshire man, whom by their statutes they are bound to preferr before anie other.

The fellowes of that Colledge are to nominat two, and the visitor within six weekes must elect the one of them to be President.

Upon marriage with the Lady Poliuizena,[5] Sir Henry Crom-

---

[1] This " Mr. Oliver Cromwell " was in truth, according to other writers who have mentioned him, Sir Oliver Cromwell, stated to have been knighted by Queen Elizabeth in 1598, created K.B. at the coronation of King James, and uncle to his namesake the future Protector. An ancestor of his in the reign of Henry VIII. is described by Mr Carlyle as " a vehement, swift-riding man." (Cromwell's Letters and Speeches, i. 42, ed. 1846.) Sir Oliver seems to have inherited some of the ancestral qualities.

[2] Translated from Worcester 1597 ; died 1616.

[3] Widow of Secretary Walsingham.

[4] Dr. Arthur Yildard died 1st Feb. 1598. Dr. Ralph Kettell " was nominated and admitted by Thomas Bilson, Bishop of Winchester, 12th Feb. 1598." (Hardy's Le Neve, iii. 572.)

[5] " Lady Poliuizena " was Anne dau. of Giles Hoofman or Hooftman, of Antwerp, mentioned in p. 51, and widow of Sir Horatio Palavicini, a well known native of Genoa settled at Daberham, in co. Cambridge. Sir Horatio died 6th July 1600 : his lady, fulfilling the customary obligations of her widowhood to the very letter, was married to Sir Oliver on the 7th July 1601. Sir Henry Cromwell who is mentioned in this paragraph was the Golden Knight ; father of Sir Oliver and grandfather of

well conueyed his lands vnto his sonne Mr. Oliuer in marriage. Soe Mr. Oliuer with his owne and his ladyes living is the greatest esquire living in those partes, thought to be worth neere 5000*l.* per annum. There liues a housefull at Hinchingbrooke, like a kennell.

Mrs. Mary Androes, daughter and heir to Mr. Androes of Sandey, was married to one Mr. Mayne of Grayes In; had 1000*l.* present, and yf Androes have issue, to have an other. Mayne had but 150*l.* per annum.

I hear that the yong Lord North was married to Mrs. Brocket, Sir Jo. Cutts his Ladies sister, being constrayned in a manner through want of money while he liued in Cambridge; he had some 800*l.* with hir. Shee is not yong nor well fauoured, noe maruaile yf he loue hir not.[1]

On Easter day Dr. Chamberlaine was at Sir Henry Cromwells, and ministered the communion, but without booke.

15.

I was with my cosen in Kent, and he told me that there is one [2]   , a rich broker in London, whose first wife had such a running strong conceit in hir head that the sherifes sought still to apprehend hir, that noe perswasion to the contrary preuayling with hir, first shee cutt hir owne throate, and that being cured, she brake hir necke by leaping out at hir garret windowe.

the Protector. He died in January 1603-4. In the April before his death, Sir Oliver, being in possession of his father's lands under the arrangement mentioned in this paragraph, received King James at Hinchinbrooke on his way from Scotland to take possession of the throne. There is no mention of Sir Henry having been present on that occasion.

[1] The young gentleman here alluded to, who was just twenty years of age, was Dudley the third Lord North, who succeeded to that title on the death of his grandfather, the second Baron, on 3rd Dec. 1600. Dugdale informs us that the lady alluded to was Frances daughter of Sir John Brockett of Brockett Hall, co. Hertford, and that there was issue of the marriage four sons and two daughters. Lord North himself died on the 6th Jan. 1666-7, being then 85 years of age. (Baronage, ii. 394.)

[2] Blank in orig.

Jo. Vermeren a Dutchman, of kin to my cosens first wifes sisters husband, had issue a daughter married to one Niepson. Their daughter was married to one Hoofman, a notable rich man, whoe in his beginning was but a pedler of pottes, yet after, by his good fortune and industry, he proued soe wealthie that he gaue 10,000*l.* with his daughter in marriage to Sir Horatio Poliuizena, now deceased, and the widdowe married to Mr. Oliuer Cromewell, the sonne and heir of Sir Henry Cromwell. This marriage, and certaine land he had from his Uncle Warrein,[1] cleared him out of debt.

My cosen concluded with William Tunbridge of Ditton to give him 115*l.* for a leas of Ditton ruffe for 25 yeares.

fo. 38.
18 Aprill, 1602.

16.

Dr. Parry told howe Dr. Barlowe, nowe one of hir Majesties chapleins, received a checke at hir Majesties, because he presumed to come in hir presence when shee had given speciall charge to the contrary, because shee would not haue the memory of the late Earl of Essex renewed by him, who had preached against him at Paules. " O, Sir," said shee, " wee heare you are an honest man! you are an honest man, &c."

Hir Majestie merrily told Dr. Parry that shee would not heare him on Good Friday; " Thou wilt speake against me, I am sure," quoth shee; yet shee heard him.

Duke de Neveurs a Frenchman departed for France this day.

18.

My cosen told me that Vicars, King Henry the 8. his Sergeant Surgeon, was at first but a meane practiser in Maidstone, such a

19.

---

[1] Sir Henry Cromwell's first wife was Jane daughter of Sir Ralph Warren, Lord Mayor of London in 1536 and 1544. Sir Ralph had an only son named Richard, who was seated at Claybury, Essex. This was the uncle Warren here alluded to. On his death Lady Cromwell was his heir, and upon her decease uncle Warren's lands would descend to Sir Oliver.

one as Bennett there, that had gayned his knowledge by experience, untill the King advanced him for curing his sore legge.

A light hand makes a heauy wound.

20.

I rode to Dr. Parryes. Shee[1] said there was noe greater evidence to proue a man foole then yf he leaue the University to marry a wife.

fo. 38ᵇ.
21 Aprill.

Dr. Parry told howe his father was Deane[2] of Salisbury, kept a sumptuous house, spent aboue his reuenewe, was carefull to preferr such as were men of hope, vsed to haue showes at his house, wherein he would haue his sonne an actor to embolden him.

He shewed me the sermon he made at Court last Good Fryday; his text was, "My God, my God, why hast thou forsaken me?" It was right eloquent and full of sound doctrine, graue exhortacions, and heauenly meditacions. *Vox horrentis*, forsaken; *Vox sperantis*, My God; *Vox admirantis*, Why hast thou, &c. Mee! There was in Christ *Esse naturæ*, *Esse gratiæ*, *Esse gloriæ*. God's presence 2ˣ [*duplex?*] by essence, by assistance; dereliction, withdrawing, and retyring.

I returned to Bradborne.

Shee[3] would have sent a part of a gammen of bacon to the seruants; my cosen said he loued it well, &c.; and, because he wold not send that she would, shee would not that he would, and grewe to strange hott contradiction with him. After, when shee sawe him moued (and not without cause) shee fell a kissing his hand at table, with an extreeme kinde of flattery, but neuer confest shee was to violently opposite.

---

[1] So in MS.

[2] Not Dean, but Chancellor. He was collated in 1547, deprived during the reign of Queen Mary, but restored shortly after the accession of Queen Elizabeth. He died in 1571. (Hardy's Le Neve, ii. 651, 652.)

[3] Evidently his cousin's wife.

The *fleur de luce*, as we call it, takes his name, I thinke, as Fleur de Lis, which *Lis* is a river in Flanders neere Artoys.

I came from my cosens to London.

Perpetuityes are so much impugned because they would be preiudiciall to the Queenes proffit, which is raysed dayly from[1] fines and recoueryes.

One Parkins of the Inner house a very complementall gentleman; a barrester but noe lawyer.

In the Star Chamber the benche on that part of the roome where the Queenes armes are placed is alwayes vacant; noe man may sitt on it, as I take it, because it is reserued as a seate for the Prince, and therefore before the same are layed the purse and the mace as notes of autority.

*   *   ●   *

Those which name such as they ought not, and such as they knowe to be vnfitt, to be Sheriues of London, doe but goe a woll-gathering, purposing to fleece such men. (*Cosen Onsloe.*) And they goe a fishinge for some 100*l.* or 2, as they nominated my cosen this yeare.

30

One Mr. Ousley of the Middle Temple, a yong gallant, but of a short cutt, ouertaking a tall stately stalking caualier in the streetes, made noe more a doe but slipt into an ironmongers shop, threwe of his cloke and rapier, fitted himselfe with bells, and presently cam skipping, whistling, and dauncing the morris about that long swag-gerer, whoe, staringly demaunding what he ment; "I cry you mercy," said the gent., "I tooke you for a May pole." (*Ch. Da. nar.*)

---

[1] for in MS.

9.   Sniges nose looked downe to see howe many of his teethe were lost, and could neuer get up againe. (*Th. Ouerbury of Sniges crooked nose.*)

Sir Frauncis Englefields house ouerthrowne by the practice of Mr. Blundell of the Middle Temple, whoe, being put in speciall trust, tooke a spleen vpon a small occasion against the heir, and presently in his heate informed the Earl of Essex, that such a conveyaunce was made of soe goodly an inheritaunce in defraud of the Queen, and soe animated him to begg it, to the vtter ruine of that house. (*Mr. Curle nar.*)

One told a jest, and added, that all good wittes applauded it; a way to bring one to a dilemma, either of arrogance in arriding, as though he had a good witt too, or of ignoraunce, as thoughe he could not conceiue of it as well as others.

fo. 40.
10 Oct. 1602.

AT PAULES CROSSE.

Dr. Spenser [1] preached. He remembred in his prayer the Companie of the Fishmongers, as his speciall benefactors while he lived in Oxford; his text the 5 of Isay, v. 4.

We are soe blind and peruerse by nature, that wee are soe farre from the sence of our owne imperfections and the terror of our synn, that either not seing or not acknowledging our owne weaknesses, wee runne headlong into all wickednes, and hate soe much to be reformed, that God is fayne to deale pollitikely with vs, propounding our state vnto vs in parables, as it were an others case, that thereby drawing man from conceit

---

[1] Dr. John Spenser, fellow-student with Hooker at Corpus Christi College, Oxford, and president of that college from 1607 to 1614. Wood states (Ath. Oxon. ii. 145) that he was " a noted preacher and a chaplain to King James I." It was to him that upon Hooker's death his MSS. were delivered over for completion of the Ecclesiastical Polity. The sermon of which Manningham took such copious notes was printed in 1615, after Dr. Spenser's death, under the editorship of Hamlet Marshall, his curate. The author of the Christian Year speaks of it as " full of eloquence and striking thoughts ; the theological matter almost entirely, and sometimes the very wordes, being taken from those parts of Hooker in which he treats of the visible church." (Hooker's Works, ed. Keble, i. xxiii.)

of himselfe, which would make him partiall, he might draw an uncorrupt iudgment of him self from him selfe. Soe dealt the Lord with David by the parable of the poore mans sheepe, and soe here he taketh up a comparison of the vine, to shewe Israell their ingratitude.

Parables are proportionable resemblances of things not well understoode; they be vayles indeed, which couer things, but being remoued give a kinde of light to them which before was insensible, and makes them seeme as though they were sensible.

The things considerable in the text are, first, The churche, resembled by the vine. 2. Gods benefits towards the Churche expressed in the manner of his dressing the vine. 3. The fruit expected, grapes, iudgment and rightcousnes. 4. The fayling and ingratitude, by bringing forth sower and wylde grapes; oppression and crying. 5. God's judgment, vers. 6.

In the Church he considered, what it is, and where it is.   fo. 40ᵇ.

The Churche is compared most aptly to the vyne, for neither of them spring naturally. *Non sumus de carne, nec voluntate hominis, sed beneplacito Dei.* 2. Both spring, and growe, first in weakenes, yet then they claspe their little hands and take hold on of an other, and soe going on *crescunt sine modo*, the increase without measure, as Pliny sayth. 3. Noe plant more flourishing in the summer, none more poore and bare [1] in winter. All followe the Church in prosperitie, and the rich, the mighty, the wise, in persequution fall away like leaves. 4. Bring forth fruit in clusters, which cheres the hart. God and men and angels reioyce when the Church aboundes in workes of rightcousnes and true holines. 5. Both have but one roote, though manie branches; Christ is the true foundacion, other then this can no man lay. 6. The branches are in-grafted, and as in planting all are tyed alike with the outward bond, yet all proue not alike, soe all haue the same profession and outward meanes, yet all growe not nor fructifie alike : but it is the inward grace that maketh the true branche; as he is a Jewe that is one within. Rom. ii. 28, 29.

2. The Lord's vineyard is not to be knowne by the fruit (for wo reade here that it bringeth forth wyld grapes), but where the roote is planted,   fo. 41. where Christ is professed, there the Church is; it is nowe universall, not yed to a nic place ; we reade of 7 Churches in the Reuelacions, though all

[1] " here Naked " is interlined in the MS. as another reading.

not aliko pure, yet all churches: Israell is his eldest sonne, though a prodigall : as betwixt man and woman after a publique contract celebrated, though the woman play the harlot and bring forth children of fornicacion unto hir husband, yet continues shee his wife whose name shee beares vutill a publique divorce be sued. Some churches are soare, some sicke, some soe leprous that noe communion ought to [be] continued with them, yet churches still. Yf anie aske, as manie papists use to doe, where our church was before Martin Luther was borne, we aunswer that it is the same churche that was from the beginninge, and noe newe on as they terme it, for the weeding of a vyneyard is noe destroyinge, nor the pruning any planting ; for we have remoued but idolatrie and a privat masse of ceremonies, which with the burying the author[?] of life in a hidden and unknowne language had almost put the heavenly light out of our candlesticke; and when the trashe of humaine inventions had raysed themselues to soe high esteeme, it was tyme to say, "Yf Ephraim play the harlot, yet lett not Israell synn."

fo. 41ᵇ.   Jerusalem litterally is the mother Churche of all.

The Churche, like the vine that hath many branches but one roote, may haue severall members, but all knit together with the vnity of three bonds— one Lord, one fayth, one baptisme. But nowe Rome, usurping over his fellowes, speakes like Babilon in the 18 Reuel. "I cannot erre," and have encroched an article vpon the Creede, that must be beeleeved upon payne of damnation, that there is one visible heade of the Churche (which must be the Pope). And yet in an œcumenical Counsell of 330 Catholike Bishops it was decreed that Constantinople should have equall authority with Rome ; which plainely confuted their usurped universall supremacy. Yet the Popes, by the assistaunce of the Emperours, haue, like ivy, risen higher then the oke by which it climed: soe much that our countriman Stapleton doubts not to call his Holines *Supremum in terris numen.*

3. The benefites and manner of dressing the vine: Genesis is but the nurse of it; Exodus, the removing; Leviticus, the ordering and manner of keeping it; Josua, the weeding, &c. God soe loued it that he gave his onely Sonne to redeeme it, and when he gave him, what gave he not with him ?

Might not the Church use the wordes of the leeper in the Ghospell :

" Lord, if thou wilt, thou canst make me cleane;" and why then com-
playnest thou ?

True it is, yf we consider his power : for he that is able to rayse vp fo. 42.
children to Abraham of stones, to make the iron sweate, &c. can purifie
our corruptions yf wee regard his power, and that without our meanes ;
but God hath tyed himself to ordinary meanes, by his eternall decree :
and he that will not heare Moses and the prophets neither will he beleeve
though one should rise from the dead. Many were foule with the leprosie
in Nathans [Elishas?] tyme, yet none cured but Naman.

4. The fruit. All things, euen the meanest, imitate the Creator in doing
something in their kind for the common good, not themselves alone ; the
olive doth not anoint itself with its owne oyle ; the trees and plants which
spend themselues in bringing forth some fruit or berry holds it noe
longer then till it be ripe, and then letts it fall at his masters feete; the
grape is not made drunke with its owne iuyce.

" He that receiveth a benefit hath lost his liberty," saith Seneca ; and,
since we have received such benefits of God as we can not, we would not
renounce, lett us glorifie him in our bodies whose we are, not our owne.

Aeternitie cometh before we worke, therefore our workes merit not
eternall life : and infants incorporat into the mysticall vyne are sauced
though they dy before they are able to bring forth anie good worke.

Our good workes growe as it were in a cold region ; the best of them,
even our prayers, scarce come to perfection throughe the imperfection of
our nature.

Good workes to be performed for mutuall helpe, and though we holde
ourselves sufficient, yet they are to be done, even as every thing bringeth fo. 42b.
forth something yf for noe other purpose yet to continue in its owne
state ; like the spring, which, because it yeildeth water, is therefore continually fed with water.

Bona opera sunt via regni, non causa regnandi. (Bernard.)

The fruits brought forth ; wyld grapes : an heavy sight to a carefull
husbandman, to haue noe better reward of his paynes.

I pray God the Church of England may not justifie the synns of Sodome and Judas. Couetousnes, the roote of all wickednes, maketh men
desyre to be greate rather then good, and this desyre causes them to

sucke even the lyfe from one another. There is a synn amongst us which
hath not bin heard of amongst the Gentiles, that wee should robb God,
and that is in tithing. Howe manie desyrous that the labouring man,
the minister, might be put out, that themselues might haue the inheritaunce. It is the corruption of the ministery that all the dores of entraunce are shut up but the dore of symony, soe that the most and best
places are for the most possessed by the worst; and, yf anie of the better
be forced to come in, they are constrayned to make shipwracke of a good
conscience.

If it be true which is published in the names of the popish faction, the
Pope hath sent a dispensation that the popish patrons may sell their pre-
sentations, soe be it the money come to the maintenance of the Jesuites.
And will Peters successor thinke it lawefull to sell the guifts of the Holie
Ghost? Will Simon Peter become Simon Magus? But he will nowe become a fisher for men; because he findes in their mouthes greater peices
fo. 43.   then twenty pence. The ministers are like the hart and liver, from whence
are derived lyfe and nourishment by sound doctrine and good example into
the members of the Church, and yf these be corrupt it is much to be
feared the whole body is like to languishe in a dangerous consumption.

In defrauding the ministery, we pull downe the pillers of the house wee
dwell in.

fo. 43ᵇ.   The Lord Zouche, Lord President of the Marches of Wales,
11 October,   begins to knowe and use his authoritie soe muche that his iuris-
1602.
diction is allready brought in question in the Common place, and the
Cheif Justice of that bench[1] thinkes that Glostershire, Hereford-
shire, &c., are not within his circuit.

When he came to sitt on the benche at Ludlowe, there were, as it
was wont, two cushions layd, one for the Cheife Justice Leukenour,
another for the President, but he tooke the on, and casting it downe
said, one was enough for that place.   (*Tho: Overbury.*)

Sir Walter Rhaleighs sollicitor, on Sheborough, was verry mal-

---

[1] Sir Edmund Anderson; 1582—1605.

apert and saucy in speacho to Justice Walmesley[1] at the bench in the Common place; soe far that, after words past hotly betwixt them, he said he thought it fitt to commit him for his contemptuous behauiour, but the other iudges were mum. *Quantus ille!* His wordes, " Before God, you do not well to lay their practises vpon us. You knowe me well enough. If you list, &c."

*   *   *   *

I heard that Sir Robert Cecile is fallen in dislike with one of his Secretaries of greatest confidence (Mr.[2]   ,) and hath discarded him, which moues manie coniectures and much discourse in the Court. This Secretary was a sutour to be on of the clerkes of the signet, as a place of more ease and lesse attendaunce then a clarke of the counsell, which it is though[t] he might haue.

fo. 44.
10 October, 1602.

The Irish Earle of Clanrichard[3] is well esteemed of by hir Maiestie, and in speciall grace at this tyme; hath spent lavishly since he came ouer, yet payes honestly. (*Mr. Hadsor.*)

The Earl of Ormond[4] is purposed, and hath licence, to marry his daughter to one of his cosens, not to the Lord Mountioy as was thought. (*Idem.*)

. Evill companie cuttes to the bone before the fleshe smart. It is like a fray in the night, when a man knowes not howe to ward. (*Ch. Dauers booke.*)

The libertines from the rose of *Sola fides*, sucke the poyson of security. (*Idem.*)

---

[1] Mr. Justice Thomas Walmesley, puisne Judge of the Common Pleas 1589—1611. (Foss's Judges, vi. 191.)   [2] Blank in MS.

[3] Richard of Kinsale, the fourth Earl, 1601—1635.

[4] Thomas, the tenth Earl, 1546—1614. The young lady here mentioned, who was the Earl's only child, was ultimately married, through the influence of King James I. to Sir Richard Preston, subsequently created Earl of Desmond.

A souldier being challenged for flying from the camp said, *Homo fugiens denuo pugnabit.*

· Booth being indited of felony for forgery the second time, desyred a day to aunswere till Easter terme; " Oh !" said the Attorny, " you would haue a spring; you shall, but in a halter." (*Ch. Da.*)

* * * * *

25.

I heard that Sir Richard Basset is much seduced, indeed gulled, by one Nic. Hill, a great profest philosopher, and nowe abuseth this yong knight by imagined alchymic.[1] (*Jo. Chap.*)

fo. 44b.
12 October,
1602.

The Earle of Sussex keepes Mrs. Syluester Morgan (sometyme his ladies gentlewoman) at Dr. Daylies house as his mistress, calls hir his Countesse, hyres Captain Whitlocke,[2] with monie and cast suites, to braue his Countes, with telling of hir howe he buyes his

[1] Antony Wood tells several strange tales about Nicholas Hill, who was one of the astrologers and alchemists whom the Earl of Northumberland gathered round him during his long imprisonment in the Tower. Ben Jonson laughed at

" those *atomi* ridiculous,
Whereof old Democrite and Hill Nicholas,
One said, the other swore, the world consists ;"

and the world at large seems to have entertained a very mean opinion of the modern up-holder of those doctrines. His end, according to a hearsay commemorated by Wood, was very unhappy, and was connected with the other person mentioned in our text. It is said that he fell into a conspiracy with " one Hill of Umberley in Devonshire, descended from Arthur Plantagenet, Viscount Lisle, a natural son of King Edward IV., who pretended some right to the crown." Being forced to fly into Holland, Hill practised physic at Rotterdam, in conjunction with his son Laurence, on whose death he went into an apothecary's shop, swallowed poison, and died on the spot. (Ath. Oxon. ii. 86.)

[2] Capt. Edmund Whitelocke, a brother of Sir James Whitelocke, father of Bulstrode Whitelocke. The Captain was one of the gayest and wildest of men, a great traveller, "well seen in the tongues," "extreme prodigal," a fellow of infinite merriment, and suspected of being concerned in half the plots and duels of his day. He was in trouble with the Earl of Essex, and again about the Powder Plot, and probably knew familiarly all the prisons in the metropolis. He died about six years after the time with which our Diarist is dealing, at Newhall, in Essex, the seat of his friend the Earl of Sussex. The Earl attended his funeral, and laid him honourably in the chapel of the Ratcliffes. See *Liber Famelicus of Sir James Whitelocke*, (*Camden Society*,) pp. iv. 10. The Earl of Sussex here alluded to was Robert the fifth Earl of the family of the Radcliffes, 1593—1629.

wench a wascote of 10*l.*, and puts hir in hir veluet gowne, &c.: thus, not content to abuse hir by keeping a common wench, he striues to invent meanes of more greife to his lady, whoe is of a verry goodly and comely personage, of an excellent presence, and a rare witt. Shee hath brought the Earle to allowe hir 1700*l.* a yeare for the maintenaunce of hir selfe and hir children while she liues apart. It is coniectured that Captain Whitlocke, like a base pander, hath incited the Earl to followe this sensuall humour,   *   *
    *   as he did the Earl of Rutland. (*J. Bramstone nar.*) The Countesse is daughter to the Lady Morrison in Hartford-shire, [1] with whom it is like she purposeth to liue.   *   *
    *   A practise to bring the nobilitie into contempt and beggery, by nourishing such as may prouoke them to spend all vpon lechery and such base pleasures.

When there came one which presented a supplicacion for his master to the Counsell, that vpon sufficient bond he might be released out of Wisbishe Castle, where he lay for recusancy, that he might looke to his busines in haruest, the Lord Admirall [2] thought the petition reasonable, but the old Lord Treasurour, Sir W. Cecil, said he would not assent, " for," said he, " I knowe howe such men would vse vs yf they had vs at the like aduantage, and therefore while we haue the staffe in our handes lett us hold it, and when they gett it lett them vse it." (*Mr. Hadsor nar.*)

Out of a Poeme called " It is merry when Gossips meete." S. R. [3]
Such a one is clarret proofe, *i. e.* a good wine-bibber.

fo. 45.
October, 1602.

    There's many deale vpon the score for wyne,
    When they should pay forgett the Vintner's syne.
       *   *   *   *

[1] Bridget, daughter of Sir Charles Morison of Cashiobury, Herts. She was aunt to the wife of the celebrated Lord Falkland.

[2] Lord Charles Howard, Earl of Nottingham.

[3] These initials, inserted by a later hand, indicate " Samuel Rowlands," the author of this very popular little volume. The first edition bears date in 1602, and had probably just been published when it attracted the attention of our diarist.

A man whose beard seemes scard with sprites to have bin,
And hath noe difference twixt his nose and chin,
But all his hayres haue got the falling sicknes,
Whose forefront lookes like jack an apes behind.

A gossips round, thats every on a cup.

Mr. Steuen Beckingham of Hartfordshire was brought into the Kings benche at the suit of two poore ioyners whom he hath undone; they seeled his house, which came to a matter of some 80*l.* and they could hardly obtain anie thing by suit. A man of a hott collerick disposicion, a creaking loud voyce, a greasy whitish head, a reddish beard, of long staring *mouchetons ;* wore an outworne muff with two old gold laces, a playne falling band, his cuffs wrought with coloured silk and gold, a sattin doublet, a wrought wastcote, &c. *vt facile quis cognoscat haud facile si cum alijs convenire posset, qui voce, facie, vestitu ita secum dissidet.* One of his witnesses would not aunswere any thing for him vntill he were payd his charges in the face of the court. Soe little confidence had he in his credit, whoe had dealt soe hardly with his ioyners.

On Fossar, an old ioyner dwelling [in] Paules Churchyard, a common and a good measurer of ioyncrs work.

Mr. Prideaux, a great practiscr in the Eschequer, and one that usurpes vpon a place certaine at the barr, left his man one day to keepe his place for him, but Lancaster of Grayes In comming in the meane tyme, would needes haue the place, though the man would haue kept it. " For," said L. " knowes thou not that I beeleue nothing but the reall presence? " meaning that he was a Papist; and besydes, " could not thinke it to be *corpus meum* except Mr. Prideux himselfe were there." (*Mr. Hackwell nar.*)

When Mr. Dodridge,[1] in his argument of Mr. Darsies patentes, and

¹ This anecdote derives some little *vraisemblance* from the circumstance that Sir John Doderidge, who was a justice of the King's Bench from 1612 to 1628, was looked upon

soe of the prerogatiue in generall, he began his speache from Gods gouernment. " It is done like a good archer," quoth Fr. Bacon, " he shootes a fayre compasse."

There was an action brought to trie the title of one Rooke an infant for a house and certaine land. " All this controversye," said the attorny, " is but for a little rookes nest."

\An Epitaphe upon a bellowes maker.

Here lyes Jo. Potterell, a maker of bellowes,
Maister of his trade, and king of good fellowes ;
Yet for all this, att the houre of his death,
He that made bellowes could not make breath. (B. J.)[1]

Mr. Bodly, the author, promoter, [and] the perfecter, of a goodly library in Oxford, wan a riche widdowe by this meanes. Comming to the place where the widdowe was with one whoe is reported to haue bin sure of hir, as occasion happened the widdowe was absent; while he was in game, he, finding this opportunity, entreated the surmised assured gent. to hold his cardes till he returned. In which tyme he found the widdowe in a garden, courted, and obteined his desyre; soe he played his game, while an other held his cardes.[2] He was at first but the sonne of a merchant, vntill he gave some intelligence of moment to the counsell, whereupon he was thought worthie employment, whereby he rose. (Mr. Curle.)

as a man of a philosophical character of mind, and of very large acquirements. Fuller remarks that it was hard to say whether " he was better artist, divine, civil or common lawyer " (Worthies, i. 282), and Croke, that he was " a man of great knowledge as well in common law as in other human sciences and divinity." (Reports, Car. 127, cited in Foss's Judges, vi. 309.)

[1] These initials are by a more recent hand. The lines do not appear in the published works of Ben Jonson.

[2] The lady alluded to was Anne Carew, daughter of a merchant of Bristol and widow of a person named Ball. She had a considerable fortune.

fo. 46ᵇ.
24 October.

Mr. Dr. King,[1] preacher at St. Andrews in Holborn, at Paules Crosse, this daye.

His text 2 Peter ii. v. 4, 5, 6, 7, 8, 9. The length of his text might make some tedious semblance of a long discourse, but the matter shortly cutt itself into two parts, example and rule; one particular, the other generall; the one experiment, the other science; the one of more force to proue, the other to instruct. The argument is not *a posse ad esse,* but *ab esse ad posse;* it hath bin, and therefore may be; nay by this place it shalbe, for *lege mortali quod vnquam fuit, et hodie fieri potest;* but *lege æterna,* that which hath bin shalbe agayne. Here is an acted performaunce, a demonstracion, το ὁτι, which are most forceable to persuade, being of all thinges sauing the thinges themselves neerest our apprehension, leading from the sense to the vnderstanding, which is our certaynest meane of acquiring knowledge, since philosophie teacheth *quod nihil est intellectu, quod non prius fuit in sensu; sicut audiuimus, et fecerunt patres nostri.* Hystory and example the strongest motives to imitation. Rules are but sleeping and seeming admonitions. Thomas would not beleeue vnles he thrust his fingers into Christes sydes, and felt the print of his nayles; and we are so obstinat, wee will hardly beeleue except Godes judgments thrust fingers and nayles into our sydes.

fo. 47.
Oct. 1602.

The examples are bipartite : each containing contrary doctrines, like the language of them in the last chapter of Nehemias, half Jewishe, half Ashdoch; like the bands of the Levites, that parted themselves one companie to one mount to blesse, the other to an other to curse, the people; soe the one part denounceth judgment, the other declareth mercy: they may be compared to the cleane beastes, Deut. xiv., which had parted hoofes, and chewed the cudd; soe here on the one syde is the old world drowned, on the other Noach saved; on the one Sodom burned, on the other Lott preserved. They are three of the strangest and fearefullest examples in nature; the fall of the Angells, the drowning of the world, the burning of

---

[1] Dr. John King, styled by King James the King of Preachers, Queen Elizabeth presented him in 1597 to the rectory of St. Andrew's in Holborn, and to a prebend in St. Paul's in 1599. He was Bishop of London from 1611 to 1621. (Newcourt's Report. i. 211, 275; Hardy's Le Neve, ii. 303.)

Sodome ; they stretch from one end to an other, alpha and omega, heaven and earth, men and angels, the most excellent payre of God's creatures, and the deluge œcumenicall and universall. But God in his punishment, like a wise prince, will begin at his owne sanctuary, at his owne house, *non habitabit mecum iniquus,* I will not suffer a wicked person to dwell in my house, and therefore first turned the angels from his habitacion. Angels in their creacion, *vere δεύτερον,* the second light, the eyes and eares of the great king, continuall attendantes in his court and assistauntes of his throne; they are farr above the greatest saint, for wee shalbe but like them, and they are next to the Sonne of God, otherwise he had said nothing when he said, to which of the angells sayd he at anie tyme, &c. *Heb.:* they were *in summo non in tuto,* or rather *non in summo sed in tuto,* untill they synned. But what their synne was, I may safely say I knowe not. One sayth *non seruarunt principatum,* and St. Jo. sayth, *non steterunt in veritate,* their synn was treason, [they] continued not in their allegeaunce and fidelity ; an other, *et in angelis vacuitatem, prauitatem, infamiam reperiit;* an other, though an absurd opinion, that it was fleshly lust, and concupiscence, by carnall copulacion with women upon earth, and this they would lay upon these wordes, and the Sonnes of God tooke the daughters of men ; but of this it was sayd, *perquam noxium audire et credere.* And yet it became as common as it was absurd, because men thereby thought they might sooth themselves in that synn, and thinke it tollerable when angells had done the like before them.

fo. 47ᵇ.
October, 1602.

An other opinion more probable, that it was noe carnall, but spirituall luxury that overthrewe them, a kinde of selfe love, when they overvalued their owne excellency, and forgat their Creator ; and this opinion that their synn was pride is the most recciued and most like, because after his fall the first temptation that he made was of pride to Adam in paradise, *enim similis altissimo.*

The Diuel neuer desyred to be like God in his essence, for that being impossible he could never conceiue it, and that is neuer in appeticion which was not first in apprehension. Yet he may be sayd to affect it *desyderio complacentiæ, non efficaciæ,* because he might please himself with such conceits, not conceaue howe he might attaine to those pleasures, and

fo. 48.
October, 1602.

to this purpose some there be that write as though they had been taken up into the third heaven, and heard and seene the conflict betwixt Michael and the diuel : and will not stick to affirme that Michael had his name because when the diuel like a great giant bellowed out blasphemie against the most highest, denying that he had any creator or superior, Michael should resist and tell him, *Quis ut Deus*, which is the interpretacion of Michael ; soe though it be incertaine what was the synn of angells, yet is it most certayne that they fell from the highest happines to the lowest wretchednes ; the fall was like lightning suddein, and the place of it not possible to be found ; it passeth the capacitie of man to expresse it by comparison soe perfectly that he may say *hoc impetu ;* and for their payne it is *transcendens, et transcendentia transcendit,* it is invaluable, incomprehensible, passeth all hyperbole ; there was a present amission of place, grace, glory, the fruition of Godes presence, &c. which is the greatest of

fo. 48ᵇ.
October, 1602.

miseries, *felicem fuisse :* but there remaines a fearefull expectacion of future miseries, *et Nihil magis adversarium quam expectatio ; et Quo me vindicta reservas ?*

It was the opinion of Origen long since condemned for erronius, that the diuels might be saued, and his reason was because they had *liberum voluntatis arbitrium,* which might perhaps change and encline to the desyre of good, and soe through repentaunce obteyne mercy ; but the diuels are soe obdurate in their malice that though they may have *stimulum consciencie,* yet they can neuer come *ad correptionem gratie,* and in that opinion Origen is said Πλατονιζειν non Χριστιανιζειν. Another prop to his opinion was Jacobs ladder, where he imagined the descending and ascending of angels could meane nothing but the fall and restitution of angels.

The second example is the drowning of the world, a descent from heaven to earth in judgments. The world is termed κοσμος of the Grecians, from the excellent beauty thereof, and of the Lattynes *mundus, quia nihil mundius,* but here it is used to expresse the universalitie of the destruction, as the hystorie declares it Gen. vi. 7, etc. vii. 21, 22, 23, 24 : God destroyed euery thing that was vpon the earth from man to beast, to the creeping thing, and to the foule of the heaven, onely the fishes

escaped, and the reason one rendreth was because the sea onely was un-
defiled at that tyme; there was then noe sayling upon that element, noe
pyracie and murder committed upon it, noe forrein invasion intended over
it, noe trafficque with the nations for straunge comodities, nor for one an
others synnes and vices; all the other creatures were polluted by man, and
were [to] be purged with thatfloud. The ayre as farr as our eyes could looke
and fascinate, even the foules as far as our breath could move, were infected with the contagion thereof; all were uncleane, all were to be
clensed or punished. The greatnes of their number cannot excuse, but
aggrauates the offence. A multitude may synn and their synn is more
grievous, *qui cum multitudine peccat, cum multitudine periet;* and for the
most part, the most are the worst. It is noe sound argument, it is well
done because many doe so. The fox brings forth many cubbes, and the
lyon hath but one whelpe at once, yet that is a lyon, and more then manie
foxes. The harlot boasts that shee had manie moe resorted to hir house
then Socrates to his schole, but hir followers went the way of darknes.

"And brought in the floud:" and therefor a miracle supernaturall
wrought by the finger of God, not as some imagine by the conjunction of
waterishe planets, soe atributinge all to and confirming all by naturall
meanes, they say the world shalbe destroyed by fire, as it was by water,
when there shall happen the like conjunction of firy, as there was of
watery planets; but beleeve God, whoe sayth *Ego pluam.* And this was
against nature to destroy hir owne workes. The length of the rayne, forty
dayes, the continuaunce of the waters for twelve monethes, the dissolucion
of soe muche ayre with water as should make a generall deluge. These
are directly against the rules of naturall philosophie, besydes the influence
of a planet never stretcheth beyond his hemisphere, all which shewe
plainely, that it was the miraculous worke of God, not effected by the
course of nature. This was not *imber in furore missus,* to destroy or
famishe some particular city or country, of which kinde of baptismes our
land hath within fewe yeares felt many, but this made the sea, which before made but one spheare with the earth, as man and wife make but one
flesh, breake the boundes of modesty and overflowe the whole; that which
before was the girdle of the earth, nowe girt it, but in such a fashion,
that it stiffled all. It was such a dropsie in the world, that our simples

fo. 49.
October, 1672.

having lost their former virtue, we were permitted to eat flesh for the prescruacion of our liues, which before were prolonged with the naturall herbes and fruits of the earth, more hundreds then nowe they can bee scores with our best helpes of art or nature.

But it may be said, What, will God punishe the goode with the wicked? Will he drownd, all together, the righteous and the bad? Will he say *Pereant amici, modo pereant inimici?* Will he command *stragem tam amicorum quam hostium?* Shall his judgments be like the nett in the Gospell, that catcheth good and bad togither? Noe, for he punished the old world. This floud was his sope and nitar to scoure of the filth, to seuer the good from the euill, the wheat from the chaffe. He brought the floud upon the ungodly, but he "saued Noah, the eighth person;" a small number, a child may tell them, a poore number, *pauperi est numerare,* but eight persons saved. Those tymes were euil, but there are worse dayes not instant but extant, wherein iniquitie prescribes hypocrisie, settes hir hand to manie false bills, settes downe one hundred for ten, the whole is overflowne with all wickednes, &c. The second part is God's mercy, but he "saued Noah" like a ring on his finger, he kept him as writing in the palme of his hand, as the apple of his eye, and as a scale on his heart. He built him a castle stronger then brasse, and lockt him up in the arke like a jewell in casket. He preserved him safe in a wodden vessell amongst the toppes of mountains, in a world of waters, without card, taclcing, or pilot. He was saued between judgment and judgment, like Susanna betwixt the twoe elders, like the Children of Israell betweene two walles of water in the Red Sea, like Christ betweene the two theiues; soe that it may be truly sayd, it was noe meaner a miracle in sauing Noah, then in drowning the whole world.

But "saued Noah, the eight person, a preacher of righteousnes." Here is a banner of hope to all that feare God. When Justice was running hir course like a strong giant to haue destroyed the whole world, Mercy mett, encountered, and told hir that she must not touch Gods anoynted, nor doe his prophetes anie harme. There was Noah, "a preacher of righteousnes," and he must be spared, he was a preacher, not a whisperer in corners, singing to himselfe and his muses. This Noah was the hemme of the world, the remnant of the old, and the element of the newe: he was

communis terminus, the first shipwright, and yet "a preacher of righteousnes." Nowe concerninge the estimacion of preachers in auncient
tymes, and the contempt of that calling in these dayes, their high account
with God, and their neglect with men, from hence he said he could
paradox manie conclusions which tyme forced him to ouer slip. But in
this age lett a preacher be as aunciently discended and of as good a parentage, bee as well qualified, as soundly learned, of as comely personage, as sweete a conversation, have a mother witt, and perhaps a
fathers blessing to, lett him be equall in all the giftes and ornamentes of
nature, art, and fortune to a man of an other profession, yet he shall be
scorned, derided, and pointed at like a bird of diuers strange colours, and
all because he beares the name of a preacher.

Tymes past were so liberall to the clergy that for feare all would have
runne into their handes there were statutes of mortmaine enacted to re-
strayne that current : but devotion at this day is grown soe cold, that the
harts and hands of all are a verry mortmaine it self; they hold soe fast
they will part from nothing ; noe, not from that which hath bin of auu-
cient given to holie uses. There are in England aboue 3000 impropria-
cions, where the minister hath a poore stipend ; their bread is broken
amongst strangers, the foxes and their cubbes liue in their ruines, the
swallowe builds hir nest and the satyres daunce and revill where the
Leuites were wont to sing, the Church liuings are seised vpon and possessed by the secular ; it was the old lawe, that none should eate the bread
of the aultar but those that wayted at the altar, those things which were
provided for the pastors of our soules, with what conscience can they
receive, which are not able to feede them. *O miseram sponsam talibus
creditam paranymphis.*

fo. 50ᵇ.
October, 1602.

It is strange that that abhominable synn of Symony should be so common, that it is no strang thing for a learned man to purchase his promo-
tion ; but the honest must say to their patron, as Paule to the lame, *aurum
et argentum non habeo, quod habeo dabo.* I will liue honestly, I will preach
diligently, I will pray for you deuoutly, but that *quid dabitis* liveth still
with those of Judas his humor. They thinke all to much for the preacher,
nothing to much for themselves ; it must be enacted tha' they may not
haue to much for feare of surfetting ; they would haue them, according to
the newe dyet, brought downe to the skin and bone, to cure them. "All

their speaches and actions tend to our impouerishment," saith he, " as though wee were onely droanes and they the bees of the State. The Lord commaunded to bring into his tabernacle, but these strive whoe may carry out fastest, and blesse themselves in the spoile, saying with that Churche robber, *Videtis quam prospera nauigatio ab ipsis dijs immortalibus sacrilegis detur*, but the hier of these labourers, this field of Naboth, &c., will cry out against them. Christ, when he was vpon the earth, wipped those out the Church which bought and sold in the Church, what will he doe with those which buy and sell his church itselfe? I speake not this, because I would perswade you to give your goodes unto ns; *non vestra, sed vos*, nay, *non nostra sed vos, quero*. I doe but advertise you to consider whether the withholding the tenth may not depriue you of the whole, the spoiling the Churche of hir clothes may not strip you of your living, the impropriating hir benefices may not dispropriat the Kingdome of Heaven to you.

" A preacher of righteousnes " or a righteous preacher, such a one as Jo. Baptist was; he preached, as all ought to doe, by his lyfe, by his hands. By his lyfe; *vel non omnino vel moribus doceto*. He preached amendement from synn, he preached the lawes of nature and the judgments imminent, and as some thinke he preached Christ alsoc. And wee preache the lawe of nature : doth not nature teache you, &c. Wee preache faythe : then being justified by faythe. Wee preache the lawe of

Moses: Christ came not to breake but to fulfill the lawe. We preach righteousnes, *semen et germen*, embued, endued, active, and contemplative, justificacion and sanctificacion, primitiue and imputed, the one in Christ absolute, the other in us. Righteousnes acted by Christ and accepted by us, which is the true justifying rightcousnes, and abouc all the others.

The third example of Sodome and Gomorrhe. They were not condemned onely, but condemned to be ouerthrowne, and soe ouerthrowne that they should be turned, not into stones which might come togither againe, but into ashes; neither soe onely, for there had bin some mitigacion, yf they might soe have perished that they should not haue bin remembred, but they must be an example to all posteritle. Their remembraunce must not dye.

The cuntry is said to have bin a verry pleasaunt and fruitfull soyle, but *terra bona, gens mala fuit*, and therefore it was destroyed with fyre from a seven tymes hotter myne then that seven times heated ouen. It was hell-fyre out of heaven, fire from coales that were neuer blowne, it rayned fyre. As Kayne was sett as a marke to take heede of bloudshed, soe are those places an example to the ungodly; there remaines untill this day such a noysom water that some call it the Diuels Sea; others the Sea of Brimstone, for the ill savour; the Dead Sea, for noe fishe can liue in it, soe foule that noe uncleane thing can be clensed in it, soe thicke a water that nothing can sinke into it. There are certaine apples fayre to the eye which being touched *in fumum abeunt, tanquam ardent adhuc, et olet adhuc incendio terra.* There is seen a cloud of pitche and heapes of ashes at this daye, their woundes are not skinned ouer, they appeare for ever.

fo. 52.
October, 1602.

"And deliuered just Lott." The word signified a kinde of force, as though he had pulled him out; here is Lottes commendacion that he liued amongst the wicked, and was not infected with them; *bonum esse cum bonis non admodum laudabile; nihil est in Asia non fuisse, sed in Asia continenter vixisse, eximium.* Soe was Abraham in Chaldea, Moses in the Court of Pharao, and yet noe partakers of the synnes of those places, "vexed with the uncleane conversacion." *Non veniat anima mea in consilium eorum!* The justice of Lott was professed enmity with the wicked. When Martiall asked Nazianzeene but a question, Nazianzeene told him he would not answere *nisi purgatus fuerit.* Wee must not say soe much as "God saue them!" to the wicked. But our stomakes are to strong; wee can digest to be drunke for companie, to rend the ayre with prodigious oathes in a brauery, but not rend our garmentes in contrition of heart; wee can telle howe to take 10 in the 100, nay 100 for 10, with a secure conscience; this syhne of usury is a synn against nature, like the synn of Sodome. Wee will dissemble with the hyppocrite, temporise with the politician, deride with the atheist. Men thinke nowe a dayes that Arrianisme, Atheisme, Papisme, Libertinisme, may stand togither, and like salt, oyle, and meale be put togither in a sacrifice. Their conscience is sett in bonde, like Thamar when shee went to play the harlott. They had rather haue the shrift of a popishe priest then heare the holsome admonicion of a preacher; they have Metian, Suffetian myndes; *Vertumni, Protei;* any relligion, every relligion will serve their turne. Rome, that second Sodome, which still battlith our Church and relligion, lett it charge hir

fo. 52ᵇ.
October, 1602.

wheirein the Gospel hath offended this 44 yeares, and at last it will appeare all hir fault wilbe noe more but innocence and true godlines.   *Est
mihi supplicii causa fuisse piam*, &c.

God's mercy in particuler to our nation, in prosperity, in trade, auoy-
daunce of forrein attempts, appeasing of inbred treasons and dissensions,
&c. soe that wee may say these 44 yeares of hir Majesties happie government is the kalender of earthly felicity wherein the Gospell hath growne
old, yf not to old to some which begin to fall out of love with it, but were
it as newe as it was the first day of hir Majesties entraunce, wee should
hear them cry " Oh, howe beautifull are the feete of those that bring glad
tydyngs of salvacion !"   *Eamus in domum Domini*, &c.   And lett us pray
to Christ that, as the Evangelist writes he did, soe the Gospell may
crescere ætate et gratia.

" The rule followeth," saith he, " which I promised, but tyme and order
must rule me.   It is but the summe of the examples, it is the same liquor
that ranne from those spouts and is nowe in this cysterne.   It runnes like
that violl in the Gospell with wyne and oyle, wherewith Christ cured the
wounded travailer; it runnes like Christes syde, with water and bloud,
judgment and mercy; punishment and comfort," &c.

Consciencia est coluber in domo, immo in sinu.

fo. 53.
28 October,
1602.
In the Chequer, Mr. Crooke,[1] the Recorder of London, standing
at the barr betweene the twoe Maiors, the succeeding on his right
hand, and the resigning on his left, made a speache after his fashion,
wherin first he exhorted the magistrates to good deserts in regard of
the prayse or shame that attends such men for their tyme well or
ill imployed; then he remembered manie hir Majesties fauours to the
Citie, their greate and beneficiall priviledges, their ornaments and
ensignes of autoritie, their choise out of their owne Companies, &c.
" Great, and exceeding great," said hee, " is hir Majesties goodnes
to this City," for which he remembred their humble due thanke-

---

[1] Afterwards Sir John Croke, Recorder of London from 1595 to 1603. Speaker of the
House of Commons in 1601, and a Judge of the King's Bench under James I. (Foss's
Judges, vi. 130.)

fulnes; next he briefly commended the resigning Sir Jo. Jarrett, [1]
saying that his owne performances were speaking wittnesses for him,
and the succeeding, for the good hope, &c.: and then, showing howe
this maior, Mr. Lee, had bin chosen by the free and generall assent
of the Citye, he presented him to that honourable Court, praying
their accustomable allowaunce.

The Lord Chief Baron Periam comended the Recorders speache,
and recommended hir Majesties singular benefits to their thankefull
consideracions, admonished that their might be some monethly strict
searche be made in the Cytie for idle persons and maisterles men,
whereof there were, as he said, at this tyme 30,000 in London;
theise ought to be found out and well punished, for they are the very
scumme of England, and the sinke of iniquitie, &c.

The Lord Treasuror, L. Buckhurst,[2] spake sharpely and earnestly,
that of his certaine knowledge there were two thinges hir Majestie
is desyrous should be amended. There hath bin warning given often
tymes, yet the commaundement still neglected. They are both
matters of importaunce, and yf they be not better looked vnto the
blame wilbe insupportable, and their answere inexcusable. The
former is, nowe in this time of plenty to make prouision of corne to
fill the magazines of the Citie, as well for suddein occasions as for
prouision for the poore in tyme of dearth: this he aduised the maior
to have speciall care of, and to amend their neglect by diligence,
while their fault sleepes in the bosome of hir Majesties clemency.
The other matter was the erecting and furnishing hospitals. Theise
were thinges must be better regarded then they have bin: otherwise,
howesoever he honour the Cytie in his priuat person, yet it is his
dutie in regard of his place to call them to accompt for it.

fo. 53ᵇ.
28 October
1602.

---

[1] Sir John Garrett or Garrard.
[2] Thomas Sackville, poet and statesman; Lord Buckhurst, 1567—1604, Earl of Dorset,
1604—1608, and Lord Treasurer, 1599—1608.

fo. 54.   Thou carest not for me, thou scornest and spurnest me, but yet,
27 Oct. 1602. like those which play at footeball, spurne that which they runne
after. (*Hoste to his wife.*)

Wee call an hippocrite a puritan, in briefe, as by an ironized
terme a good fellow meanes a thiefe. (*Albions England.*)

He lives by throwing a payre of dice, and breathing a horse
28.   sometyme, *i. e.* by cheatinge and robbinge. (*Towse nar.* [*?*]).

In Patres Jesuitas.
> *Tute mares vitias, non uxor, non tibi scortum,*
> *Dic Jesuita mihi, qui potes esse pater ?*

When there was a speach concerning a peace to be made with
Spayne, a lusty cauallier at an ordinary swore he would be hangd
yf there were a peace with Spaine, for which words he was sent
for to the Court, and chargd as a busie medler, and a seditious fellowe; he aunswered, he meant noe such matter as they imagined;
but he ment plainely that because himselfe was a man of armes, yf
wee should haue a peace he should want employment, and then
must take a purse, and soe he was sure he should be hanged yf there
were a peace with Spaine. (*Mr. Gorson.*)

One said the Recorder was the mouth of the Cytie; then the City
hath a black mouth, said Harwell, for he is a verry blacke man.

fo. 54ᵇ.   OCTOBER 31. AT PAULES

Dr. Dene [?] made a Sermon against the excessiue pride and vanitie of
women in apparraile, &c., which vice he said was in their husbands power
to correct. This man the last tyme he was in this place taught that a
man could not be divorced from his wife, though she should commit
adultery.
He reprehended Mr. Egerton, and such an other popular preacher, that

their auditory, being most of women, abounded in that superfluous vanity of appa[raile].

AT THE TEMPLE CHURCH

One Mr. Irland, whoe about some three yeares since was a student of the Middle Temple, preached upon this text : " Thy fayth hath saued the, goe thy waye in peace."

The Persians had a lawé, that when any nobleman offended, himselfe was neuer punished, but they tooke his clothes, and when they had beaten them they gave them vnto him againe; soe when mans soule had synned, Christ took our flesh upon him, which is as it were the apparaile of the soule, and when it had been beaten he gave it us againe.

In the afternoone Mr. Marbury of the Temple, text xxi. Isay. 5 v. &c. But I may not write what he said, for I could not heare him, he pronunces in manner of a common discourse. Wee may streatche our eares to catch a word nowe and then, but he will not be at the paynes to strayne his voyce, that wee might gaine one sentence.

I love not to heare the sound of the sermon, except the preacher will tell me what he says. I thinke many of those which are fayne to stand without dores at the sermon of a preacher whom the multitude throng after may come with as greate a deuotion as some that are nearer, yet I beleeve the most come away as I did from this, scarse one word the wiser. *fo. 55.* *Octob. 1602.*

↘ A preacher in Cambridge said that manie in their universitie had long beards and short wittes, were of greate standing and small vnderstandinge; the world sayth *Bonum est nobis esse hic,* and *Soluite asinum,* for the Lorde hath neede of him; the good schollers are kept downe in the vniuersitie, while the dunces are preferred. (*Cosen Willis narr.*) *fol. 55ᵇ.* *1 Nov. 1602.*

One Clapham, a preacher in London, said the diuell was like a fidler, that comes betymes in the morning to a mans windowe to call him vp before he hath any mynde to rise, and there standes scraping a long tyme, till the window opens, and he gets a peece of syluer, and then he turnes his backe, puts up his pipe and away; soe the diuel waites in Gods presence till he hath gotten some imployment, which he lookt for, and then he goes from the face of God.

2.   Suspicion is noe proofe, nor jealousy an equall judge.

1.   Dr. Withers, a black man, preached in Paules this day, his text Mark ix. 2, &c.

Of the transfiguracion of Christ : whereby, first, we learne to contemne earth and the pleasure thereof, in regard of the heauenly glory wee shall receiue. 2ndly. by the hope of this glorie the paynes of this lyfe are eased. 3dly. by this transfiguracion of Christ wee are taught that he suffered the indignitie of the Crosse not by imposed necessitie, but of his owne good will and pleasure.

In that he tooke but three disciples it may be collected that all thinges are not at the first to be published to all men, but first to some fewe and after to others.

fo. 56.   He tooke them vp into a mountaine, to shewe their thoughtes and hopes
1 Nov. 1602. must be higher then the earth; lifted vp to the heauens like a cloud. The mountaine was high and alone. Two principall points of regard in a fortificacion ; that it be difficult of accesse, and far from an other that may annoy it. The glory of Christ's kingdome is hard to be attayned, the way is steepe and high, *facilis descensus Averni, sed revocare gradum superasque euadere ad auras, hic labor, hoc opus est,* and it can not be equalled by anie.

The lyfe of a Christian is like Moses serpent, which was terrible to looke vpon in the forepart, but take it by the tayle and it became a rodd to slay him; soe yf we consider onely the present miseries of this lyfe, which usually accompanied a true Christian, it would terrifie a man from the profession; but take it by the tayle, looke to the ende and glory that wee hope for, and it is lyfe incomparably most to be desyred.

Paule sayth our body shall rise a spirituall body, not a body that shalbe a spirit, for spirits are noe bodies : but a body glorious, nimble, incorruptible as a spirit.

"At that day," sayth the Prophet, "the moone shall shine as the sunne, and the sunne shall be seven times as bright ;" the unconstant condicion of man is compared to the moone, and Christ is the sunn of righteousnes, &c.

Christ carried them into a mountayne apart, for commonly the multitude is like a banquet whether every one brings his part of wickednes and vice, and soe by contagion infect one an other.

fo. 56^b.
Nov. 1602.

It was a wonder howe the glorious diuinity could dwell in flesh, and not showe his brightnes; but it was the pleasure of the Almightie to eclipse the splendor with the vayle of our body, but here like the sunne out [of] a cloud he breaketh forth, and his glory appeareth.

Barker told certaine gent. in the buttry that one of the benchers had sometime come downe for a lesse noyse: "Soe he may nowe too, I think," said Whitlocke, "for I thinke he may finde a lesse noyse anie where in the house then here is."

fo. 57.
4 Nov.

Mrs. Gibbes seing a straunger's horse in their yard, asked a thrasher, "Whose horse?" He told hir. "Wherefore comes he?" "Wherefore should he come," said he, "but to buy witt?" (viz. a clyent to the counsellor.) (Mr. Gibbes.)

5.

*   *   *   *   *

Mr. Curle told me he heard of certaine that Mr. Cartwright[1] comming to a certaine goodfellowe that was chosen to be Maior of [a] towne, told him soe plainely, and with such a spirit, of his dissolute and drunken life, howe vnfit for the office to governe others when he could not rule himselfe, &c. that the man fell presently into a swound, and within thre dayes dyed. Whether Cartwrightes vehemency, the manes conceit, or both wrought in him, it was verry straunge. Happened in Warwickshire.

5.

---

[1] Qu. Thomas Cartwright, the leader of the Puritans. He was at this time master of a hospital at Warwick, where he died in 1603.

Mr. Hadsor [1] told Mr. Curle and me that he heard lately forth of Irland, that whereas on Burke, whoe followes the Lord Deputy, had obteyned the graunt of a country in Irland in consideracion of his good scruice, and this by meanes of Sir Robert Cecile, vpon Sir Robert Gardneres certificat vnder his hand, and all this after passed and perfected according to the course in the courts in Irland. Nowe of late an other Burke, one of greate commaund and a dangerous person yf he should breake out, hearing of this graunt, envyed, grudged, and vpbrayded his owne deserts, intimating as much as yf others of meaner worth were soe well regarded and himselfe neglected, he ment perhaps to give the slip and try his fortune on the other party. The Lord Deputy having intelligence hereof, and foreseeing the perilous consequence yf he should breake out, sent for the otheres patent, as desyrous to peruse the forme of the graunt, but when he had it he kept it; and, upon aduise with the Counsaile, cancelled both the patent and the whole record, to preuent the rebellion like to ensue upon the graunt. A strange president.

Sir Robert commends none but will be sure to haue the same under the hand of some other, on whome, yf it fall out otherwise then was suggested or expected, the blame may be translated. (*Idem.*)

He told further that Mr. Plowden [2] had such a checke as he neuer chanced [?] of, for saying to a circumuenting justice of peace, upon demand made what were to be done in such a case, that by the lawe neither a justice nor the counsell could committ anie to prison without a cause, vpon their pleasure.

---

[1] Richard Hadsor, of the Middle Temple, occurs frequently among the State Papers of James I. and Charles I. as a person in communication with the government on Irish affairs. We shall find further particulars respecting him hereafter.

[2] Probably Edmund Plowden, the author of the Reports, whose connection with the Middle Temple is commemorated by a range of buildings which bears his name.

Mr. Gardner of Furnivales Inne told howe that Mr. King, preacher at St. Androes in Holborne, beinge earnestly intreated to make a sermon at the funerals of [a] gent. of their house, because the gent. desyred he should be requested, made noe better nor 'other aunswer, but told them plainely he was not beholding to that house nor anie of the Innes of Chauncery, and therefore would not. He is greived it seemes because the gents. of the Innes come and take up roomes in his churche, and pay not as other his parishioners doe. He is soe highly esteemed of his auditors, that when he went to Oxeford[1] they made a purse for his charges, and at his return rode forth to meete him, and brought him into towne with ringing, etc.

fo. 53.
3 Nov. 1602.

6. I heard that the Earl of Northumberland liues apart againe from his lady nowe shee hath brought him an heire, which he sayd was the soder of their reconcilement; he liues at Sion house with the child, and plays with it, being otherwise of a verry melancholy spirit.[2]

A gentlewoman which had bin to see a child that was sayd to be possessed with the diuel, told howe she had lost hir purse while they were at prayer. "Oh," said a gent. " not vnlikely, for you forgott halfe your lesson; Christ bad you watch and pray, and you prayed onely; but, had you watched as you prayed, you might have kept your purse still." (*W. Scott nar.*)

---

[1] He was of Christ Church. The occasion alluded to was perhaps on his proceeding D.D., which he did in this year, 1602. Wood says that he had so excellent a volubility of speech that Sir Edward Coke would often say of him that he was the best speaker in the Star Chamber in his time. (Ath. Oxon. ii. 295.)

[2] Henry, the ninth Earl of Northumberland, known as the Wizard Earl, and remembered for his fifteen years' imprisonment in the Tower. His wife was Dorothy, daughter of Walter Devereux, the first Earl of Essex of that family, and widow of Sir Thomas Perrott. The child here alluded to must have been Algernon, the tenth Earl, who is stated by Collins to have been baptised on the 13th Oct. 1602. (Peerage, ed. Brydges, ii. 346.)

5. "I was muzeled in my pleading," said Mr. Martin, when he was out, and could not well open.

"He will clogg a man with a jeast, he will neuer leaue you till he hath told it." (*Of Mr. L.*)

fo. 58ᵇ. Mr. Overbury, telling howe a knaue had stolne his cloke out
November 6. of his chamber, said the villeine had gotten a cloke for his knauery.

One said of a foule face, it needes noe maske, it is a maske it selfe. "Nay," said another, "it hath neede of a maske to hide the deformitie."

I heard that Dr. Redman, Bishop of Norwiche,[1] Dr. Juel, professor at . . . . .[2] in the Low Cuntryes, and Mr. Perkins of Cambridge,[3] all men of note, are dead of late.

The preacher at the Temple said, that he which offereth himselfe to God, that is, which mortifieth and leaueth his pleasures and affection to serue God, doth more then Abraham did when he offered to sacrifice his sonne, for there is none but loues himself more dearly then his owne children.

10. The embasing of the coyne for Irland hath brought them almost to a famine, for the Queen hath received backe as muche as shee coyned; they haue none other left, and for that none will bring anie victuall vnto them. (*Mr. Curle nar.*)

I heard that the French King hath reteined the Sythers [Switzers?] for 8,000*l.* present and 3,000*l.* annuall, [and] hath sold

[1] Dr. William Redman, Bishop from 1594 until his death on 25th Sept. 1602. (Hardy's Le Neve, ii. 470.)

[2] Blank in MS. ( )

[3] William Perkins, of Christs Church, Cambridge, and minister of St. Andrew's in that town; the well-known Calvinistic divine.

divers townes to the Duke of Bulloine, whoe means to be on the part of the Archduke for them.

" I was brought up as my frends were able; when manners were in the hall I was in the stable," quoth my laundres, when I told hir of hir saucy boldnes.

Mr. Curle demaunded of Wake a marke which he layd out for him when they rede with the reader; his aunswere was he lived upon exhibicion, he could not tell whether his friends would allowe him soe much for that purpose. (*Sordide.*) fo. 59. 10 November.

Soe soone as they began to rate the charges at St. Albans awaye startes hee. " He did justly, a dog would not tarry when you rate him," said L.

Mr. Blunt, a great gamester, marvellous franke, and a blunt cauelier.

* * * * * 8.

Mr. Bacon, in giving evidence in the Lord Morleys case for the forrest of Hatfield, said it had alwayes flowne an high pitche; *i.e.* hath bin allwayes in the hands of greate men.

The first Lord Riche was Lord Chauncellor of England in Edward VI.'s tyme [1] (*Bacon.*)

* * * * *

In the Starr Chamber, when Mr. Moore urged in defense of attournies that followed suites out of their proper courts, that it was usuall and common ; the Lord Keeper said, " *Multitudo peccantium pudorem tollit, non peccatum.*" 12.

" Ha ! the divel goe with the," said the Bishop of L. to his boule when himselfe ran after it. (*Mr. Cu.*)

" Size ace will not, deux ace cannot, quater tree must," quothe fo. 59b. November, 1602.

---

[1] Robert Lord Rich, Lord Chancellor from 1547 to 1551.

Blackborne, when he sent for wine ; a common phrase of subsidies and such taxes, the greate ones will not, the little ones cannot, the meane men must pay for all.

The old Lord Treasurors witt was as it seemes of Borrowe English tenure, for it descended to his younger sonne, Sir Robert.

A nobleman on horsebacke with a rable of footmen about him is but like a huntsman with a kennell of houndes after him.

     *   *   *   *   *

The Dutch which lately stormed the galleys which our ships had first battered, deserve noe more credit then a lackey for pillaging of that dead body which his maister had slayne. (*Sir Robert Mansell.*)

Sequitur sua pœna nocentem.

Bacon said that the generall rules of the lawe were like cometes, and wandring stars. Mr. Attorney [Coke] said rather they were like the sunne; they have light in themselves, and give light to others, whereas the starrs are but *corpora opaca.*

The Attorney said he could make a lamentable argument for him in the remainder that is prejudiced by the act of the particular tenant; but it would be said of him as of Cassandra, when he had spoken much he should not be believed.

A difference without a diuersitie, a curiosity.

Vennar, a gent. of Lincolnes, who had lately playd a notable cunnicatching tricke, and gulled many under couller of a play to be of gent. and reuerens, comming to the court since in a blacke suit, bootes and golden spurres without a rapier, one told him he was not well suited; the golden spurres and his brazen face uns[uited?]

fo. 60.
November,
1602.

A vehement suspicion may not be a judicial condemnacion: the Lord Keeper said he would dimisse one as a partie vehemently suspected, then judicially condemned [*sic*].

The callender of women saynts was full long agoe.

* * * * *

A womans love is river-like, which stopt doth overflowe,
But when the river findes noe lett, it often runnes too lowe.

An hypocrite or puritan is like a globe, that hath all in *conuexo*, nihil in *concauo*, all without painted, nothing within included. (*Mr. Curle.*)

14.

About some three yeares since there were certayne .rogues in Barkeshire which usually frequented certaine shipcoates every night. A justice having intelligence of their rablement, purposing to apprehend them, went strong, and about midnight found them in the shipcoate, some six couple men and women dauncing naked, the rest lying by them ; divers of them taken and committed to prison. (*Mr. Pigott.*)

Posies for a jet ring lined with sylver.

" One two :" soe written as you may begin with either word.

" This one ring is two," or both sylver and jet make but one ring; the body and soule one man; twoe frends one mynde.

" *Candida mens est*," the sylver resembling the soule, being the inner part.

" *Bell' ame bell' amy*," a fayre soule is a fayre frend, &c.

" Yet fayre within."

" The firmer the better;" the sylver the stronger and the better.

Mille modis læti miseros mors una fatigat.

* * * * * 1

Yf foure or five assist one which kills another, the lawe sayth

---

¹ We have here ventured to omit seven pages of extracts from an academical oration by Thomas Stapleton the controversialist, " *An Politici horum temporum in numero Christianorum sint habendi*," printed among his works.

they shall all be hanged, because they have deprivd the Queene of a subject; but is this a way to preserve the Queens subjects, when there is one slayne already, to hang up four or five more out of the way? ' Is this to punishe the fact or the State? (*Benn.*)

16.

Goe little booke, I envy not thy lott,
Though thou shalt goe where I my selfe cannot.

18.

One would needes knowe of a philosopher what reason there was that a man should be in love with beauty ; the other made noe other answer, but told him it was a blind mans question. Soe one wondered what sweetenes men found in musicke they were soe much delighted in, an other said it was but the doubt of a deaf man, &c.

" *Flumen orationis, micam vero habuit rationis,*" hee had a streame of wordes, but scarce a drop of witt.

Beauty more excellent then many virtues, for it makes itselfe more knowne : noe sooner seene but admired, whereas one may looke long enough upon a man before he can tell what virtue is in him, untill some occasion be offered to shew them.

23.

Captaine Whitlocke, a shuttlecock: flyes up and downe from one nobleman to an other, good for nothing but to make sport, and help them to loose tyme. [1]

**fo. 65.
14 November,
1602.**

DR. DAWSON *of Trinity in Cambridge,* AT PAULES CROSSE.

His text, vii. Isay. 10. All the while he prayed he kept on his velvet night cap untill he came to name the Queene, and then of went that to, when he had spoken before both of and to God with it on his head.

Yf Godes words will not move us, neither will his workes. If *dixit* will not perswade, neither can *fecit* induce us.

A regall not a righteous motive.

Puts on the visard of hypocrisie.

Omne bonum a Deo bono, as all springs from their offspring the sea.

[1] See page 60.

Judge the whole by part, as merchants sell their wares, the whole butt by a tast of a pint, &c.

Jobs patience compared to Gods not soe muche as a drop to the sea, or a mote to the whole earth.

Sinfull man approching Gods presence is not consumed as the stuble with the fyre, because man is Gods worke, and Gods mercy is ouer all his workes.

What will you make me like unto, or what will you make like unto me, saith God.

Scriptura discentem non docentem respicit, and therefore penned in a plaine and easie manner.

Essentia operis est potentia creatoris. Here he stumbled into an invective against contempt of ministers, and impoverishing the clergy. Pharoes dreame is revived, the leane kine eate up the fatt, and were never the fatter. Laymens best liuings were the Church livings ; yet the gentry come to beggery.

Magnum solatium est magnum supplicium a magno impositum; but intollerable when the basest make it their cheife grace to disgrace the ministers.   fo. 65^b. *[fo. 65ᵇ.]* 14 November, 1602.

Christ calls them the light of the world, and they are the children of darknes that would blowe it out.

Pride is a greate cause of unthankefullnes, when he shall thinke *omne datum esse tuum officium et suum meritum.*

Bishop Bonner made bonefires of the bones of saints and martyres in Queen Maries days.

Praysd our happy gouernment for peace and religion ; and soe ended.

Though a fashion of witt in writing may last longer then a fashion in a sute of clothes, yet yf a writer live long, and change not his fashion, he may perhaps outlive his best credit. It were good for such a man to dy quickly. (*Of Dr. Reynolds; Th. Cranmer.*)   fo. 66. 21 November, 1602.

Reynolds esteemes it his best glorie to quote an author for every sentence, nay almost every syllable; soe he may indeede shewe a great memory but small judgment. Alas, poore man ! he does as yf a begger should come and pouer all his scraps out of his wallet at a riche mans table. He had done what he could, might tell where he had begd this peece and that peece, but all were but a beggerly shewe. He takes a speciall grace to use an old worne sentence, as though anie would like to be served with cockcrowen pottage,[1] or a man should like delight to have a garment of shreeds. (*Cra. and I.*)

The old deane of Paules, Nowell, told Dr. Holland that he did *onerare*, not *honorare*, *eum laudibus*.

That which men doe naturally they doe more justly; subiects naturally desire liberty, for all things tend to their naturall first state, and all were naturally free without subjection; therefore the subiect may more justly seeke liberty then the prince incroach upon his liberty. (*Th. Cran.*)

Lucian, after a great contention amongst the gods which should have the first place, the Grecian challenging the prioritie for their curious workmanship, though their stuff were not soe rich, the other for the richnes of their substaunce, though they were less curious; at last he determines, the richer must be first placed, and the virtuous next. (*Th. Cran.*)

fo. 66 ᵇ.
21 Nov. 1602.

Jo. Marstone the last Christmas he daunct with Alderman Mores wiues daughter, a Spaniard borne. Fell into a strang commendacion of hir witt and beauty. When he had done, shee thought to pay him home, and told him she though[t] he was a poet. " 'Tis true," said he, " for poets fayne and lye, and soe dyd I when I commended your beauty, for you are exceeding foule."

Mr. Tho. Egerton, the Lord Keeper's sonne,[2] brake a staff gallantly

---

[1] "Cock-crown. Poor pottage. *North.*" Halliwell, Arch. Dict. i. 260.

[2] Perhaps grandson, son to Sir John Egerton, the Lord Keeper's eldest son and successor. Sir Thomas Egerton, the Lord Keeper's eldest son, died in Ireland in 1599. It may be doubtful whether the " Tho." in the MS. was not intended to be erased.

this tilting; there came a page skipping, " Ha, well done yfayth !" said he, " your graundfather never ranne such a course." (*In novitatem.*)

" His mouth were good to make a mouse trap;" of one that smels of chese-eating.

A good plaine fellowe preacht at night in the Temple Churche; his text, lxxxvi Psal. v. 11, " Teache me thy wayes, O Lord, and I will walk in thy truth."

1. Note David's wisdome in desyring knowledge before all things. 2. Our ignoraunce that must be taught. 3. Our imperfection. David was an old scholler in Gods schole, and yet desyred to be taught. 4. Thy wayes; not false decretals, &c. nor lying legends, &c.

Soe soone as the Arke came into the Temple the idol Dagon fell downe and brake its necke; when God enters into our harts our idol synnes must be cast out.

AT PAULES CROSSE

Mr. FENTON, reader of Gray's Inn. His text, Luke xix. 9, " This day is salvacion come unto this house: insoemuch as this man also is become the sonne of Abraham." This is an absolution, and a rule of it, 1. He that pronounceth the absolution is Christ; 2. The person absolued is Zachee. An example that may most move this auditorie to followe Christ; since this man was rich and a ruler of the people, whereas the most of them that followed Christ had nothing to loose; 3. The ground of his absolucion, that he was the sonne of Abraham, which he proved to Christ by his fayth, to the world by his works. He observed 5 parts : 1. The nature of the absolution, that it is a declaracion of saluacion. 2. By whom it is declared, viz. by Christ. 3. How far it extended, to Zachee and his family. 4. Upon what ground, that is, his fayth and repentaunce. 5. Howe soone, " This day."

fo. 67.
21 Nov. 1602.

Saluacion is come; wee are not able to seeke it; therefore Christ sayd, " Enter into thy fathers joy ;" for wee' are not capable that it should enter into us; but enter into that joy as the bucket into the fountayne.

Yf he should endeauour to prefix a preface for attention, he could not finde a better then to tell them he must tell them of saluation. None under the degree of an angell was thought worthie to publishe the first tydinges of it to a fewe shepheards.

Noe preacher able to giue his auditorie a tast of saluacion. It is one thing to forgive, another thing to declare forgivenes of synnes; the former is personall, and that Christ carried to heaven with him, the other ministeriall, and that he left behinde to his disciples and apostles; " Whose synnes you binde shallbe bound, whose synnes you remitt shalbe loosed."

The raysing of Lazarus, a resemblaunce of absolucion. Lazarus had layen three dayes when Christ came to rayse him ; he bad him come out; here is his voyce, which being seconded by divine power restored him to lyfe; soe the word of God preached to a synner, being seconded with divine grace, rayseth the synner.

Popishe priests and Jesuites play fast and loose with mens consciences.

Jesuites come into riche mens houses, not to bring them salvacion, but because there is something to be fisht for. Jesus and the Church wee knowe ; but whoe are these? Soe they are sent away naked and torne, like those presumptuous fellowes that would have cast out diuels in Christs name without his leaue, and the God of heaven will laugh them to scorne.

Not all poore blessed, but the poore in spirit onely; nor all rich cursed, but the riche in this world onely; for here is Zache blessed. Howsoever Christs words import a greate difficulty for rich men to enter into heauen, when, after he had compared heauen gate to a needles eye, and the rich man to a cammel, hee aunswered his disciples words, that all things are possible with God, and as though it were a miracle with men. Hardly can he runne after Christ when his hart is lockt vp in his coffer.

But the scripture tells us there is a rich Abraham in heaven, as well as a Dives in hell. Yf anie have inriched themselves by forged cauillacion lett them not despayre, for soe did Zache. Yf anie have a place that he must have vnder him as many officers as Briareus had hands, through whose hands many things may be ill carried, lett him not be discouraged, for soe had Zache. Yf anie be branded with infamie lett him yet be comforted by the example of Zache, for soe was hee, and yet became a true Christian.

Saluacion came unto Zache by a threefold conveyaunce : 1. By his riches, which to the good are sacramentes of His favor. 2. That himself being conuert, his whole family was soe; the servants and attendants are the shaddowes of their master; they moue at his motion. 3. That all his household was blessed for his sake ; such are the braunches as the roote ; the whole lumpe was made holie by the first fruits.

Thrice happie land, whose prince is the daughter of Abraham, crowning it with the sacraments of temporall blessings. Add, O Lord ! this blessing, that hir dayes may be multiplied as the starres of heaven.

To become the sonne of Abraham is to receive the image of Abraham. He hath two images, his fayth, and his workes. Imitate him : 1. In rejoycing in God, as Simeon did when he had Christ in his armes, and this joy made the burden seeme light to the lame man when he carried his bed, after Christ had cured him. 2. In hospitallitie he received angels, and amongst them God, for one was called Jehoua. 3. In de- spising to growe rich by ill meanes. Sodome could not make him rich, because he would not have it said that the diuel had made him riche.

fo. 68 b.
21 Nov. 1602.

There is none but would spend the best bloud in his body, and stretch. his verry hart strings, to be made sure of his salvacion ; but the matter is easier, you must stretch your purse-strings, and restore what you have gotten wrongefully, otherwise noe security of saluacion.

A peremptory to conclude before his premisses.

What motives to restitution. Should I propound the rigor of the lawe, you will say that is taken away by the gospell. Should I sett before you the commendable examples of such as professed restitution, you will alledge your owne imperfection—they were perfect and rare men, wee must not look for such perfection. Shall I tell you there are but four crying synnes, and this is one of them—"The syn of them that have taken from others by fraud or violence cryeth before the Lord of Hosts," as though nothing could appease but vengeance. Yet, you will say, though the syn be heynous, yet the mercy of God is over all his workes, and there is more virtue in the seede of the woman to heale then there can be poison in the serpent to hurt us. And

God forgiueth all upon repentaunce. 'Tis true God absolueth the penitent, but upon condicion that he restore the pledge that he withheld, and that which he hath robbed. But may not this be dispensed withall by the gospell? The shaddowe points at the truthe. In the v. of Numbers, 7 [v.] besides the ransom for the attonement, the goods that were deteyned must be restored. Christ resembleth the ram, &c. *Ob.* Hath not Christ paid all our debts for us? Yes, but such as thou couldst not pay thyselfe; he hath satisfied God for thy syn, and thou must satisfie thy brother for the wrong thou hast done him yf thou beest able, otherwise thou must look for noe absolucion, for without repentaunce and amendment noe absolucion, and without restitution no true repentaunce. It may be you will say you are sorry for that you have gayned wrongfully, and meane to doe soe noe more. This is noe true sorrowe nor sufficient repentaunce, for soe long as you reteine the thing, there is a continuaunce of the syn, for thou holdest that willingly which was gotten wrongfully. Surely yf a theife had taken your purse, and should tell you he were sorry, but could not finde in his heart to give you it againe, you would thinke he did but mocke you. But be not deceived, God will not be mocked. Glaunces make noe impression. There is a worldly sorrowe, and there is a godly sorrowe. Soe long as the goods are reteined *pœnitentia non agitur sed fingitur.* But *pœnitentia vera non est pœnitenda.* But you will say, yf I should make restitution I should empty manie of my bags, and make a greate hole in my lands, and this would make me sorry againe; but this is worldly. Soe there would followe a certaine kinde of shame upon restitucion; but the point is to resolve first to restore, and then doubt not but the wisdome of God will cause you to restore without shame, as the cunning of the diuel made you gett without shame.

This day. When God came to reprehend and denounce judgment against Adam in Paradise, it is sayd he walked; but when he comes with saluacion he comes with hindes feet swiftly. This day. Against procrastinacion and deferring repentaunce. It is a fearefull saying, they shall striue to enter in and cannot, because they came not soone enough; too many think they have the Spirit of God in a string, and are able to dispatch all while the bell is tolling. But God sayth, they shall cry, but I will not hear them; then they shall seeke me earely, but they shall not finde me,

Margin notes:
fo. 69.
21 Nov. 1602.

fo. 69 ʰ.
21 Nov. 1602.

because they cry and seeke too late. The example of the theife on the crosse is noe example. It was a miracle, that Christ might shewe the power of his diuinity in his greatest humiliacion: besides, the theife had moe and greater graces then manie of the disciples at that time, for some had forsaken and none durst confesse him. And besydes, he were but a desperat theife that would presume because the prince had graunted one pardon.

Outward actions of Christ point at inward and spirituall matters; the raysing of Lazarus that had bin dead three dayes was with great difficulty. Christ was fayne to cry out and grone ere he could get him up. And the disciples could not cast out the diuel that had possessed the man from his infancy. And when Christ cast him out it was with wonderfull tormentinges to the possessed; soe dangerous delay, for the difficulty to repent, syn growing as deare as old, &c.

I heard that one Daniel, an Italian, having appeached one Mow- fo. 70. bray, a Scott, of treason against his King, Mowbray challenged the 22 Nov. 1602. combat, and it was appointed to be foughten.

Lord Cheife Baron Manwood[1] understanding that his sonne had 25. sold his chayne to a goldsmith, sent for the goldsmith, willed him to bring the chayne, enquired where he bought it. He told, in his house. The Baron desyred to see it, and put it in his pocket, telling him it was not lawefully bought. The goldsmith sued the Lord, and, fearing the issue would proue against him, obtained the counsels letters to the Lord, whoe answered, "*Malas causas habentes semper fugiunt ad potentes. Ubi non valet veritas, prevalet authoritas. Currat lex, Vivat Rex*, and soe fare you well, my Lords;" but he was committ. (*Curle.*)

Take heed of your frend;
You are in the right—
Your foe strikes by day,
Your freind in the night.

[1] 1578—1603. (Foss's Judges, v. 516.)

Mr. Nichols, of Eastwell in Kent, wrote a booke which he called the Plea of Innocents;[1] wherin it seemes he hath taken vpon him the defense of Puritans more then he ought, for I heard that he is deprived, and must be degraded for it, besides imprisonment and perpetuall silence, before the High Commissioners at Lambeth.

Women, because they cannot have their wills when they dye, they will have their wills while they live.

27.   Dum spero pereo. (*J. Couper's motto.*)

＊   ＊   ＊   ＊   ＊

John Sweete : wee shine to:—a companie of stars about the moone. (*His devise.*)

fo. 70ᵇ.   There were called to the bar by parliament, Shurland, Branstone,
27 Nov. 1602. Bradnum, Bennet, Gibbes, Jeanor, Rivers, Paget, Horton, and Crue.

The diuine, the lawyer, and the physicion must all have these three things, reason, experience, and autority, but eache in a severall degree; the diuine must begin with the autoritie of scripture, the lawyer rely upon reason, and the physicion trust to experience.

The happiest lyfe that I can fynd,
Is sweete content in a setled mynd.

＊   ＊   ＊   ＊   ＊

Serjeant Harris, standing on day at the common place barr with the other sergeants, and hauing scarce clients enough to hold motion,—" They talke of a call of sergeants," said he, " but for ought I can see wee had more neede of a call of clients."

[1] The title of the book is " The Plea of the Innocent: wherein is averred That the Ministers and People falslie termed Puritanes are iniuriouslie slaundered for enemies or troublers of the State." 12mo. 1602. The author, Josias Nichols, was instituted to the rectory of Eastwell in 1580, deprived 1603, but buried there May 16, 1639. Hasted's Kent, fol. edit. iii. 203.

When one said that Vennar the graund connicatcher had golden spurres and a brasen face, " It seemes," said R. R., " he hath some mettall in him."

A proud man is like a rotten egge, which swymmes above his betters.

AT PAULES,

Mr. TOLSON of Queenes Colledge in Cambridge; his text in Ephes. v. 25: "As Christ alsoe hath loved the Church, and hath given himself for hir, that he might sanctifie it."

The blessinges of God to man are infinit and exceeding gracious; many being giuen which we knowe not of, many before wee aske them, manie which wee are unthankefull for; but of all this gift is most admirable, most inestimable, Christ gave himselfe.

He considered the person giving, the party receiving.

There is noe creature soe base and little but if it be considered with reason it may shewe, as were written in greate caractars, that there is a God.

God is infinit and eternall, therefore can be but one in essence. One person doth not differ from another really in the essence of deity. Yet each person differeth really from other, and haue their proper personall operacions not common to all. Soe here Christ is said to have giuen himselfe, that is, the person of the sonne of God, perfect God and perfect man; he gave not his body, nor his soule, nor his whole humanitie onely,— for if all the creatures in the world were heaped up togither to be giuen, they were noe sufficient sacrifice to satisffie the justice of God,—but he gave himselfe, his whole person.

But two deaths of the soule, synn and eternall damnacion; to affirme that the soule of Christ suffered either were horrible blasphemie.

Woe must soe worship God as a trinity in vnity, and an vnity in trynity, otherwise we worship but our owne fastasie.

Christ was *et sacerdos et sacrificium*, he gave himselfe.

Christus totus mortuus est, non totum Christi, the whole person of Christ and both his natures suffered; his deity and soule being mortall could not, but his whole person, wherein both natures are indissolubly united. *Christus homo in terra, deus in cœlo, Christus in utroque.*

Christ not made in nor by the Virgin, but of the Virgin; therefore perfect man, not an essence of a nature above the angels but inferior to the Godhead : but the splendor or brightnes of Gods glory, the engraven forme of his person, (Hebr. i. cap.) therefore perfect God.

He gave himselfe not for all men, but for his Church; he died for all *sufficienter non efficienter;* he would have all men saued, *revelata non occulta voluntate,* or rather, as a Father sayth, *Deus vult omnes salvos fieri, non quod nullus hominum sit quem non velit salvum fieri, sed quia nemo salvus fit nisi quem velit;* he saveth whom he pleaseth, and they are saved because he will.

Christ gave himselfe for the Church, and hence growes the greate quarrell betwixt Papists and us Protestants, for, this gift being soe precious that none can be saved without it, every one is ready to intitle himselfe thereunto, and challeng his part therin; noe heretike so damnable, but would hold he was of the Churche, but the point is whether they bee what they pretend, or haue what they arrogate. And here, because, as he said, the text gaue him occasion, and he had direction from the superuisor of this sea, he spake some thinge against the common enimye.

Ecclesia, dicitur απο τοῦ εκκαλεῖν, *ab evocando,* because it is a people called from the rest to be sanctified by Christ.

fo. 72.
28 Nov. 1602.
The Church is compared unto the moone for fayrenes and to the sonne for brightnes, therefore the church is not a companie of reprobates, and idolatrous hereticks, as Rome is. Christ is not the head of such a body. Those which give him such a body doe, as the poet sayth, *humano capiti cervicem adjungere equinam,* but if they define the Church such a congregacion, the[y] may easily mainteane theirs to be one.

The Papists have a trick of appropriatinge the name of the Church to themselves onely; as they reade the Church, it is theirs dead sure; but this is but the fashion of Cresilaus of Athens, a franticke fellowe, that would board all ships that arrived, searche and take account of all things as they were his owne, when poore fellowe he was scarse worth the clothes on his backe.

The Papists call their masse a bloudles sacrifice, but yf wee look backe but [to] the late tymes before hir Majesties happie entraunce, wee may see tokens and wittnes enough, that it is the most bloudy kind that ever was invented.

Christ gave himselfe: noe virtue that is not voluntary : he gave himselfe willingly, soe saith he, "I lay downe my life, and noe man taketh it
from me," though the Jewes layd violent hands upon him, which made
them inexcusable; yet because yf he would have resisted, they could not
have effected their malice, therefore his subjection to their violence was
voluntary.

Nowe from informing your understandings, give me leave, said he, to
proceede to the reforming your wills and affections.

fo. 72ᵇ.
28 Nov. 1602.

Vses. Since Christ hath giuen himselfe for vs, such worthles creatures,
such nothings indeed, let us dedicate our soules, ourselves, our thoughts,
and actions to his service for a reasonable sacrifice. Christ gaue his whole
person for vs, wee must give our whole selues to him; not as some which
are content to be present at his seruice, but haue their myndes about
other matters; or as others which will say they haue given their mynds
to God, and serue him in their soule, though their bodies be present
where he is most dishonored, as the yong degenerat trauayler that can be
content, be present, and perhaps partaker at a masse, and yet thinke he
can be sound at the hart for all that. But wee must apply both body
and soule to Christs seruice. Most trauaylers returne, either worse men
or worse subjects; caveat in permitting to many trauailers. Some can be
content to be feruent and zealous in the halcion dayes of the gospell, as
Peter, but lett the sword, persecution, be once drawne out the[y] strait
withdrawe them selves and leaue their maister. Yf the[y] think they spie a
tempest but comming a farr of, strait they runn under hatches. Yf Judas
come with a kisse, and a companie with swordes and staues, they are
gone. All were hott and zealous against the Papist in the beginning of
hir Majesties raigne; all cold, as it were asleepe, nay dead, in these tymes.

Some slaunder the Court as though they were neuters, some the
universities as yf inclining to Popery, many looking for a tolleracion; but
whither shall wee goe? here is the word of lyfe.

MR. LAYFEILD AT ST. CLEMENTS.

fo. 73.
5 Dec. 1602.

His text, 2 Cor. iii. 7: "Whoe hath alsoe made us fitt ministers of the

Newe Testament, not of the letter, but of the spirit: for the letter killeth, but the spirit quickeneth."

He had preached heretofore of this text, and had in that sermon ob-serued out of this place that the duty of a Christian and a fitt minister are severall and distinct. Nowe he considered the object whereabout the office of a minister is imployed, which is the Newe Testament, and to this purpose he shewed the difference betwixt the Old and Newe Testa-ment, the old lawe and the newe, which consisted not onely in this (which the Papists make to all), that the newe is more plaine then the old, and that Moses was the writer of the first and Christ of the latter; but this the true essentiall difference, the old was a covenant; a mutuall sponsion and stipulacion; a promise upon condicion; something to be performed on either part. *Fac hoc*, sayth God to man, this is the lawe to be observed by man, *et vives*, and I will give thee lyfe; trust me with that. But the gospell, the Newe Testament, is a covenant absolute, like that "I have made a covenant with myne eyes," and that "I have made a covenant with David that I will not fayle :" a promise on Gods part onely, like a testament in this, that it is a free donacion without condicion precedent, all meerely of grace and favour from God. Noe merit from us. When he assended he gave gifts unto men.

When man had entered into covenant with God, and by breaking of it became soe farre his debtor that he had forfayted body and soule for his synn, God dealt mercifully with him, and tooke a sacrifice of some living beast as a bond which deferred, not satisfied, the debt, and this to con-tinue till Christs comming, whose death should be a discharge of that obligacion, and the whole debt alsoe for soe manie as could obtaine Christs favour.

fo. 73 ᵇ.
5 Dec. 1602.
In the afternoone, the same man at the same place. After a briefe recapitulacion of what he had deliuered in the forenoone, he proceeded to shewe the office of a minister of the Newe Testament, with the difference betweene the preists of the Old and the ministers of the Newe Testament. The office of those was to teache the covenant, to denounce the curse, and to take sacrifices of synners as obligacions and testimonies against the synner that he had soe often forfayted his soule and body ; the office of

the minister of the New Testament is to preache both the lawe to deject and humble the synner by the operacion of the spirit; and the gospell to rayse and comfort him, that he may not despayre and dye, but beeleeve and be saved; their office is alsoe as executors of Christs testament to dispose of his legacyes, his promises; that is, to remitt synnes to every penitent beleeving synner; and lastly, to impart and confirme the graces by ministring his blessed sacraments.

The letter killeth, for that sayth in the lawe, Thou must doe this, thou must not doe that, otherwise God must be satisfied; thou must be punished, or els thou must have pardon. Man could not obserue them; man was not able to abide the punishment—was like a man in prison, could not gett forth to sue for pardon; was like a poor man deepely indebted, had noe meanes to make satisfaction. The gospell likewise in the letter sayth, Thou must repent, thou must beleeue, or els thou canst not be saued; and yet none of them is in our power. But the spirit quickeneth; that shewes vs Christ hath satisfied, and giues vs grace to beleeve it, &c.

The lawe of the Old Testament is not abolished by the Newe, but the old covenant, the condicion of the lawe, is taken awaye; for the lawe continues and hath a singular vse in the ministry of the Newe Testament, to make a synner knowe and confesse himselfe such a one, for before he finde his synnes greuous he hath noe neede of a sauiour; as Christ sayd, " I came not to call the righteous but synners to repentaunce," and " Come vnto me, all ye that are weary, and I will easye you," and " The whole neede not the physitian."

Yf the minister dispense Christs legacyes to a counterfayt and dissemblinge penitent, yet they haue done their duty. And as Christ sayd to his disciples, " When you enter into anie place, say peace be with you, and yf the Sonne of peace be not there, your peace shall returne againe vnto you."

Christ made his testament, bequeathed legacyes, made his executors the disposers of them : therefore there must be certaine markes and notes, as certaine as the names of persons to knowe the persons to whom the legacyes are bequeathed, otherwise the executors cannot knowe howe [to] dispose of them. And these markes are fayth and repentaunce, for to euery one that repenteth and beleeueth remission of syn is giuen : and

fo. 74.

5 Dec. 1602.

therefore it followeth, against the doctrine of the Church of Rome, that a man must beleeue, and knowe that he beleeueth, hath fayth and repentaunce, for that generall fayth of that church in generall is noe more but to beleeue noe [more ?] but this, that all that is in the Scripture is true, that all that beleeue shall be saued, and that noe man knoweth whether he beleeue or repent. But, on the contrarie, we hold that beleeue and fayth must be in particuler, and then such a person is become a legatary certaine in Christs testament, and capable of the disposicion of the promise.

fo. 74ᵇ; In Justice Catlines[1] tyme one Burchely brought a Replegiar
7 Dec. 1602. " *quare averia cepit et injuste detinuit,*" et declare " *quod cepit et detinuit unam vaccam,*" and soe it was recorded. After, when Meade came to argue, he pleaded this in abatement; and Burchely, perceuing the recorde was faulty, entred the words *et vitulum,* and then said there was a calfe in the case in the roll (an Essex case). Justice Catline demaunded to see the record, and, the wordes being written soe newely that they were not dry, "It is true," sayd he, "your cowe hath newly calved, for shee hath not lickt the calfe dry yet." (*Colebrand.*)

The abuse of the Statute for reforming errors in the Kings Bench, &c. hath frayed the clients from their suites, when they see they can haue noe judgment certaine or speedy.

* * * * *

Three men's opinions preferred before five, yf not all togither; as in a writt of error in the Kings Benche to reverse a judgment in the Common place. Yf there be three of one opinion to reverse, and the fourth would haue it affirmed; nowe regarding the judgment in the Common place, with this mans opinion there are five on the on syde, and but three on the other, yet those three shall prevaile.

[1] There were two contemporary Judges of this name, but this was probably the one who was Lord Chief Justice of the King's Bench from 1559 to 1574. (Foss, v. 471.)

Out of a little book intituled *Buccina Capelli in laudem Juris :*[1]
Lawe hath God for the author, and was from the beginning.

Jurisprudentia est naturæ effigies, ut Demosthenes; humanitatis initium, ut Isocrates; libertatis fundamentum, ut Anaxagoras ; recte viuendi norma, ut Diodorus ; æqui bonique ars, ut Ulpianus. Confert divitias, quibus egenos fulciant, amicos sublevent, patriam vel labentem sustineant, vel præcipitantem erigant, vel florentem augeant; honores, quibus illustrati familiam suam obscuram illustrent, novam exornent, insignem decorent, facultatem qua inquinatam improborum vitam retundant et comprimant, et optimorum optimè traductam muneribus et mercede digna et laudabili ornent et illustrent, ut majores dicantur.

Quid aliud vult sibi legis nomen quam hoc, ut velit quicquid sit insolutum ligare, quicquid dissolutum legis severitate devincire, quicquid corruptum, quicquid inquinatum, illud resecare vel resarcire. Cuidam percontanti quomodo respublica florere, et statu fælicissimo quam diutissimè permanere possit, respondet Solon, " Si illi quos fortuna ad infimam plebis sortem depresserat penderent a præscripto magistratuum, et quos fortuna ad altiorem dignitatis gradum crexerat penderent a præscripto legum."
Literis incumbunt juuenes ut fiant judices.

Scio qualis fuerim, immo qualis fuisse non deberem ; cognosco qualis sum, timeo qualis futurus sim, et magis timeo quo minus doleo; utinam magis dolerem, ut minus timerem.

Doleo quia semper dolens dolere nescio.

Quo modo nisi per dolores sanabitur, qui per delectationes infirmatur? Doce me salutarem dolorem.

Dunne [2] is undonne; he was lately secretary to the Lord Keeper, and cast of because he would match him selfe to a gentlewoman against his Lords pleasure.

On Munday last the Quoene dyned at Sir Robert Secils [*sic*] newe house in the Stran. Shee was verry royally entertained, richely presented, and marvelous well contented, but at hir departure shee

---

[1] We have not found any other trace of this "little book." It was probably a work of one of the celebrated French Protestants of the name of Cappel. (*La France Protestante*, iii. 198.)

[2] Donne the poet. His marriage to the Lord Keeper's wife's niece, the daughter of Sir George More, is a well-known circumstance in his history.

*

strayned hir foote. His hall was well furnished with choise weapons, which hir Majestie tooke speciall notice of. Sundry deuises; at hir entraunce, three women, a maid, a widdowe, and a wife, eache commending their owne states, but the Virgin preferred;[1] an other, on attired in habit of a Turke desyrous to see hir Majestie, but as a straunger without hope of such grace, in regard of the retired manner of hir Lord, complained; answere made, howe gracious hir Majestie in admitting to presence, and howe able to discourse in anie language; which the Turke admired, and, admitted, presents hir with a riche mantle, &c.

fo. 76.
12 Dec. 1602.

AT ST. CLEMENTS.

A plaine plodding fellowe, sometimes of Queenes Colledge in Cambridge, his text Heb. cap. xi. v. 8. He noted the fayth of Abraham, and the fruit thereof, his obedience; he shewed the kindes of fayth, and sayd this fayth of Abraham was not hystoricall, not miraculous, not a momentary fayth; such lasts noe longer then prosperitee, &c. but it was the true justifieng fayth, which was a firme beleife of Christs comminge, with the application of his merits. He named fayth to be the gift of God, because Abraham is said to be called. God performeth his promises in his due tyme, or in a better kind. He promiseth long lyfe to the godly: yet oftentymes he takes them away in the floure of their age, but he gives them a better lyfe for it.

Abraham went into a straunge country; therefore trauailing lawefull, soe it be either specially warranted by Gods call, or to profitt the country, not to see and bring home ill fashions, and worse consciences.

He was called, therefore euery one must [take] upon him some calling and profession, and this calling must be allowed of God; therefore the trade of stageplayers vnlawefull.

The land of promise given to Abraham for the syn of the people; lett vs leave synning least our land be given into the hand of a strange people againe, as it was sometyme to the Romans, and lastly to the Normans, for a conquest.

1 The mention of this "device" enables us to correct a little mistake of the otherwise ost careful and accurate editor of Chamberlain's Letters, temp. Elizabeth, (Camden Soc.) p. 169. The "device" was not the composition of John Davies of Hereford, but of John Davies, the future Sir John, author of the poem on the Immortality of the Soul.

AT THE BLACK FRIARS.

Mr. Egerton, a little church or chappell up stayres, but a great congregacion, specially of women. After " God be mercifull," reade after the second lesson; having sat a good tyme before in the pulpit, willed them to sing to the glorie of God and theire owne edifying, the 66 Psal. 2 part; after he made a good prayer, then turnd the glas, and to his text, Acts vii. 23, &c. Here he made a recapitulacion of that he had deliuered the last Sabboth, and soe he came to deliuer doctrines out of this text. When he had said what he thought good of it, he went to catachise; it seemes an order which he hath but newely begun, for he was but in his exordium questions; then he prayed, sung a plasme [psalm], gave the blessing, and soe an end.

He remembred out of his former text these notes, v. 17: That God performes his promises not in our tyme, but in his tyme, which is best, because he is wisest. 2. The pollicy of man folishnes with God. They may maliciously oppose themselves therein, but cannot alter his decree. 3. God makes our enimies become our frends, and causeth them to do good vnwittingly. 4. Parents ought to giue their children educacion, as well as foode and rayment, and rather bring them up in learning and trades, then proud inheritances with wronge. 5. Moses a good orator and a good warrior, mighty in wordes and in deedes, yet modest in all.

Then in his text: Not dispaire of calling, for Moses was 40 yeares old before he thought of this busines. 2. God put the motion in his heart. 3. Lawefull to protect the wronged and reproue them that doe ill, though a man be hated for his labour. 4. The good rejoyce and are glad to see the magistrate, and euery good Cristian and true subiect glad to see the principall magistrat with a gard about, as well to reward and protect the good, as to reuenge the wronged, glad like [1] one that in a hott sunshine sees a fayre leauy tree, which promiseth a shaddowe yf he be sunburnt; such is the prince to the good subject.

Those which come to sermons and goe away vnreformed are like those which looke in a glas, spie the spott in their face, but will not take the pains to wipe it off.

He defined catechising to be a breife and familiar kinde of teaching the principles of relligion, in a plaine manner by way of question and

---

[1] There is here a superfluous repetition of " glad like a glad as " in the MS.

aunswere, either publiquely by the minister, or privately by the maister or
mistres of the family. Herein noted the difference betwixt preaching and
catechising, that that is a large continued course of speache, and may
be performed onely by the minister.

It is the custome (not the lawe) in Fraunce and Italy, that yf
anie notorious professed strumpet will begg for a husband a man
which is going to execution, he shal be reprieved, and she may
obteine a pardon, and marry him, that both their ill lives may be
bettered by soe holie an action. Hence grewe a jeast, when a
scoffing gentlewoman told a gentleman shee heard that he was in
some danger to haue bin hangd for some villanie, he answered,
" Truely, madame, I was a feard of nothing soe much as you would
have begd me."   *   *   *

In England it hath bin vsed that yf a woman will beg a condemned person for hir husband, shee must come in hir smocke onely,
and a white rod in hir hand : as Sterrill said he had seen.
Montagne tells of a Piccard that was going to execution, and
when he sawe a limping wenche coming to begg him, " Oh, shee
limps ! she limps !" sayd hee, " dispatch me quickly,". preferring
death before a limping wife.

fo. 77ᵇ.
12 Dec. 1602.

J. Cooper demaunded of Nic. Girlington, whoe is lately returned
from Fraunce, what thing he tooke most delight in, in all his tra-
vail. He told him to see a masse in their churches, it was performed
with such magnificent pomp and ceremonie, in soe goodly a place,
as would make a man admire it. The Hugonots are coupt up in
barnes, as it were, in regard of the Papists churches.

I heard that Geneva is beseiged by the Duke of Savoy.

16.

Mr. Hadsor told me that the Earl of Ormonds daughter is come
to our Court, and that shee shall be married to yong Ormond, cosen
german to the old Earle, which yong man was in prison here in
Engl[and,] but is nowe to be released.

Mr. Girlington told me there was on Blackewell brought ouer as

apprehended and sent over by Sir Thomas Parry, Embassador in
Fraunce, because he had confessed under his hand that he came
from the Spanyard to murder hir Majestie or burne the Navy.

17.

Heard that certaine in ragged apparrell, offring their seruice
in the Navy, were apprehended as suspected, and found worthy
suspicion.

18.

fo. 78.
16 Dec. 1602.

I brought in a moote with Jo. Bramstone.

I was with Stowe the antiquary. He told me that a modell of
his picture was found in the Recorder Fleetewoods study, with this
inscription or circumscription, JOHANNES STOWE, ANTIQUARIUS
ANGLIÆ, which nowe is cutt in brasse and prefixed in print to his
Survey of London.[1] He sayth of it, as Pilat sayd, " What I have
written, I have written," and thinkes himselfe worthie of that title
for his paynes, for he hath noe gaines by his trauaile. He gaue me
this good reason why in his Survey he omittes manie newe monuments: because those men have bin the defacers of the monuments
of others, and soe thinks them worthy to be depriued of that memory
whereof they have injuriously robbed others. He told me that the
Cheife Citizens of London in auncient tymes were called Barons,
and soe divers kinges wrote unto them " *Portegrevio et Baronibus
suis London.*," and the auncient seale had this circumscription,
" SIGILLUM BARONUM LONDONIARUM."

18.

fo. 78ᵇ.

I heard that Dr. Smith, Master of Clare Hall,[2] is Vice Chauncellor
of Cambridge this yeare. It was told me by one of St. Johns
Colledge that Dr. Playfare[3] hath bin halfe frantike againe, and
strangely doted for one Mrs. Hammond, a gentlewoman in Kent, is
nowe well reclaimed, and hath reade some lectures since. A mad
reader for divinity! *proh pudor, et dolor !*

18 Dec. 1602.

---

[1] " *Ætatis suæ* 77, 1603.'' This now rare engraving was carefully copied by John
Swaine, and republished in the Gentleman's Magazine for Jan. 1837.

[2] Dr. William Smith, master of Clare Hall from 1598 to 1612, when he became Provost of King's College. (Hardy's Le Neve, iii. 671, 683.)

[3] Dr. Thomas Playfere of St. John's College was Lady Margaret's Professor of Divinity
rom 1596 to 1609. (Hardy's Le Neve, iii. 654.)

Mr. Perkins was buried verry neere with as great sollemnity as Dr. Whitaker.[1]

The Lord Mountjoy in Ireland will never discourse at table; eates in silence.   Sir Robert Gardner mislikes him for it, as an unsosiable quality (*Hadsor*); but great wisdome in soe captious a presence, especially being such a man as desyres to speake wisely.

Mr. Bramstone told howe he sold his bed in Cambridge.   Mr. Pym[2] sayd he did wisely, for he knewe those that kept their beds longe seldome prove riche.

21.

One Merredeth, a notable coward, when he was in field, and demaunded why he did not fight and strive to kill his enemies? He, good man, told them, he could not finde in his heart to kill them whom he never sawe before, nor had ever any quarrell with them.

fo. 79.
19 Dec. 1602.

AT PAULES.

One with a long browne beard, a hanging looke, a gloting eye, and a tossing learing jeasture; his text " Take heede of false prophets which

---

[1] " His funeral was solemnly and sumptuously performed at the sole charges of Christe College, which challenged, as she gave him his breeding, to pay for his burial ; the Vniversity and Town lovingly contending which should express more sorrow thereat.   Dr. Montague, afterwards Bishop of Winchester, preached his funeral sermon, and excellently discharged the place, taking for his text, *Moses my servant is dead*." This is Fuller's description of the honourable way in which Perkins was brought to his grave. (Holy State, ed. 1840, p. 71.)   Whitaker died in 1595, and was buried in St. John's College, whereof he was master. (Ibid. p. 53.)

[2] Doubt has existed whether Pym the statesman was a member of one of the Inns of Court. The allusion to him in our text has led to inquiries which have enabled us to place this point beyond a question. J. E. Martin, Esq. Librarian of the Inner Temple, has sent us an extract from the books of the Middle Temple, which proves that " Mr. Johannes Pym, filius et heres Alexandri Pym nuper de Brymour in comitatu Somerset, ar. defuncti," was admitted " generaliter " into the Society of the Middle Temple on the 23rd of April 1602. His relation Mr. Francis Rowse and Mr. William Whitaker were his sureties, " et dat pro fine ad requisicionem Mᵈ Gybbes, unius Magistrorum de Banco hujus hospicii, nisi, xxˢ."

come to you in sheepes clothinge, but within are rauening wolves; you shall know them by their fruits."

False prophets *qui veritatem laudant sed amant mendacia* preache truely but liue wickedly. He ran over manie heresies, and concluded still to take heede of them ; false prophets which soothe up in synn by pardons for past, and dispensacions for synn to come.

The sheepes clothing, pretended innocency, simplicity, and profitt; they come onely to teache us the auncient universall, and that relligion which our fathers lived and dyed in; that ours is scarse an hundred yeares old, received but in a corner or twoe as it were of the world.

But ours is auncient, theirs newe, all since 600 yeares after Christ, as their universall vicarage. 2. Their singing by note in the churche. 3. Their lifting up of the breade. 4. Auricular confession and universall pardon, &c.

The multitude noe signe of the churche, for Noah and his family in the old world, Lott in Sodome, &c.

fo. 79 ^b.
19.

And a true note of the true church, that it hath bin allways persecuted, and the false the persecutor. Abel slayne, &c. This cruelty the property of wolves.

His whole sermon was a stronge continued invectiue against the papists and jesuites. Not a notable villanous practise committed but a pope, a cardinall, a bishop, or a priest had a hand in it; they were still at the worst ende.

They come, they are neuer sent, they come without sending for.

In the afternoone, at a church in Foster Lane end, one Clappam, a blacke fellowe, with a sower looke, but a good spirit, bold, and sometymes bluntly witty; his text Salomon's Song, iv. ca. 3 v.: "Thy lips are like a thred of skarlett." For the exposicion of this text he said he would not doe as' many would after the fancy of their owne braine, but according to the Scripture, expound it by some other place, and that was ii. of Josua, where he findeth the same words, a skarlet thred, v. 21, " Shee bound the skarlet threed in the windowe." He told a long story of Rahab before he came to the threed ; and after almost all his sermon was some allusion to that story. Rabby Shulamo makes this comparison,

fo. 80.
19 Dec. 1602.

that the lips are said to be like a threed of skarlett, to signifie such person in the churche whose promises are performaunces, whose wordes are
workes, as the red threed was a simbole and a signe unto Rahab. Rahab
was a tauernes, and it signifies alsoe an harlot, because such kinde of
people in that country used to sell their honesty with their meate. Like
scarlett; the colour sheweth life within, as palenes death.

Joshua a type of Jesus, and the wordes the same in seuerall languages.
Moses could not bring the children of Israel into the land of promise, but
that was the office of Joshua; the lawe could not be our saviour, but
Christ is he that must bring us to heauen. Joshua sent two spies; Christ
obserued the same number, and alwayes· sent two disciples togither. 3.
What the spies undertooke and promised according to their commission
was firme and ratified by Joshua; whose synnes the disciples, and nowe
the ministers, according to their power, remitt or binde on earth, shalbe
remitted or bound in heaven.

There are enough of Rahab's profession in euery place; a man may
finde a greate many more then a good sorte. "I would not giue a penny
for an 100 of them," said he.

Rahab beleeved and shewed it by hir workes. Every one will say he
beleeues, but except he can showe it to me by his workes, I will not giue
two strawes for it; lett him carry it to the exchange and see what he can
gett for.it.

An harlot is like a pantofle or slipper at an inne, which is ready to
serue for every foote that comes.

Paule, like the spies, was lett downe out at a windowe, and ouer a city
wall too. Wee promise in babtisme to fight against Sathan; but, alas,
will some say, I finde that I haue often strooe with him, and still I finde
I goe away with some wound or other. "Be therefore comforted," sayd he,
" for these woundes are signes of your fighting."

When God deliuered his people from the Aegiptians he led them with
a pillar of light, but caste a darke cloud betwixt, "and soe the blinde
buzards," said he, "ran up and downe, they knewe not about what."

When he shewed that Salmon was the husband of Rahab, he said
" Yf anie nowe, after 44 yeares preaching, and the bible being in English,
were ignorant of that, it were a horrible shame." And here he sett downe

a posicion that none could soundly interpret or vnderstand the Scripture without genealogy, which he commended verry highly.

Of love; they wilbe at your commaundement. But you may doe it yourselfe. You shall commaund and goe without.

When Dr. Colpeper, warden of New Colledge in Oxford,[1] ex- ^{fo. 81 b.} pelled one Payne of that house for some slight offence, this Payne ^{22 Dec. 1602.} recited that verse alluding to their name.

  Pæna potest demi, Culpa perennis erit. (*Rous.*)

I tooke my journey and came to Bradborne.   24.

John Kent told me of a pretty cosenning connycatching trick of late used in London. On that was in execution for debt at the suit of a gent. that dwelt in a far country, procured one of his acquaintaunce to surmise that his creditor was deade, dyed intestate, and he the next of kin, and thereupon to procure letters of admi-nistracion, by coulour whereof he might have good opportunity to discharge the party, which was effected accordingly.

My cosen told me that the county of Kent hath compounded, by the mediacion of the justices of peace, with the Greene clothe to be discharged of the purueyors for the Queenes house for all victualls, &c. except timber and carriage, with the price of wheate raised to 20*d.* the bushell, which before was but 10*d.*, and for this to pay 2100*l.* per annum, for which the parishes rated, and East Malling at 5*l.*

We have good cardes to shew for it, said a lawyer to the old ^{27.} Recorder Fleetewood: "Well," said he, "I am sure wee have kings and queenes for us, and then you can have but a company of knaues on your syde."

I tooke my journey about my cosens busines, to have a sight of ^{fo. 82.} certaine bondes in Mrs. Aldriche handes, as executrix to hir husband, ^{29 Dec. 1602.}

[1] Dr. Martin Culpeper, warden 1573 to 1599. (Hardy's Le Neve, iii. 555.)

wherein my cosen G. Mannyngham, deceased, and his executors, &c. with William Sumner, stoode bound; which bonds, by the meanes of my cosen Mr. Watts, I had a sight of, and finde that eache of them is in 500*l.* The condicion of one of them is to pay to Mr. Aldriche during his lyfe 100*l.* yearely at severall feasts. And yf William Sumner fayle in payment, or not put in nue suretyes upon the death of anie, then to stand in force. Nowe Sumner sayth he did not pay allwayes at the day, and it is apparent that noe sureties are put in since the death of my cosen, nor since the death of one Savil an other obligor. The condicion of the other was, whereas Mr. Aldriche had deputed William Sumner to exercise his office, that he should not comitt any thing which might amount to a forfayture of the letters patents whereby Mr. Aldriche held his office, and alsoe that William Sumner should performe all covenants conteyned in a payre of Indentures bearing the same date with the obligacion, all dated the 20 of June *A° Reginæ* 37, *A° Dni.* 1595. These I was to have a sight of, that yf the legataries sue my cosen, as executor in the right of his wife, he might pleade these obligacions in barr.

I lay at my cosen Chapmans at Godmerrsham.

I dined at my cosen Cranmers at Canterbury, and by him understoode howe Mr. Sumner had submitted himselfe to the arbitrement of Mr. Rauens and another, but the arbitrators, not regarding their authority, shuffled it vp vpon a sudden betweene Mrs. Aldriche and Sumner, whereas the submission and obligacion was betweene one of Mr. Aldriches sonnes and Sumner; and soe, by their negligent mistaking, all was was voyd. The cause of controversy was, Mr. Aldriche dyed some 2 or 3 dayes before the day of payment, his widdowe executrix desyred the whole, Sumner denied all, yet, in regard that Mrs. Aldriche should cancell his bondes and make him a generall acquittaunce, he offred 20 markes, and the arbitrators gaue but 20*l.*, which Sumner refuseth to pay, and therefore the widdowe threatenes either to sue the bondes or bring an accion of accompt against Sumner for all the monies he receiued as deputy; but Sumner told me he hath generall acquittances for all accompts, except the last quarter.

This night I lay at my Cosen Watts, by Sandwich, and he rode with me the next morning to Canterbury.

Sir Wa. Rawley made this rime upon the name of a gallant, one Mr. Noel,

fo. 83.
30 Dec. 1602.

> The word of deniall, and the letter of fifty,
> Makes the gent. name that will never be thrifty. (*Noe. L.*)

and Noels answere,

> The foe to the stommacke, and the word of disgrace,
> Shewes the gent. name with the bold face. (*Raw. Ly.*)

My cosen Watts told me that the Bishop of Yorke, Dr. Hutton,[1] was esteemed by Campion the onely man of all our divines for the fathers.

That opinion which some hold that Paule did not publishe his writings till he and they were confirmed by Peter, as the head of the Apostles, is plainely everted by the 1 and 2 chapters to the Ga[lla]thians, where it is apparant that Paule withstoode and contradicted Peter, &c.

Dyned with my cosen Watts, at my cosen Cranmers in Canterbury. In discourse howe obstinate some are, that they will not confesse a fact, wherefore they were justly condemned, my cosen Cranmer remembred this story. Not long since one Keyt a Kentishe man had made [his] will, whereby he bequeathed a great legacy to one Harris, but after, being displeased, he gave out that he would

31.

---

[1] Dr. Matthew Hutton, Archbishop of York, 1595-1606. (Hardy's Le Neve, iii. 115.)

revoke his will, and Harris should have nothing, whereupon Harris, thinking to prevent his purpose, hired a thrasher to murther him. This poore knave having effected this villany began to grow resty, could not endure to worke any more, but would be maynteyned by Harris for this feate, otherwise most desperatly he threatened to reveall the matter. Thus the fellowe fedd soe long, and spent soe lavishly upon himselfe and his queanes, out of Harris's purse, that Harris, growing weary of the charge, began to thinke howe he might conceale the first by practising a second murther; which he plotted in this manner, he would invite the knave to a dynner at Maidstone, and procure some to murther him as he should come through the woodes. But the fellowe, fearing the worst (because they had bin at some hott words before) imparted his feare to his whore whome he kept, told hir that yf he were murthered shee should accuse the Harrisses, and wisht hir to looke in the bottome of his deske, and there shee should finde that would be sufficient to hang them. As he feared it happened, for he was murthered; the queane brought all to light, and those papers in his deske shewed the whole manner of the former murther of Keyt, whereupon the Harrises were indited, found gilty, and adjudged to be hanged. The former tooke it upon his death that he was guiltles of the latter murder, but the other confest it as he was tumbling from the ladder.

When certaine schollers returning from Italy were at the Bishops of Canterbury, amongst other they came about my cosen Cranmer with their new fashioned salutacions belowe the knee. He, like a good plaine honest man, stoode still, and told them he had not learned to dissemble soe deeply.

Hee told mee what dissembling hyppocrites these Puritanes be, and howe slightly they regard an oath : Rauens having a booke brought unto him by a puritane to have his opinion of it, the booke being written by B. Bilson, Rauens as he had reade it would needes be

shewing his foolishe witt in the margent, in scoffing at the booke.
When the fellowe that had but borrowed it was to carry it home again,
he swore it neuer went out of his hands.   After, when it was shewed
him what had bin written in it when himselfe could not write, he
confessed that Ravens had it; then Rauens forswore his owne hand.

fo. 84ᵇ.
7 Jan. 1602.

I came from Canterbury to Godmersham.

Cosen Jo. Chapman takes the upper hand and place of his elder
brother Drue.

Mr. Jo. Cutts, Sir John Cutts sonne and heire, was married some
two yeares since to Mr. Kemp of Wye his daughter; keepes
foure horses, foure men, his wife a gentleman and a mayde, and hath
but 200*l.* per annum in present ; mary his meate and drinke and
horse meate is frank with Mr. Kemps.   He shall be heir to Sir Henry
Cutts of Kent; is like to be worthe some 1,500*l.* per annum, after
his father and mother and Sir Henry Cutts and his ladyes death.

Stafford, that married Sir John Cutts daughter hath brought his
yonger brother to this composicion, that there is 300*l.* per annum
for his children, 200*l.* of it for his wife during hir life, and 100*l.* for
hir husband, shee to keepe hir selfe and children, he to be soe
limited because too prodigall.

fo. 85. ⎫ nil.
fo. 85ᵇ. ⎭
fo. 86.
30 Jan. 1602.

AT PAULES CROSSE.

One BARLOWE, a beardless man of Pembroke Hall in Cambridge.
After his prayer and before he came to his text, he made a large exordium after this fashion; that yf Paule sayth of himselfe that he was
amongst the Corinthians in weaknes, in feare and trembling, much more
might he say the like of himselfe : whoe was weake in deliveraunce and
methode, &c.   Yet he entreated they would not heare, as some say they
will heare, the man, but that they would regard the matter.   Of all parts of
Scripture the book of the Preacher may seeme most befitting a preacher,

wherein is lively depainted the vanity of the world and all things therein:
wherof at this time he intended to speake, but not out of the Preacher, but
out of the words of St. Paule, and those were written in the viiith chapter
to the Romans, the 19, 20, 21, and 22 verses. His distribution of this
text, or rather context as he called it, because he said it was like Christs
garment soe wouen togither that it might not be parted, was into five
points : 1. That the creature is subject to vanity, v. 20. 2d. The reason of this subjection, by reason of him which hath subdued it vnder hope.
3. That the creatures shall be delivered, and hope for deliveraunce. 4. The
effects of the subjection to vanity : every creature groneth with us, v. 22.
5. The effect of hope, the feruent desyre of the creature wayteth, &c. v. 19.
He said this place of Scripture is accounted the hardest in all Paules
Epistles. For the first, that the creature is subject to vanity, he interpreted the word by " creature " is ment, in this place, the heavens, the
fo. 86ᵇ. elements, all things made of them, or conteyned in them, except men and
angells. The vanity of the creature is in two points, 1. In the frustracion
of their end, which is twoefold, the service of God, that made them; 2d.
and the service of good men, for whom he made them. The 2d vanity,
that they are subject to corruption, not of annihilacion of matter, but de-
caying in force and virtue.

The creatures, yf they had their owne will, would destroy the wicked
and save the godly alone. As the earth would open hir mouth and
swallowe them quicke, as it did Datham and Abiram. The lyons would
devoure them, as it did the accusers of Daniel, but shutt their mouths
against the innocent. The fier would burne them, as it did those which
cast the three children into the furnace. It hath bin obserued that as well
the influence of the heauens as the fertilnes of the earth is decayed, and
that the whole world is the worse for wearing, the heavens themselves
growing old as doth a garment.

2. God hath subdued the creature, for it is he alone that maketh the
sunne shine, and powreth downe rayne as well upon the good as the bad, &c.
and the reason of this subjection is the synn of man; for all these being
created for mans vse, when he synned they were punished with him.

3. They shall be delivered from this bondage when there shalbe a newe
heaven and a newe earth ; not that the substance of these shalbe abolished,

but a newe forme and perfection added, when they shall enjoy their ends and be of religion. The elements shall melt with fyre, a comparison from mettall which is melted not to be consumed, but to be purified and put in forme. fol. 87.
Jan. 1602.

The morall uses ; 1. patiently to endure the afflictions of this life, for as thoughe the Apostle should laye them in a balance to weighe them, he sayth that the momentary afflictions of this lyfe are not worthy the waighte of glory that is layed vp for us in the life to come.

We may truely say that the afflictions of these tymes wherein we liue are not worthy the glory, for these are non, wee living in abundant prosperity and peace, but tymes of persecution may come, wherein these may be comfortable arguments; and, he said, that for ought he could see the crosse was the proper badge and cognisaunce of a Christian. There are soe many kindes of takinge; of takinge bribes, monie, gifts, &c. that there be fewe will take paynes with the creatures.

The creatures travayle togither with us, a metaphore taken from travayle with child : which is caused from syn, and is a desyre to be delivered.

When the sonnes of God shall be reuealed, *i. e.* when the number of the elect be called, for whose sake the dissolucion of the world is deferred. The Jewes must be conuerted before the world can be dissolued. He that before the dissolucion of abbies had foretold what was to happen unto them for their fault and wickednes which liued in them, yf they had thereupon repented and entred into a new course of lyfe, though this could not perhaps haue stayed their dissolucion, yet it might haue saued themselves in some better state; soo when men are foretold of the dissolucion of the world, which is hastned and caused for our synnes, though our repentaunce and amendment of lyfe cannot hinder the dissolucion, yet may it be good for ourselves. fo. 87ᵇ.

IN THE AFTERNOONE, AT ST. PETERS BY PAULES WHARFE, MR. CLAPHAM. GEN. IV. 8. fo. 88.
30 Jan. 1602.

"Yf a man doth not well, synn lieth at the dore," like a dog, sayd he, that will snap him by the shins.

By primority of birth Kaine had the inheritaunce of land, and the rule of his brother Habel. He was Lord over him, and did domineer, a title

that was used, and is allowed by all to temporall persons, but by some
fantasticall curious heads of late denied to the ecclesiasticall governors.
A sort of busie superstitious and factious braines there be, and some in
this city, that are afrayed of they know not what, would haue something
if they could tell what it ment : they are like a goose that stoopes when
it comes in at a barne dore, though it knowe not wherefore. These forsoothe
crye into the eares of those auditors that like and followe them, that there
must be noe such title as Lord given to anie ecclesiastike person, because
Christ sayd to his disciples ; " Be ye not called Lord," and " The rulers of
the Gentiles beare dominacion, but you not soe," Math. xx.   Indeede the
Scripture talkes after that manner, but not that meaning, and at last
they come out with a place, and tell the people they read, Luke xxii. 25.
" The kings of the Gentiles be called Gracious Lords, but ye shall not be

fo. 88ᵇ.
Jan. 1602.

soe :" and this they say cuts home indeede, just as a leaden sawe ; for
they may well say they reade so : but I dare say they cannot reade soe in
the Scripture, they bely Christ when they say he said soe ; he never spake
those words; it is a punishment for our synnes that wee cannot reade
right in this age.   They are unlearned malitious that reade soe.   The
word in the text originall is ενεργεται, derived of the particle εν, good,
and the other verbe εργαζομαι to worke ; in Latin they are called Bene-
factores, we may call them Good Workers, a title which the kings of the
Southerne Nations, those which Daniel describeth to be the kingdome
that stands upon black legges, when they had done some little good to
their state, they would arrogate; soe Ptolome Energetes, and soe it is
forbidden by way of arrogancy for good deedes : because the glory
must be ascribed to God.

And by their reason they might as well deny the name of Maister, and
Father, for both are forbidden, as well as the other, and soe they might
quickly be amongst the Anabaptists, and overturne all difference and
jurisdicion.   Lord is a name sometyme of place, and sometyme of
grace ; and soe the ecclesiastike may haue it as well as the temporall, for
to the temporall it is a name of place onely, but the ecclesiasticall by their
merit may haue it of grace.   Neither is it soe strange a title ; Jacob useth
it to his brother Esau, and the prophet Isay takes it, my Lord, Adoni ;
Christ acknowledged the name, and some of the Apostles did not refuse it.

"Then Kain spake to Habell ;" it is not sett downe what he said : yet some have adventured to say that he said *Transeamus in campos*, but whatsoever it was it is not here mentioned, but left to be conceived, as in iii. Gen. v. 22, least he put forth his hand [and] take alsoe of the tree of lyfe : it is left what he resolved. Not that yf Adam had tasted of the tree of lyfe that he should have liued for ever, noe more then he that receives the Sacrament vnworthily shall be a member of Christs body, but that was spoken *ironice*.

It is like he spake fayre words, being in the house in presence of his father and mother, and that he used dissembling flattering speaches to draw him to such a place where he might with aduantage execute his purpose. A common practise in this world, and an old one, you see, a Machiuilian tricke. They will match the diuel in this age, to carry fayre countenaunce to him whome they meane to overthrowe; to glose and insinuate, to offer hart roote and all, till he may take him at such a vantage that he may cutt his throate or breake his necke, a familiar fashion amongst the nobility in Court, not altogither unusuall amongst the Clergy.

And when they were in the feild Kain rose up against his brother and killed him, a pittifull and a wonderfull matter, will some say, that God will suffer the wicked thus to murther the good; pittifull indeed, but not wonderfull, for the synnes of the best have deserved greater punishment.

A strang thing those which were soe great frends, went arme in arme, nowe mortall enimies upon the suddein. A maruelous strang thinge that he should knowe he could kill his brother, that he could dy, for he never sawe any man dye before; but manie things are done, both good and evil, by a secret instinct whereof a man sawe no reason til after the thing performed, as Moses when he slewe the Agyptian.

Murder an auncient synn, the first open offence after the fall that was committed in the world. Here a notable pollicy of the diuel to have dammed up Gods glory and mans relligion, both at once.

Noe murderer at this day but is guilty of this murder of Kain, and all since, since iniquity is sayd to be a measure which every synner in his kinde by adding his synne striues to make full, and soe assents to all before acted, like a conjuror that subscribes with his bloud.

"Where is Habel thy brother ?" The Lord careth for the righteous.

"Whoe answered, I cannot tell." He flaps God in the mouth with a ly at the first word, a generall rule that after murder lying followeth, they are links togither, ahd commonly noe syn committed but a lye runnes after : for none is soe impudent to confesse it, euery one would have the face of virtue.

"Am I my brothers keeper?" See a Kings sonne, the heir of the world, what a lob [1] it is! Howe like a clowne, a clunche,[2] an asse, he aunswers. A synner is the verryest noddy of all. This Kain was the verriest duns in the world. He thought to have outfact God with [a] ly, and then would excuse it; "Am I my brothers keeper?" I marry art thou, as thou wast
fo. 90.   his brother in love, his elder in government, as the prince is the keeper of his people, the minister of the congregacion, every one of an other! The greate ones would keep the minister poore and beggerly that they might not tell them of their faults, but stopp the preists mouth with a coate or a dynner; "but," sayd he, "the diuel take dynners giuen to such a purpose!"

fo. 90ᵇ.   The Papists make a forril [3] [?] of the Scripture; they souc up the
30 Jan. 1602· mouth of it. (*Clapham the other Sunday, as Mr. Peter* [?] *told me.*)

Scottish taunts.

> Long beardes hartles,
> Painted hoodes wittles,
> Gay coates gracelles,
> Makes England thriftles.[4]

5 February.   Mr. Asheford told me these verses under written are upon a picture of the nowe Lord Keeper, Sir Thomas Egerton, in the Lord

---

[1] Lob, a clown, a clumsy fellow. (Halliwell's Archaic Dict.)

[2] Clunch, a clod-hopper. (Halliwell.)

[3] This word in the MS. is somewhat blotted and in consequence doubtful. The "forel" was the cloth or canvas covering in which it was at one time customary to wrap up a book; see Prompt. Parvulorum, p. 171. Mr. Way there gives a quotation from Horman, who says "I hadde leuer haue my boke sowed in a forel than bounde in bourdis."

[4] Camden prints these lines in his Remaines (ed. 1637, p. 194) and assigns them to the reign of Edward III. They have since been quoted in many places, and frequently assigned to the Scots, although Camden does not give them that origin.

Chief Justice Pophams lodging: —

> *In vita gravitas, vultu constantia, fronte*
> *Consilium, os purum, mens pia, munda manus.*

A gentleman without monie is like a leane pudding without fatt.
(*J. Bramstone.*)

Justice Glandville [1] upon a tyme, when fidlers pressed to play
before him, made them sing alsoe, and then askt them yf they could
not cry too; they said his worship was a merry man; but he made
them sad fellowes, for he caused them to be vsed like rogues as they
were. (*Ch. Dauers.*)

There is best sport always when you put a woman in the case.
(*Greene.*)

The Attorney Generall [Coke] put a case thus in the Kings
benche;—" Yf I covenant to stand seised to the use of my bastard
daughter—as I thanke God I have none"—and blusht.

There were 11 Sergeants-at-lawe called this day; two of the Middle
Temple, Mr. Phillips and Mr. Nicholes ; five of the Inner Temple,
Crooke the Recorder of London, Tanfeild, Coventry, Foster, and
Barker; three of Lyncoln's Inn, Harris and Houghton; one of
Grayes Inn, Mr. Altam.
When the Queene was moved to have called another to have
made up twelve, she refused, saying she feared yf there were
twelve there would be one false brother amongst them.
Sergeant Harris when he heard that Barker was called, " It is
well," said he, " there should be one Barker amongst soe manie
byters."
This day at dynner Mr. Sprig tooke Mr. Nicholes by the hand and

fo. 91.
1 Feb. 1602.
[?]

---

[1] Justice of the Common Pleas, 1598—1600. (Foss's Judges, v. 494.)

led him up from the lower end of the table, where his place was, and
seated him on the benche highest at the upper end.

3.

I heard by Mr. Hadsore the lawyers recusants are admitted to
plead at the barr in Irland ; that one Everard is preferred of late to
be a Justice in the Kings Bench there, where there are but two,
and yet he a recusant, but an honest man.

4.

It is said Mr. Snig offers 800*l.* to be Sergeant, whereupon Mr.
Sergeant Harris said that he doubted not but he should shortly
salut his deare brother Mr. Snig.

Argent makes Sargent.

fo. 91ᵇ. *Out of a poeme intituled The Tragicall History of* MARY QUEEN OF
4 Feb. 1602. SCOTTS *and Dowager of Fraunce.*[1] *Hir Ghost to Baldwyne.*

[4.]   In swiftest channell is the shallowest ground,
            In common bruite a truth is seldome found.

[1] The poem from which the following lines were extracted remained unpublished for
two centuries after the time of our Diarist. It was written in the style of the Mirror for
Magistrates, and was clearly intended for insertion in some subsequent edition of that
popular work, but there were obvious reasons connected with its subject-matter which
would operate against its publication in the reign of Elizabeth and in that of her successor, and after that time the Mirror had fallen out of fashion, another style of poetry
had come into vogue, Queen Mary and her sorrows had lost for a time their hold upon the
public mind, and the Tragicall History was consequently entirely lost sight of. In 1810
it was found by Mr. John Fry in a manuscript belonging to a gentleman named Fryer, and
was published by Mr. Fry in a volume entitled " The Legend of Mary Queen of Scots and
other ancient Poems, now first published from MSS. of the 16th century." (Lond. 8vo.)
At the end of the principal poem there occurs in Mr. Fryer's MS. the date of the 10th
July 1601, with the name of the supposed and, in all probability, the real author, Thomas
Wenman. He is thought to be the person of those names who contributed one of the
commendatory poems prefixed to the second part of Browne's Britannia's Pastorals, published in 1616. Wenman was of the Inner Temple. He was Public Orator of the University
of Oxford from 1594 to 1597 (Wood's Athenæ, ii. 365. Fasti, i. 251. Hardy's Le Neve,
iii. 534,) and, as may be gathered from Mr. Fryer's MS., was a Roman Catholic. We
doubted whether the extracts given by our Diarist should be printed, the whole poem

[5.]   A slight defence repells a weake assault.

[6.]   But soe unhappy is a princes state
        That scarce of thousands which on them depend
One shall be found, untill it be too late,
        That solid truth shall in their counsell fend [lend],
But all theyre vainest humours will defend;
Till wee, alas! doe beare the guilt of all,
And they themselves doe save, what ere befall!

[12.]   I will not shewe thee howe my body lyes,
A senceles corps by over hastned death.

[13.]   I might bemoane the hap that fell to me
That yet in graue must still accused bee.

[14.]   Lett the faults upon the guilty light.

[19.]   But fatall was my Guyssian kin to mee;
        Who built their hopes on hazard of my bloud,
Like iuy they did clyme up by my tree,
        And skathed my growth in many a likely bud.
Theyre ouer kindenes did me little good,
        Whose clyming steps of theyre unbridled mynde
    Makes me, alas! to blame them as unkinde.

[20.]   They gave us courage quarrels to pretend
Gainst neighbours, kings and friends, for whom of right
Our interest and bloud would wish us fight.

fo. 92.

[21.]   Soe did the wise obserue my tyme of birth
To be a day of mourning, not of mirth,

having been included in the volume edited by Mr. Fry, but after consideration we have come to the conclusion that it was best to do so: 1, Because Mr. Fry's impression was an extremely small one, and the poem is consequently very little known, even to poetical antiquaries; and 2, Because many of the lines here quoted supply other readings, and in many cases correct obvious misreadings, in the edition of Mr. Fry. The tenour of the writer's opinions upon the moot points of Queen Mary's history may be gathered even from our Diarist's disjointed extracts. The numbers added in the margin within brackets refer to the stanzas of the poem as printed by Mr. Fry.

22.   For death deprived two brothers that I had,
        Both in a day, not long ere I was borne,
        So that a mourning weede my cradle clad.

24.   A greivous chaunce it is to meanest sort
            To leaue a widdowe in a forrein land,
        A child whose yeares cannot herselfe support,
            A suckling babe which can ne speak nor stand
        But must depend upon a tutors hand;
        But greatest mischief is it to a king
        Then which noe hap can greater hazard bring.

25.   Ill to the prince, and to the people worse,
        Which giveth meanes to the ambitious mynd
        By rapine to enrich their greedy purse
        By wreak [wrack] of commonweale, whilst that they blind
        The peoples eyes and shewe themselves unkinde
        To pupil princes, whom they doe accuse
        As cause of such disorders they doe use.

33.   Pride, wealth, and lust, and gredines of mynde
            The finest witts we see doth often blynde.

*The choise of the Regent was the beginning of their broyles. Duke
Hamilton a worthie, wise prince, chosen Regent, purposed a
marriag twixt Q. Mary and Ed. 6., interrupted by the Clergy,
and matched with the Dauphine of Fraunce.*[1]

fo. 92ᵇ. 41.   Thus to and fro, I, silly wretch, was tost,
        And made the instrument of either side,
        Turmoyled with stormes, with wilfull wynde and tyde.

47.   The Cardinall of Lorraine bare the purse,
        The Duke of Guyse the Civil Wars did nurse.

[1] This is given by Manningham as the substance of stanzas 34 to 40.

Our Queene offered hir 30,000 crownes per annum soe she would not marry a forreyner.[1]

67.   In heaven they say are weddings first decreed,
All though on earth they are solemnized.

70.   Soe most unhappy is a princes state
Who must have least respect them selves to ease,
Barr'd of the right men have of meaner state,
Whose choyse is cheife theyr eyes and mynde to please;
Noe outward pompe can inward grief appease;
A sheepherds lyfe with calme content of mynde
Is greater blisse then many princes finde.

78.   God graunt in safety long his life may stay
That riper years may yeild a plenteous crop
Of virtues which doe kingdomes underprop.

81.   Not civil but unciuil wars they were,
Twixt man and wife, which jealousy did breede.

82.   But if my mynde which was not growne soo base,
Or Dauis yeares unfitt for Ladyes loue,
As fitt excuses might have taken place.

Dauis hir secretary gave counsell, that shee should not crowne hir husband, Lord Darly.[2]

85.   Whose rule was like for to eclipse my power.

86.   Not any hate unto the Prince he had,
Not unbeseeming loue to me he bare.

88.   But as they clyme whom princes doe aduaunce
Eache tongue will trip, and envyes eye will glaunce.

89.   To be aduanced from a base estate
By virtue is indeede a happy thing;

fo. 93.

---

[1] Manningham's abstract of stanzas 48 to 66.   [2] Abstract of stanzas 83 and 84.

CAMD. SOC.   R

But who by fortune clymes will all men hate,
Unles his lyfe unlookt for fruit doe bring
Wherewith to cure the wound of envies sting,
But seldome-tymes is found soe wise a man
That gayneing honour well it governe can.

Of the murther of Davies.

94. I would have wisht some other had him stroke,
And in a place more farther from my sight,
Or for his right arraigned he had spoke,
Or of his death some other sense had light.

95. A Princes presence should a pardon bee,
A ladyes shout should moue a manly mynde,
A childwifes chamber should from bloud be free,
A wife by husband should not slaunder finde.

101. To disvnite their league I went about,
For cables crack like threds when they vntuist.

*That not the Queen but others procured Bothwell to murther
Lord Darly.*[1]

118. It stoode them well upon to finde a way
To rid a foe whose power they well might feare;
They knewe the King did watch reuenging day,
And Bothwell did them litle likeing beare,
They knewe ambition might his malice teare,
They knewe the hope of kingdome and of me
Would win him to the Kings decay agree.

119. To fayne my hand to worke soe greate effect
They would not stick to haue their lives assured.

109. Howe ere it was, by whose soeuer fact,
The breache of peace betwixt us growne of late,
Our parted bed, my loue which somewhat slackt,

---

[1] Abstract of stanzas 102 to 117. The numbers in this and the following page are
printed as in the MS.

Some letters shewed as myne importing hate,
With the slender shewe I make in mourners state [1]
Conferred with my match which did ensue,
Makes most suppose a false report for true.

110.   With equall mynde doe but the matter weigh,   fo. 93ᵇ.
       And till thou heare my tale thy judgment stay.

114.   I craue noe priuiledge to shield my cause,
       Lett only reasons balance triall make,
       A guiltles conscience needes not feare the lawes.

My Nay might answer well a bare suspect,
But likelyhoodes of thinges shall me protect.

That she mourned not.

122.   I must accuse the custome of the place,
       Where most our auncestors themselves doe want
       Due monuments theyr memoryes to plant.

130.   Soe hard it is to virtue to reclayme
       The mynde where pride or malice giueth ayme.

132.   Noe cause soe bad you knowe, but colours may
       Be layd to beautifie what princes say.

135.   A fetch soe foule as to report I shame,
       Euen to depriue the life I lately gave,
       And shed the bloud I would have dyed to save.

136.   A dangerous thing it is once to incur
       A common bruit or light suspect of ill,
       Fame flyeth fast, the worse she is more farr
       She goeth, and soone a jealous head will fill;
       What most men say is held for Ghospell still.

---

[1] This line does not occur in Mr. Fry's publication.

Of hir favors.

148.   My suit did crave but liberty to liue
Exiled from those at home which sought my bloud;
Hir bounty did extend further to giue,
With lyfe, eache needefull thing with calling stood,
And such repayre of frends as me seemed good;
Which had I used as did a guest beseeme
I had not bin a prisoner, as I deeme.

149.   But winged with an over high desyre.

fo. 94.   150.   Small provocations serue a willing mynd,
Soe prone wee are to clyme against the hill,
If honour or reuenge our sayles [soules?] doe fill,
But woe is me I ever tooke in hand
That to decide I did not understande!

The cause that moued hir to stir sedition.

151.   It was the thirst I had both crownes to weare,
And from a captiues state my selfe to reare.

159.   Guyse whoe did lay the egges that I should hatch
Sawe subjects hearts in England would not bend
To treason, nor his force noe hold could catch
To bring to passe the thing wee did entend,
He therefore caused the Pope a pardon send
To such as should by violent stroke procure
Hir death whose fall my rising might procure.

Tyborne tippets, i. e. halters.[1]

163.   At length, by full consent of Commonweale,
In Englishe Parliament it was decreed,
By cutting of a withered branche to heale
Theyre body burdened with a fruitles weede,

---

[1] Note of Manningham on a phrase in stanza 160.

Which was by hir it touched most indeede
Withstoode by pitty, which could not take place
Because it did concerne a common case.

165.   In body yet wee Adams badge doe weare,
And to appeare before Gods throne doe feare.

Appeald to forrein princes.

167.   For of releif I promises had store,
But when, alas! it stoode my lyfe upon
I found them fayle ; my life and all was gone.

168.   Proofes were produced; it seemed I should confes
A murder purposed, and some treacherousnes
Against a queene, my cosen and my frend,
Whoe from my subiects sword did me defend.

170.   And soe the cause did seeme to stand with mee,   fo. 94 ᵇ.
That ones decay must others safety bee.

172.   Thus I convict must satisfy the lawe,
Not of revenge which hatred did deserue,
But of necessity, by which they say [sawe ?]
My onely death would hir in lyfe preserve,
Which I reioice soe good a turne did serve,
That haples I might make some recompence
By yielding vp the life bred such offence.

173.   I did rather others facts allowe,
Then sett them on to actions soe vnkinde,
Though many tymes myselfe was not behinde
To blowe the fyre which others seemed to make.

174.   To doe or to procure, to worke or will,
With God is one, and princes hold the same.

179.¹   What favour should I from my foes expect
If soe vnkindely frends did deale with me ?

¹ 184, Fry.

> If that my subiects doe my faults detect,
> I cannot looke that straungers should me free ;
> They should have propt or bent my budding tree
> In youth, whilst I as yet was pliant wood
> And might have proued a plant of tymber good.

180.[1]   Howe seldome natures richest soyle doth yeild
> A bower where virtue may hir mansion build.

182.[2]   Tell them that bloud did always vengeance crave
> Since Abel's tyme untill this present day,
> Tell them they lightly loose that all would haue,
> That clymers feete are but in ticle stay,
> That strength is lost when men doe oversway,
> That treason neuer is soe well contrived
> That he that useth it is longest lyved.

*   *   *   *   * [3]

At the Temple Churche, Dr. Abbottes,[4] Deane of [Winchester. [5]]

His text, 59 of Isay, v. 12: "For our tresspasses are many before thee, and our synnes testify against us, for our trespasses are with us, and we knowe our iniquities."

He began with a commendacion of this prophet for the most eloquent and evangelique, in soe much that St. Jerome said he might rather be placed amongst the Evangelists then the Prophets.

---

[1] 179, Fry.   [2] 181, Fry.

[3] We have omitted here the mottoes in a Lottery, drawn upon the occasion of a visit paid by Queen Elizabeth to Lord Keeper Egerton, which have been printed already by the Percy and Shakespeare Societies and in Nichols's Progresses.

[4] Dr. George Abbot, Dean of Winchester, from 1599-1600 to 1609, when he was appointed Bishop of Coventry and Lichfield, and in 1611 translated to the see of Canterbury. (Hardy's Le Neve, i. 26, 556, iii. 22.)

[5] Blank in original.

All men are synners. " Our trespasses." When Christ taught his disciples to pray, it was one peticion, "Forgive us our trespasses:" to lett them knowe that they were his chosen disciples, yet they were not without synn.

Some may say they have liued *sine crimine, sine querela, sed nemo absque peccato.*

Hence we must learne not to be presumptuous, but to worke out our salvacion with feare and trembling, since all are synners. 2. Not to de-spayre, since the best haue synned.

Our synnes are before God, his eyes are 10,000 tymes brighter then the sunne, nothing hid from his knowledge. Synne is like a smoke, like fyre, it mounteth upward, and comes even before God to accuse us; it is like a serpent in our bosome, still ready to sting us; it is the diuels daughter. A woman hath hir paynes in travaile and delivery, but re-joyceth when she seeth a child is borne; but the birth of synn is of a con-trary fashion; for all the pleasure [is] in the bringing forth, but when it is finished and brought forth, it tormenteth us continually; they haunt us like the tragicall furies.

In the afternoone, MR. CLAPHAM; his text, Math. xxiv. 15.

fo. 96ᵇ.
6 Feb. 1602.

" Lett him that readeth consider it." He said this chapter is not to be understoode of doomesday, but of the destruction of Jerusalem; and that the 28 v. " Wheresoever the dead carcase is, thither doe the eagles resort, " cannot be applied to the resurrection and congregacion of the saints into state of glory with Christ, as some notes interpret, but of the gathering togither of Christes people in the kingdome of grace : for Christ in his kingdome of glory cannot be sayd a carcase, but nowe he may, because he is crucified. And the 29 v. " The sunne shall be darkened, and the moone shall not give hir light, and the stars shall fall from heaven," he expounded thus, That the temporall and ecclesiasticall state of the Jewes in Jerusalem, and the starres, *i. e.* their magistrates, shall loose their authority.

He expounded the opening the seven seales in the Revelacion to have reference to sundry tymes, and the 6. to the destruction of Jerusalem.

7 tymes 7 makes a weeke of yeares, the Jewes true Jubilee, wherein 7 trumpets should be blowne.

The best expositor of the Revelacion a nobleman in Scotland,[1] whoe hath taken Christian and learned paynes therein, yet fayled in the computacion of the beginning of the yeares.

The Revelacion might be better understood if men would better studye it; and that it may be understood, and hath good use, he alledged the word, 1. 3. "Blessed is he that readeth, and they that hear the wordes of this prophesy, and keepe those thinges which are written therein;" which were vayne unles it might be understoode.

fo. 97..
Feb. 1602. Towards the end of his sermon he told his auditory howe it had bin bruited abroade, as he thought by some Atheists or Papists whose profest enemy he is, that this last weeke he had hanged himselfe, but some of his friends, he said, would not believe it, but said some other had done it; yet others.that like him not for some opinion, said it was noe marvaile yf he hanged himselfe, for he had bin possest of the diuel a good while, "but I thinke rather," said he, "they were possessed that said soe, and yet not soe possessed as some hold possession now a dayes, that is essentially," and here he shewed his opinion that there can be noe essentiall possession : 1. Because the diuel can effect as much without entering into the person as yf he were essentially in him, and then it is more then needes. 2. Because there cannot be assigned anie proper token or signe to knowe that anie is essentially possessed. Which signe must be apparent in all such as are soe possessed, and not in anie others. This opinion of his, he said, he would hold till he sawe better reason to the contrary.

In his sermon he told a tale of the Jewes Thalmud, which, he said, was as true perhaps as anie in the Papists legend of lyes, and it was howe Rabbi Haley had conference with Elias in a caue, and would knowe of Elias when Messias should come. Elias told him, Goe aske of the Messias himselfe. Rabbi Haley required where the Messias might be found. Elias told him he should find him at Rome gates amongst the poore; a verry

[1] Napier of Merchiston, the inventor of Logarithms. His work entitled " A plain Discovery of the whole Revelation of St. John " was printed at Edinburgh in 1593, by Waldegrave. It went through many editions and was translated into the principal languages of Europe.

scoffe and a flout, he thought, to the Papists, to shewe that Christ neuer came within their city, but they kept him out of dores, and that he was not amongst their Cardinals, but the beggars, &c.

I will not believe it, because I will not, is Tom Sculs argument, as they say in Cambrige, and a womans reason, as they say here. (*Clapham.*)

Mr. Bodley which hath made the famous library at Oxeford was the sonne of a merchant of London: was sometymes a factor for the state: after maried a riche widdowe in Devonshire or Cornewall, whose husband grewe to a greate quantity of wealth in a short space, specially by trading for pilchers; nowe himself having noe children lives a pleasing privat life, somewhile at the City, somewhile at the University; he followed the Earl of Essex till his fall. (*Mr. Curle.*)

One came to the fyre and Mr. South gave him place; " You are as kinde," quoth he, " as the South-west winde." (*Da.*) 7.

Tom Lancaster met Robbin Snig one day in the Court of Requests · " Howe nowe, old Robbin," quoth he, " what dost thou here ?" " Fayth," said he, " I came to be heard, if I can." " I thinke soe," said he; " nowe thou canst be heard in noe other Court thou appealest to Cesar." (*Dr. Cesar, Master of Requests.*) 8.

*　　*　　*　　*　　*.

Two poore men being at a verry doubtfull demurrer in the Kings benche, the Justices moved that they would referr the matter to some indifferent men that might determine soe chargeable and diffi- cult a controversy, and one demaunded of one of them yf he could be content to haue the land parted betweene them; when he shewed himselfe willing, " Doubtles," said ¯Mr. Cooke, the attorney, " the child is none of his, that would have it divided," alluding to the judgment of Solomon.

*   *   *   *   *

7.

Turner and Dun, two famous fencers, playd their prizes this day at the Banke side, but Turner at last run Dun soe far in the brayne at the eye, that he fell downe presently stone deade; a goodly sport in a Christian state, to see on man kill an other!

*   *   *   *   *

21.

He that offers to violate the memory of the deade is like a swyne that rootes up a grave.

The towne of Manitre in Essex holdes by stage playes.[1] And Rocheford, that they must come at a day unknowne into a field, where the Steward keepes Court at midnight, and writes with a cole, but the night he goes he must make knowne where he stays; those that are absent, and haue none to answer, loose theyr land ; grewe upon tenants burn[ing] Lords evidences.

fo. 98b.
12 Feb. 1602.

Ben Johnson the poet nowe lives upon one Townesend[2] and scornes the world. (*Tho: Overbury.*)

Sir Christopher Hatton and another knight made challenge whoe should present the truest picture of hir Majestie to the Queene. One

---

[1] It is stated in Heywood's Apology for Actors, that " to this day [1612], in divers places of England there be townes that hold the priviledge of their fairs and other charters by yearly stage-playes, as at Manningtree in Suffolke, Kendall in the North, and others." (Shakespeare Soc. ed. p. 61.) The Lawless Court of Rochford has been described in various places, especially in Morant's Essex, i. 272, and in Notes and Queries, ix. 11. W. H. Black, Esq. F.S.A. has made it the subject of a privately printed ballad entitled " The Court of the Honor of Rayleigh," in which it is stated that the parties assemble at a post in a close called the King's Hill, and that whatever is spoken during their proceedings is whispered to the post.

[2] Aurelian Townsend is probably here alluded to. He was at one time steward in the household of Sir Robert Cecil.

caused a flattering picture to be drawne; the other presented a glas, wherein the Queene sawe hir selfe, the truest picture that might be. (*Freewer ?*)

I heard by Mr. Hull, that, whereas heretofore the Lord Admiral used to have the tenthe of all reprisal goods, the State hath nowe thought good, for the encouragement of men to furnishe ships of war against the enimy, to forgiue that imposicion of tenth, but it is thought this indulgence comes too late, the Spaniard hauing growne soe strong in shipping that fewe dare hazard to venture in small company for incertaine booty.   **13.**

The Maysters of the Court of Requests take their place aboue a Knight. (*Whitlock.*)   **12.**

Mr. Hadsor, an Irishe gentleman of our house, was called to the barre, and tooke his oath to the Supremacy. He is shortly to goe for Ireland, there to be Chiefe Justice in Ulster, yf the troubles be pacified, as there is great hope they will bee, for the Rebbell Tyrone hath sent an absolute submission.

One Weston, a merchant of Dublin, hath bin a great discoverer.[1]

The Papistes relligion is like a beggars cloke, where there are soe many patches of pollicy sowed on, that none of the first clothe can be seene. (*B. Rud[yerd].*)   fo. 99. 15.

" I will doe myne endeavor," quoth he that thrasht in his cloke. (*E. Curle.*)

" *Non sic fuit ab antiquo,*" say the Papistes of ours; " *Non sic fuit ab initio,*" say wee of their religion. (*B. Rudyerd.*)

---

[1] Qu. of concealed lands.

14.   Impunity is the mother of contempt and impiety, and both those
the subverters of all governement. (*Lord Keeper.*)

Qui in os laudatur, in corde flagellatur.

I heard that about this last Christmas the Lady Effingham,[1] as
shee was playing at shuttlecocke, upon a suddein felt hir selfe some-
whatt, and presently retiring hir selfe into a chamber was brought
to bed of a child without a midwife, shee never suspecting that shee
had bin with child.

The play at shuttlecocke is become soe muche in request at Court,
that the making shuttlecockes is almost growne a trade in London.

Præstat otiosum esse quam nihil agere.

AT PAULES,

fo. 99ᵇ.
13 Feb. 1602.   A yong man made a finicall boysterous exordium, and rann himselfe
out almost dry before he was halfe through; his text; " He humbled himselfe to the death, even to the death of the crosse, wherefore God hath
glorified him." He spake much of humility. *Melior est peccator humilis,
quam superbus justus. Peccare non potest nisi superbus, nec penitere nisi
humilis.*   He first dilated of three meanes to knowe God ; by his greatnes,
by the prophets in the old, by his sonne in the newe Testament. Against
pride in beauty; the diuel playes the sophister whiles he perswades women
to paint that they may seeme fayrer than they are ; which painting being
discovered, makes them to be thought fouler than they are. Pride in
apparell is pride of our shame, for it was made to cover it, and as yf one
should embroyder a sheete wherein he had done pennaunce, and shewe it
in bragging manner. It is said by some that St. John Baptist for his
humility is rewarded with the place which the diuel lost for his pride.

---

[1] The lady pointed at by this anecdote was Anne daughter and heir of John Lord St.
John of Bletsoe, married to William Lord Howard of Effingham, eldest son of Charles
Earl of Nottingham, on 7th Feb. 1597-8 (Faulkner's Chelsea, ii. 124, where the lady is
inaccurately termed " Agneta"). There is mention in Faulkner of the baptism of a daughter Anne on 12th October 1605, but no allusion to the child who is said by our diarist to
have come so unceremoniously into the world.

He spake against duellisme, or single combat, and said that yf two goe into the field with purpose to fight an the one be slayne, he is a murderour of himselfe. He exhorted the judges to severity, telling them that there is more incouragement taken by one that escapes the punishment due unto him by the lawe, then there is feare wrought by the execution of an hundred.

In the afternoone MR. CLAPHAM, at his Churche by Paules Wharf.

fo. 100.
13 Feb. 1602.

Text, Gen. iv. 13. "Then Kain said to the Lord or Jehovah, My punishment is greater then I can beare, &c." but he reade it "My synne is greater then can be concealed." He noted that translators did very ill to foyst their inventions into the text and sett the originall in the margent, as commonly the common translacions have "synne" in the margent for the word "punishment" in the text, as grosse an absurdity as yf one should shutt the master out of dores, and give entertainement to his attendants.

Nowe Kayne was prest with the horror of his synn he confesseth, but with a kinde of desperacion and repining, as Judas when he confest and hanged himselfe. If a man will not confesse his faultes he shall be prest till he confesse, and when his confession comes to late he may confesse and be hanged to, well enough. For repentant confession must come while grace is offered, while it is called to-day. God deales as the debtor which tenders his money till sunne goe downe. When night is come, up goes his money and a fig for his creditor. Yf men take not tyme while grace is offered, but delay till the sunne of grace be gonne downe, there remaines nothing but horrible desperat reprobacion. A vagabond; an excommunicate person is a vagabond, turned out of the society of Gods Churche both here in earth, and in heaven too, yf it were done by the Spirit of Christ; and therefore lett not men soe lightly esteeme of this greate censure, nor thinke to excuse themselves by saying it was for trifles; but lett them take heede they deserve it not, and yf they which gave the sentence abused their authority, lett them aunswere for it, but always the censure is to [be] reverently regarded.

fo. 100b.
1 Feb. 1602.

Ther be pasport-makers that are as verry rogues as any justice rogues, noble rogues; all that live out of the communion of the Churche are noe better than rogues and vagabonds in the eye [?] of God.

Paradox. That paynting is lawefull. Fowlenes is loathesome; can it be soe that helpes it ? What thou lovest most in hir face is colour, and this painting gives that; but thou hatest it, not because it is, but because thou knowest it is. Foole, whom ignorance only maketh happie. Love hir whoe shewes greate love to the by taking this paynes to seeme lovely to thee.

Hee that weepeth is most wise. Wee come first unwitting, weeping and crying, into a world of woe, and shall wee not weepe and cry when wee knowe it?

The Reason of Reasons was seene divers tymes to weepe, but never to laugh.

Art thou a synner? Wilt thou repent? Weepe. Art thou poore? Wouldst thou be relieved? Weepe. Hast thou broken the lawes of thy prince? Hast thou deserued death? Wouldst thou be pittyed? Wouldst thou liue? Weepe. Hast thou injured thy friend? Wilt thou be reconciled? Weepe.

Laughinge is the greatest signe of wisdome. Ride, si sapis, O puella, ride. Yf thou be wise laugh, for sith the powers of discourse and reason and laughinge be equally proper to only man, why shall not he be most wise that hath most use of laughing, as well as he that hath most use of reasoning and discoursing? I have seene men laugh soo long and soo ernestly that they have wept at last, because they could weepe [laugh?] noe more. Laugh at a foolish gallant; soo shall he be knowne a man, because he laughs; a wise man, for he knowes what he laughs at ; and valiant, that he dares laugh.

To keepe sheepe, the best lyfe. The Lyfe of Man was soe affected to this lyfe, that he denyed not to crowne his deity with this title : and by this he directed his especiall charge to his especiall disciple: giving us men this best name of a beast, of the best nature of beastes. They are innocent, they are patient, soe would God have man; they

love and live together, soe would God have man. God made thee
to behold the Heaven, and to meditate the wonders thereof ; make
thyselfe a shepheard, and thou art still beholding, still meditating.
God commaundes thee to forsake the world : yf thou art a shepheard
thou dost soe, thou withdrawest thyselfe from the world. The private lyfe is the sweetest lyfe ; yf thou livest the lyfe of a shepheard,
thou livest the sweetest private. Wilt thou be a king ? Be a shepheard, thou hast subjects, thou hast obedient subjects, thou hast
sheepe, thou hast a scepter, thou hast a crooke; thy fold is thy
counsell chamber, and the greene field thy flourishing pallace.
Thy companions are the sunne, the moone, and the stars, of whom
thou makest continuall use, and from the vieue of their lights recey-
vest thy counsell and advise. Thou art more happie then other
kings, thou art freed from hate and soe from feare, thou reignest
quietly, and rulest securely; thou hast but one enemie, and thou
hast an enemy for that enemie, the dog and wolf. He that
was Gods second best beloved was a shepheard and a king; yf thou
art a shepheard thou art a king, thou art happie, nay thou art
most happie, thou art a happie king, thy subiectes living onely to
lengthen thy life, and to shorten their owne, &c.

One fee is too good for a bad lawyer, and two fees too little for a
good one.

fo. 102.
Feb. 1602.

Hee that will love a man he knowes not why, will hate him
though he knowe not wherefore.

When Sir Edward Hobby heard of Sir Henry Nevils disaster
with the Earl of Essex, he said that his coson Nevil was ambling
towardes his preferment, and would needes gallop in all the hast,
and soe stumbled and fell. (*Ch. Davers.*)

The Bishop of Bath and Wells, [1] being sent for to the Court and

---

[1] Dr. John Still, who had been Master of Trinity College, Cambridge, was Bishop of
Bath and Wells from 1592 to 1607-8.

there offered the Bishoprickc of Ely upon some condicions which he thought inconvenient, he said that Bishopricke was the onely mayden Bishopricke in England, and he would not be the first should deflour it. (*Hooper.*)

One being entreated to part a man and his wife that were togither by the eares, "Nay," quoth he, " I will never part man and wife while I live."

Dr. Rud made a sermon before the Queene upon the text, " I sayd yee are Gods, but you shall all dy like men;" wherein he made such a discourse of death that hir Majestic, when his sermon was ended, said unto him, " Mr. Dr. you have made me a good funerall sermon, I may dye when I will."

Giue the way to any that you meete ; yf he have a better horse it is duty, yf a worse in pity; yf the way be fayre you are in, commonly it is foule hard by, and soe you shall haue power to durty him that you giue the way, not he you. (*Burdett.*)

Yf you put a case in the first bookes of the lawe to the auncients, you may presume they may haue forgotten it; yf in the newe bookes, you may doubt whether they haue reade it. (*Bur[dett.]*)

fo. 102 ᵇ.
Feb. 1602.
Sir Henry Unton [1] was soe cunning a bargayner for landes that they which dealt with him were commonly greate loosers, whereupon Mr. Duns of Barkshire said that he bought lands with witt and sold them with rhetorick. (*Chute.*)

My taylor, Mr. Hill, a little pert fellowe, was upon a tyme brought before the Lord Chamberlaine, and accused that he had

---

[1] The celebrated ambassador to France. See the excellent volume of Unton Inventories, edited by Mr. John Gough Nichols, for the Berkshire Ashmolean Society, 4to. 1841.

heard one Harlestone curse the Earl of Leister in his house. But Hill denying it, the Lord Chamberlain threatning him, called him rogue and raskall, that would hear noblemen abused, and yet justifie to. Hill replyed that he was neither rogue nor raskall, but a poore artificer, that lived by his labour. The Lord demaund[ed], "What trade?" "A taylor," said Hill. "O then a theife by profession," said the Lord, "and yet yf thou beest a theife thou art but a prettie little one. But, sirra, you rogue, what say you to the matter of my Lord of Leister?" "O, my Lord," said he, "I heard noe such matter." "I will hang you, you raskall," said the Lord. "You shall hang a true man, my Lord," sayd Hill. "What, and a taylor!" said the Lord. Soe leaving Hill when he could not force him to confesse, he went to the accuser, and told him he must not come and trouble him with such trifles, which were fauls to, and yf it had bin true, yet yf he should committ every one to prison that spake evil of Leister or himselfe, he should make as many prisons in London as there be dwelling houses.

Laudo navigantem, cum pervenerit ad portum. (*Ch. Da.*)

fo. 103.
20 March.

Si præbendari, si vis in alta locari,
Consilium præsto, de sanguine præsulis esto. (*Burdett.*)

Fayth is the evidence of things not seene; as wee hold our temporall inheritance by our writinges, which we call our evidence, soe wee clayme our eternall inheritaunce in the heavens by fayth, which is our evidence. (*On King at Paules.*)

Risus potest esse causa aliqua, irrisus nulla.
Irridere bona nefas, mala crudelitas, media stultitia, probos impium, improbos sæuum, notos immanitas, ignotos dementia, denique hominem inhumanum. (*Lodou. Vives, ad Sap: intr.* 439.)[1]

---

[1] The words here quoted will be found in vol. i. p. 35, of the beautiful edition of the Works of Ludovicus Vives published at Valentia, in 8 vols. 4to. 1782—90. This particular treatise of Vives was a great favourite with our ancestors. Several editions of a translation into English, by Richard Moryson, were published by Berthelet and John Daye.

E bestijs, exiatiatis maxime ferarum est invidia mansuetarum assentatio. (Idem.)[1]

fo. 103ᵇ.
28 Feb.

One said of Rochester that it had been an auncient towne, as though it were not more auncient by continuance. (*H. Gellibrand narr.*)

*   *   *   *   *

Dr. Couels booke which he wrote as an appology of Mr. Hooker[2] may be sayd to be all heaven, butt yett Mr. Hookers sentences and discourses intermixed are the stars and constellations, the speciall ornaments of it.

One discoursing of a gentleman, Dr. Cæsars wiues first husband, that had bin imployed as a Ligier in France; "I well belleeve it," sayd another, "that he hath bin a lecher in Fraunce."

Dr. Cæsars wife was at first but a mayd servant in London; till advanct by hir first marriage. When hir Majesty dyned at Dr. Cæsars, shee gave his wife a checke, because in hir widdowhood she refused to speake with a courtier whom hir Majesty had commended to hir.

When a minister was reading the words in marriage, "Wilt thou have this man as thy wedded husband," the bryde presently cryed, "O God, I, Sir," as though shee had tarried for him.

fo. 104.
Nov. 1602.

Upon one Sunday this moneth DR. HOLLAND, Professor at Oxeford,[3] made a sermon at Paules Crosse, his text, Luke xii. v. 13, 14, &c.

---

[1] This passage seems to have puzzled our Diarist, who was probably copying from a manuscript. It stands thus in the Spanish edition above mentioned. "*Ex bestiis, exitiabiles maxime, inter feras invidia, inter mansuetas adulatio.*" (i. 42.)

[2] "A just and temperate Defence of the Five Books of Ecclesiastical Polity written by Mr. Richard Hooker, against an uncharitable Letter of certain English Protestants . . . . By Willam Covel, D.D." Lond. 4to. 1603, reprinted in the Works of Hooker, edited by Hanbury. Lond. 1830, ii. 449.

[3] Dr. Thomas Holland, Fellow of Balliol College, and Regius Professor of Divinity from 1589 to 1611. (Hardy's Le Neve, iii. 509.)

" Take heede of covetousnes, for though a man have abundaunce, his life standeth not in riches." 2 parts ; a caveat. 2. the reason. The reason by a negative, 1. Mans lyfe not in abundance. 2. by a similitude. He noted a difference between the Syriack and the Greeke. The Syriac sayth Christ spake to his disciples ; the Greeke to the brethren that strove for the inheritaunce.

In the caveat, considered 1. the giver, Christ ; 2. the brevity ; 3. the occasion, the falling out of brethren.

All that followe Christ are his disciples.

The giver is Christ, which is Amen, *verax*, omniscient, he that knowes the waye of the serpent upon the stone, of an arrowe in the ayre, and a ship in the sea. *Multa habent auctoritatem propter dicentem.* He can tell us *latet anguis in herba.* The two eyes of the lambe a great watchman to tell us the danger of synn, that it hath the face of a woman, but the sting of a scorpion.

Brevitye. One word of Christ a whole sermon—the ten commaundments are called but ten words, Deut. iv. 13. The whole have but one word, Love, of God and our neighbour, ὁ ὤν, ὁ εἰ, ὁ ἐρχόμενος, α and ω. One word of God overthrewe the whole kingdome of Assyria. Adams synn was the breach but of one commaundement, yet condemned the whole world. Relligion is one, though questions be infinit, yet all must be determined *per unum verbum domini scriptum. Verbum indicabit*, all must be resolved *per primam veritatem.* Our soule can never be quiet till it be resolved by the word of God. Neither can wee have any perfection till wee have a seed of God.

Some have gone about to shewe the truth of relligion by casting out divels. David must come out with his-two stones, the Old and the Newe Testament, before Goliah can be slayne.

He would not speake against the good use of riches. *Divitiæ nec putentur mala, quia dantur bonis ; neque bona, quia conferuntur malis.* Though-the soule neede none of these goods of riches, yet the body doth, *propter victum et vestitum*, and therefore we pray, *Da nobis hodie panem nostrum quotidianum.* God is the author of them, and soe, being the gifts of God, they cannot be evil in their nature. Diverse virtues followe and depend upon riches ; as magnificence, munificence, &c. ; hence have these goodly

fo. 104 ᵇ.

churches beene builded, famous colledges found[ed], warrs maynteyned, &c.
The use of riches is to serve our owne necessity, Gods glory; to doe
good to the poore, to lend to the needy, to reward the virtuous, to make
frend of, &c. Yet the gift cannot merrit, for yf I give all that I have,
yet yf I want charitie, &c. Yet *facta in fide Mediatoris*, they shall not
want a reward. " Come ye blessed of my Father, when I was naked you
clothed me," &c. The abuse of riches is covetousnes. Covetousnes is an
Hydra with seven heades, the diuel is the author of it. He tempted
Christ with riches, when he shewed him δόξαν, the glory of the world; the
diuel could make shewes, he was a cunning juggler.

fo. 105.
The second head, the name, which is an ill name, to covet house, land,
&c. allways taken in the ill part; *avaritia*, in Latin, *aviditas æris*, φιλαργυρία; not a good name amongst them all.

3. The daughters of covetousnes : 1. *Rapina*, robbery. 2. Φιλαργυρία.
3. *Oppressio*. 4. *Furtum*. 5. *Homicidium*. 6. *Proditio*. 7. *Fallacia*.
8. *Mendacia*. 9. *Obduratio*. Whereof more at this day then the Bishop
of Constance burnt poore people in a barne which came for a dole.
10. *Usuria*. This rangeth abroad over the whole land. 11. Bribery. 12.
Symonia, Lady Symonie, a shameles on. 13. *Sacrilegium*. The end *Su-
perbia*, which conteines all, and holds all things to base for himselfe.

Fourth head, the effects of covetousnes : 1. Hatred. 2. Misery. 3. Contempt. 4. Forgetfulnes of God. 5. *Suffocatio*, sorrowe. 6. Danger, death
of body and soule; howe many have bin slayne for riches, or dyed in them.

Fifth head, it is the roote of all evill. 1 Tim. vi. 10; it is an euill of
generality. Some nations are sicke but of one vice; but he that hath this,
hath all; it is hardly cured, it growes by continuance, *peccatum clamans*,
it is *maxime inimicum Deo*, for hee gave all by creacion to all equally, but
this strives to drawe all to it selfe most unequally. Of such a man it
is sayd *abstulit a pauperibus, congregavit, et manet in æternum ejus infamia*.

Sixth head, similitudes, all evill; it is compared to the dropsy, a dis-
quieting kinde of thirst; to leaches, which sucke till they burst.

7. The end, he gathers he knowes not for whom; the reason, mans
life consists not in the abundance of riches. 1. Because both when wee
came into the world, though wee were naked, yet wee then lived, and
fo. 105 ᵇ.
before that too. 2. Wee shall carry nothing away with us when we dye,
yet our soules shall live. 3. They cannot deliver us from death.

Riches are incertayne, and therefore Eschines compares them to Euripus, which ebbes and flowes oftentymes in a day. An other says they are winged, because the[y] passe away soe swiftly; and Fortune hir selfe is allways painted upon a wheeling stone, to note the inconstancy of riches; and certaine it is that, at last, yf they part not from us, wee must part from them.

The parable. A riche man, though he be riche, yet he must dye; for he is but a man. God would have some riche, some poore, for distinction sake, and the mutuall exercise of liberality and patience, whereby the opinion of the Anabaptists is easily confuted, whoe would have all things alike common; *admirabilis concatenatio* in the order of things and states. God made noe miraculous provision for his disciples, therefore there ought to be an ordinary provision for the ministery. As the people love the ministers for their spirituall blessings, soe the ministers love the people for their temporall commodities. The order of professions. 1. Relligion. 2. Husbandry. 3. Merchandise. 4. Souldiery.

Abuse *in acquirendo, concupiscendo, consumendo.*

The covetous man reasons with himselfe in his bed : where wee should *bonum omissum, malum commissum, tempus amissum, deflere.* David sayth, " Lord, I remember the in my bed."

" I will pull doune ;" surely he was a man of this age, pul downe colledges, churches, cyties, kingdomes; every one cryes " Downe with Jerusalem ! " An easy matter to pull downe that which was in building forty yeares ; he will build it agen, soe will not many an other doe.

The foole when his owne belly is full thinkes all the worlde hath enoughe. "Eate soule ! drinke soule ! " a hog may say as much. I will pull downe, I will build ; here is all " I," nothing but himselfe. Presumption that he shall enjoy all; whence he noted his infidelity, security, carnality, εὐτραπελία.

fo. 106.

Of the soule. The soule is the image of God, *Christi redempta sanguine, hæres cum angelis, capax cœlestis beatitudinis, simplex, immortalis, incorporea.* It useth *organa,* instruments. God giveth, not man begge[tte]th it. 21 Exod. 22. *Creando infunditur, infundendo creatur.* God is the father of soules, and the soule returneth to God that gave it ; Ecclesiastes. *Anima imago Dei, in justitia et dominio.*

Relligion of the Turk more towards their Alcoran then our[s] to the Scripture; speake but against that there it is death. He that dishonoureth his father, or disobeyeth the magistrat, every where punished, but for Gods dishonour fewe take care or vengeance.

This thought he spake to himselfe, but God puls him by the sleeve, and calls him by his name, "Thou foole!"

The godly give up their soules, but the soules of the wicked are taken from them.

fo. 106ᵇ.
March 1602.

Femme que dona s'abandona,
Femme que prende se vende,
Femme que regarde son honneur
Non veult prendre ne donner. (*My cosen.*)

My cosen told me that about some 24 yeares since the Prince of Aurange, being driven to some necessity, sent for reliefe to hir Majesty, with protestation that yf shee fayled to supply their wants he must turne pirate; and soe receyving but a cold aunswere, all they of Flushing and other parts adjoining instantly of merchants became good men of warr, and tooke our merchants fleete and forced them to lend 50,000*l.*, which was never repayd. Yet when they had served their turnes for that extremity, and after divers complaints made by our merchants to our Queen against their piracys, had receyved message from hir Majesty to desist from those courses, they presently retyred themselves on a sudden, every one to his former trade. Of soe apt a nature is that nation for any purpose.

There was a company of yong gallants sometyme in Amsterdame which called themselves the Damned Crue.[1] They would meete

---

[1] This association was not confined to Amsterdam. A club of profligates under the same name existed in London much about this time, under the captainship of Sir Edmund Baynham, a well-known young roysterer. On the death of Queen Elizabeth, Sir Edmund was committed to prison by the Council for declaring openly that the King of Scotland was a schismatic, and that he would not acknowledge him as King. In 1605 the same gentleman was sent to Rome by the Gunpowder Conspirators that he might be there, as their agent, to communicate with the Pope, after the plot should have taken effect. Garnet helped him on his way to Rome by a letter to the Pope's Nuncio in Flanders. (Jardine's Gunpowder Treason, 58, 318.)

togithcr on nights, and vowe amongst themselves to kill the next man they mett whosoever; soe divers murthers committed, but not one punished. Such impunity of murder is frequent in that country. (*My cosen narr.*)

My cosen repeated *memoriter* almost the first Booke of Virgils Æneids.   fo. 107.   1 March, 1602.

And this day he rehersed without booke verry neere the wholc second Booke of the Æneids, viz. 630 verses, without missing one word. A singular memory in a man of his age, 62.

You shall nevcr see a deares scutt cover his haunche, nor a fooles tongue his frendes secrett.

Notes of a sermon upon the xv. ch. to the Corinth. verse 22.   fo. 107b.

" As in Adam all dyc, soe in Christ shall all men be made alive." The judgement of the first disobedience was death. And in truth, God could doe noc lesse, unlesse he would be unjust, for as in wisdome he had ordayncd that man should dye when he tasted the fruit of the forbidden tree, soe in justice he was to exccute what in wisdom he had decreed.

Christ was like Adam in his preheminence, in being the cheife and having goverment ovcr all creature[s]. But yet unlike in this that Adam was the cause of death, but Christ is the cause of lyfe unto all that beleeve in him. There is a tyme for all to dye : and this act of dying is done by us, and upon us. It is a sentence which comprehendcth all, though all apprehend not it. Adam was one before all, one ouer all, and all in one, by whose synn all taynted ; soe Christ, by whom all saved. 1 Tim. ii. 4. Man is the principall cause in the course of gcneracion, but woman was in the fall of Adam. 1 Tim. ii. 14. Those which arc sicke of the wantonnes make many answerelcs, endlos, needeles questions, about the fall of Adam.

There be synnes personall, and synnes naturall ; these wee dcrive ofttymes from our parents, as a synne in us, and punishment of them. Soe adultery and drunkcnnes of father, is ofttymes punished in an adulterous and cupshott [1] childe.

Death. 3. Externall, internall, eternall. 1. Separacion of body and soule.   fo. 108.

---

[1] Drunken. " They take it generallie as no small disgrace if they happen to be cup-shottcn." Harrison's Desc. of England, p. 283, ed. 1807.

2. Of sowle from Christ, which is our lyfe, soe was that spatterlashe [*sic*] widdowe, 1 Tim. v. 6 ; dead while she lived. 3. Of body and soule in hell fyre. It was an errour of Pelagius that man should have dyed though he had never synned.

Notes of a Sermon upon Matthew v. 17.

"Thinke not that I am come to destroy the lawe, or the prophets : I am not come to destroy them, but to fullfill them." The best could not live free from slaunders, as Nehemias was charged to have rebelled, &c. and Christ himselfe could not escape the malitious censures of the wicked. When he cured the sicke of the palsy saying, Thy synnes bee forgiven thee, these whispered in their hartes, and called that speache blasphemy. When he disposs[ess]ed the man that was vexed with a deuil, they said he cast out deuils by Beelzebub the prince of the deuils. When he suffered for us they sayd he was plagued for his owne offences. But Augustine sayth well of these men ; "*Hoc facilius homo suspicatur in altero, quod sentit in seipso.*"

The lawe stretcht noe further then the outward action, but Christ layes it to the secret thought. Synnes in our thoughtes are like a snake in our bosome, which may kill us yf wee nurse it; it is like fyre to gunpowder. Wee must shake synn from our thoughts, as wee would a spark from our garments, lest yf wee be once sett on fyre. with them all our teares shall not quenche them. The divel puts synn in our thoughtes, as a thiefe thrusts a boy in at a windowe, to open the dore for the great ones. Yf syn enter into the heart it becomes like a denn of thieves, and like a cage of uncleane birds.

Synn a sly thing; it will enter at the windowe, at the casement, at a chinke of our cogitations.

The more free wee are to syn, the more slaves are wee to Sathan.

Will a thiefe steale in the sight of the Judge, and shall a man presume to synn in the sight of God ?

AT A SPITTLE SERMON.

Yf our synnes come out with a newe addicion, Gods punishments will come out with a newe edition.

Ambrose sayd of Theodosius : "*Fides Theodosij vestra fuit victoria :*" soe he of Queene Elizabeth.

*   *   *   *   *

I was at the Court at Richemond, to heare Dr. Parry one of hir Majesties chaplens preache, and to be assured whether the Queene were living or dead. I heard him, and was assured shee was then living. His text was out of the Psalme [cxvi. 18, 19] "Nowe will I pay my vowes unto the Lord in the middest of the congregacion," &c. It was a verry learned, eloquent, relligious, and moving sermon: his prayer, both in the beginning and conclusion, was soe fervent and effectuall for hir Majestie that he left few eyes drye.

The doctrine was concerning vowes, which were growne in contempt and hatred, because the Jews of old and the Papists of later tymes have used them, whereas the thing itselfe, in its owne nature, is reasonable and commendable.   Wee owe all that wee have, that wee are, vnto God; and all that wee can doe is but our bounden duty, yet those offices may seeme to please him best, and be most gratefull, [in] which even besydes those dutyes which he requires, wee doe enter of our owne will as it were into a newe, a ncere[r] bond. And he defined it to be a promise made unto God, to performe some service in such manner as we are not otherwise bound by duty to performe. It must be made to God, soe differs from other promises; it must be voluntary, and soe it differs from required dutyes; it must be deliberate, which takes away rashnes; it must be of thinges possible within our power, of things that are good, and tending to Gods glory and our bettering. And they are generally either *penitentiæ*, of a strict course of life, in punishing our synfull bodies by sparer dyet, &c.; *gratitudinis*, for benefits received; *amicitiæ*, testimonyes of our love, *dona*.

Vowes of perpetuall chastity and solitude exculed [exculcated?] because of a generall impossibility. Noe merit to be hoped by them, soe the papisticall abolished. Certaine impediments which being removed any man may walke the way without stumbling.

1. Wee cannot performe what wee are commaunded; howe can wee then add anie thing of our owne?

2. The danger of breaking them should stay us from making them.

CAMD. SOC.   U

3. They were ceremonious with the Jewes, and supersticious amongst the Papists, therefore not to be reteyned.

These were present at his sermon, the Archbishop of Canterbury [Bancroft]; the Lord Keeper [Egerton]; the ·Lord Treasurer [Buckhurst]; Lord Admirall [Howard]; Earl of Shrewsbury; Earl of Worster; Lord Gray; Sir William Knollys; Sir Edward Wootten, &c.

fo. 111.
23 Marche.
I dyned with Dr. Parry in the Priuy Chamber, and understood by him, the Bishop of Chichester, the Deane of Canterbury, the Deane of Windsore, &c. that hir Majestie hath bin by fitts troubled with melancholy some three or four monethes, but for this fort-night extreame oppressed with it, in soe much that shee refused to eate anie thing, to receive any phisike, or admit any rest in bedd, till within these two or three dayes. Shee hath bin in a manner speachles for two dayes, verry pensive and silent; since Shrovetide sitting sometymes with hir eye fixed upon one obiect many howres togither, yet shee alwayes had hir perfect senses and memory, and yesterday signified by the lifting up of hir hand and eyes to heaven, a signe which Dr. Parry entreated of hir, that shee beleeved that fayth which shee hath caused to be professed, and looked faythfully to be saved by Christes merits and mercy only, and noe other meanes. She tooke great delight in hearing prayers, would often at the name of Jesus lift up hir handes and eyes to Heaven. Shee would not heare the Arch[bishop] speake of hope of hir longer lyfe; but when he prayed or spake of Heaven, and those ioyes, shee would hug his hand, &c. It seemes shee might have lived yf she would have used meanes; but shee would not be persuaded, and princes must not be forced. Hir physicians said shee had a body of a firme and perfect constitucion, likely to have liued many yeares. A royall Maiesty is noe priviledge against death.

fo. 111ᵇ.
24 Mar. 1602.
This morning about three at clocke hir Majestie departed this lyfe, mildly like a lambe, easily like a ripe apple from the tree, *cum leue quadam febre, absque gemitu.* Dr. Parry told me that he was

present, and sent his prayers before hir soule; and I doubt not but shee is amongst the royall saints in Heaven in eternall joyes.

About ten at clocke the Counsel and diverse noblemen having bin a while in consultacion, proclaymed James the 6, King of Scots, the King of England, Fraunce, and Irland, beginning at White-hall gates; where Sir Robert Cecile reade the proclamacion which he carries in his hand, and after reade againe in Cheapside. Many noblemen, lords spirituell and temporell, knights, five trumpets, many heraulds. The gates at Ludgate and portcullis were shutt and downe, by the Lord Maiors commaund, who was there present, with the Aldermen, &c. and untill he had a token besyde promise, the Lord Treasurers George, that they would proclayme the King of Scots King of England, he would not open.

Upon the death of a King or Queene in England the Lord Maior of London is the greatest magistrate in England. All corporacions and their governors continue, most of the other officers authority is expired with the princes breath. There was a diligent watch and ward kept at every gate and street, day and night, by housholders, to prevent garboiles: which God be thanked were more feared then perceived.

The proclamacion was heard with greate expectacion and silent joye, noe great shouting. I thinke the sorrowe for hir Majesties departure was soe deep in many hearts they could not soe suddenly showe anie great joy, though it could not be lesse then exceeding greate for the succession of soe worthy a king. And at night they shewed it by bonefires, and ringing. Noe tumult, noe contradicion, noe disorder in the city; every man went about his busines, as readylie, as peaceably, as securely, as though there had bin noe change, nor any newes ever heard of competitors. God be thanked, our king hath his right! *Magna veritas et prevalet.*

fo. 112.
24 Mar. 1602.

Doubtles there was grave wise counsell and deliberacion in fact; *sed factum est hoc a Domino,* we must needes confessse, and I hope wee may truly say, *nobis parta quies.* The people is full of expec-

tacion, and great with hope of his worthines, of our nations future
greatnes; every one promises himselfe a share in some famous action
to be hereafter performed for his prince and country.   They assure
themselves of the continuance of our Church goverment and
doctrine.   Their talke is of advauncement of the nobility, of the
subsidies and fifteenes taxed in the Queenes tyme; howe much
indebted shee died to the Commons, notwithstanding all those charges
layed upon them.   They halfe despayre of payment of their privey
scales, sent in Sir William Ceciles tyme ; they will not assure themselves of the lone.   One wishes the Earl of Southampton and others
were pardoned and at liberty; others could be content some men of
great place might pay the Queenes debts, because they beleeve they
gathered enough under hir.   But all long to see our newe king.

fo. 112ᵇ.

Marche, 1602.

This evening prayer at Paules the King was publikely prayed for
in forme as our Queene used to be.

The Lord Hunsdon was in his coache at Paules Hill beyond
Ludgate, to attend the proclamacion.

It is observed that one Lee was Maior of London at hir
Majesties comming to the crowne, an[d] nowe another Lee at hir
decease.[1]

25.

This day the Proclamacions were published in print, with names
of many noblemen, and late counsellors.[2]

26.

The feares of wise men are the hopes of the malitious.

Mr. Francis Curle told me howe one Dr. Bullein, the Queenes kinsman, had a dog which he doted one, soe much that the Queene

---

[1] Persons fond of noticing such coincidences remarked also that Thursday had been
a fatal day to Henry VIII. and the succeeding Tudor sovereigns, he himself, Edward VI.
Mary, and Elizabeth having all died on that day. (Stowe's Chronicle, ed. Howes, p. 812.)

[2] As printed in the Book of Proclamations (fol. Lond. 1609, p. 1.) there are thirty-seven
signatures appended to it, headed, according to ancient custom upon such occasions, by
Robert Lee, Maior. The others were Archbishop Whitgift, Lord Keeper Egerton, Lord
Treasurer Buckhurst, and the principal nobility, officers of state and of the household
then in town. The honourable roll was closed by Sir John Popham, the Lord Chief
Justice of the Common Pleas.

nnderstanding of it requested he would graunt hir one desyre, and he should have what soever he would aske. Shee demaunded his dogge; he gave it, and "Nowe, Madame," quoth he, "you promised to give me my desyre." "I will," quothe she. "Then I pray you give me my dog againe."

A foole will not loose his bable for a [*imperfect*].

Quod taceri vis, prior ipse taceas. Arcanum quid aut celandum maxime amico quum committis, cave ne jocum admisceas, ne ille jocum ut referat occultum retegat. (Ludovic. Vives; Ad Sapient. Introd. 487.)

fo. 113.
26 Mar. 1603.

Corrumpitur atque dissolvitur officium imperantis, si quis ad id quod facere jussus est, non obsequio debito, sed consilio non desiderato respondeat. (*Agellij.*)[1]

29.

He that corrupts a Prince and perverts his government is like one that poisons the head of a conduit; all inquire after him to have him punished.

Three things which make others poore make Alderman Lee, nowe Maior,—riche, wine, women, and dice; he was fortunat in marrying riche wives, lucky in great gaming at dice, and prosperous in sale of his wines. (*Pemberton.*)

30.

At White Hall;

fo. 113b.
27.

DR. THOMPSON, Deane of Windsore, whoe at thys tyme attendes still with Dr. Parry as Chaplein, was by course to have preached this day, but DR. KING was appointed and performed that duty.

His text was the Gospell for this day, the xi. of Luke and the 14. verse, and soe forward. He prayed for the King, that as God had given

[1] Aulus Gellius; Noct. Atticæ, i. xiv.

him an head of gold, soe hee would give him a golden brest, golden legs
and feet alsoe; that as he had a peaceable and quiet entrance, soe he
would graunt him a wise and happie goverment, and a blessed ending,
whensoever he should take him from us. That it would please God to
laye his roote soe deepe that he may flourishe a long tyme, and his
braunches never fayle. The summe of his text in these parts; 1. A diuel
cast out. 2. The dumb speake. 3. The multitude wonder. 4. The Scribes
and Pharisees slander. 5. Christ confuteth. 6. A woman confesseth.
The ende of Christs comming was to dissolve the workes of the diuel,
whereof possession was not the meanest. Can there be a greater then to
take the temple of the Holy Ghost, and make it the sell and shrine of
the diuels image ?

Non requiritur intelligendi vivacitas, sed credendi simplicitas.

*Indocti cœlum rapiunt, dum nos cum doctrina nostra trudimur in in-
fernum.*

The workes of Christ, his miracles, were manifest, *posuit in sole taber-
naculum* : he cast out a diuel, they sawe it, they could not deny it, but
then, what malice could, they deprave the fact or diminishe and eclipse his
glory.

Judei signum quærunt. Julian cals it the rusticity of fayth, as though
none but the simple rude multitude beleeve.

fo. 114.   *Invidia non quærit quid dicat, sed tantum ut dicat.*
27 Mar. 1603.   The envious and malitious live onely in contradiction, like the bettle in
dung and filthines. They said not that Christ could not cast out a diuel,
and soe denyed his power, which is a synn against the Holy Ghost, but
they said himselfe was possessed, nay more that he was Belzeebub.

Beelzebub signifies an idoll of flyes : because there was soe much bloud
spilt in sacrifice before it that many flyes bred and lived upon it.

Christ confuted them by four reasons : 1. From autority; a maxime
and rule in all policy, that a kingdome divided against itselfe cannot stand.
2. From example. By whom doe your children, his apostles and disciples
he meanes, cast them out ? Yf they doe it by the finger of God, then
must I, except the same thing be not the same, yf other persons doe it.
Atticus and Ru . . . (*idem non idem si non per eundem*) unles they will
allowe the thing and condemne the person. But he said, *testes mei judices
vestri.* 3. From a similitude of a stronge and a stronger man, two

warlike men, yf one keepe possession, he must be stronger that puts him out: soe he must be greater than the diuel that can cast him out. 4. From the contrary ; the repugnancy betwixt Christ and the diuel.

He insisted most upon his first reason, of intestine discord: which he said is like a consumption; as yf the head should pull out the eye, or the mouth refuse to eate because the belly receives it, &c. This is that plague that Aegypt shall fight against Aegypt, brother against brother. In the 11 of Zacharia there are two staves mentioned, the one of beauty, the other of bonds; it is a grevous plague which is there threatened, *dissolvam germanitatem eorum*, their brotherhood of Judah and Israel. Ephraim against Manasse and Manasse against Ephraim, two tribes of the same family : the incomparable miseryes of Jerusalem by intestine sedicion. *Auxilia humana firma consensus facit.* Agesilaus shewed his armed men, a mind in consent for defence of the city, and said, *Hij sunt muri Spartæ, scutum hærens scuto, galeæ galea, atque viro vir.* Friends at discord are most deadly enimyes, and those thinges which before were *ligamenta amoris* became then *incitamenta furoris*. The greatest wrongs are most eagerly pursued ; such are commonly the causes for which frends fall out. *Quasi musto inebrientur sanguine.*

fo. 114^b.
27 Mar. 1603.

Even the diuel must have his due ; it was commendable that a legion of them could dwell togither in one man without discord amongst themselves; scarse a few in one house but some jar betwixt them. Yet their concord was not *ex amicitia, sed ex communi malitia*, like Herod and Pilat. *Aliquod bonum absque malo, sed nullum malum absque aliquo bono*, even in the diuels their essence and their order is good.

There is a tyme to gather, said he, and a tyme to scatter, but he had scattered what he had scarce any tyme to gather; his comming up to this place being *tanquam fungus e terra*, an evening and a morning being the whole tyme allotted for meditacion, and disposicion.

Wee may not be unmindefull of our late Soverayne whom God hath called to his mercy, nor ought wee be unthankefull for our newe suffected joy, by the suddein peaceable succession of our worthy king.

fo. 115.
27 Mar. 1603.

The finger of the Spirit directed the Churche, and the order of [the] Church leads me (said he) to the choise of this text, being the Gospell for this day. There are that have slandered, but they are Scribes and Pharisees; and that being the worst part of this text, he would passe over it. There were feares and foretellinges of miseries like to fall upon us at these times, but blessed be the God of peace, that hath settled peace amongst us. Blessed be the God of truth that his kingdome came unto us long since, and I hope shall continue even till the comming of Christ; and blessed be the father of lights, that wee see the truth, and be not scattered.

The miracle of dispossession. Wee have seene the exile of the diuel out of our country, his legends, his false miracles, exorcismes, superstitions, &c. and lett him goe walking through dry places, wee are watered with heavenly deawe, and wee hope he shall never returne againe; but the favour of God towards us shall be like the kindenes of Ruth, more at the latter end than it was at the beginning.

Our State hath sustayned some division of late. "I meane not," sayd he, "of the myndes of great nobles and counsellors, wherein to our good and comfort wee have found *idem velle et idem nolle,* but such a division as of the body and soule, of the vine and the branches, of the husband and the wife, of the head and the body. The prince and the land hath bin divided by hir death, a division without violence. This applying the axe to the roote made the tree bleed at the verry heart."

This Gospell makes mention of an excellent woman that sang not to hir selfe and hir muses, but went amongst the multitude, and blessed an other woman more excellent then hirselfe; yet soe blessed hir as a mother for hir babes sake. Soe there are two excellent women, one that bare Christ and an other that blessed Christ; to these may wee joyne a thrid that bare and blessed him both. Shee bare him in hir heart as a wombe, shee conceived him in fayth, shee brought him forth in aboundaunce of good workes, and nurst him with favors and protection: shee blessed him in the middest of a froward and wicked generacion, when the bulls of Bazan roared, and the unholic league, and bound themselves with oathes and cursings against the Lord and his annoynted. "And am I entred into hir prayses," said he; "and nowe is the tyme of prayse, for prayse none before their death; and then *gratissima laudis actio cum nullus fingendi aut assentandi locus relinquitur.* Yet such prayses are but like a messe of meate sett upon a dead mans grave which he cannot tast, or like a light behind a mans back which cannot him direct." He would say little, *non quod ingratus, sed quod oppressus*

multitudine et magnitudine rerum dicendarum. Onely he would say that   fo. 116.
hir government had bin soe clement, temperat and godly, that he may 27 Mar. 1603.
say *sic imbuti sumus, non possumus nisi optimum ferre.* Those which in
Theodosius the Emperours tyme went to Rome called their travel *felix
peregrinatio,* because they had seen Rome, they had seen Theodosius,
they had scene Rome and Theodosius togither; soe have and may strangers that have bin to visit our kingdome thinke them selves happie that
[they] had scene England and Queen Elizabeth, and England and Queene
Elizabeth togither. But there are panegyricks provided for hir, faythfully registred, and as she merited. Shee was *preteritis melior,* better
then those which went before hir, and may be a precedent to those that
shall followe hir; the taking hir from us was a great division, but God
hath sowed it up againe; it was a grevious sore, but God hath healed it;
he hath given us a worthy successor, a sonne of the nobles; one that is
fleshe of our fleshe. God seemes to say unto us, " Open thy mouth wide
and I will fill it with aboundant blessing;" he may say as he did to his vine,
" what should I have done that I have not done unto thee, O England ?"
Noe vacancy, noe interregnum, noe interruption of goverment, as in
Rome an[d] other places, where in such tymes the prisons fly open, &c.
but a quiet, a peaceable, and present succession of such a King, *quem
populus et proceres voce petebant;* the best wished and the onely agreed
upon. The Lord from his holy sanctuary blesse him in his throne !
It was noe shame for Solomon to walke in the wayes of his father David;   fo. 116ᵇ.
neither can it be a dishonour for our King to walke in the steps of his 27 Mar. 1603.
mother and predecessor. Lett the foster-sonne and sonnes sonne continue their glory, grace, and dignity, and never lett him want one of his
scede to sit upon his seate.

Then to the nobles for their wise menaging those greate affayres,
" *Utinam retribuat Dominus,*" said he, " and, as Nehemias prayed for himselfe, ' Remember them, O God ! in goodnes.' Your peace," said he,
" continued ours, and long may you continue in firme alledgeance to doe
your prince and country service in wisdome, honour, and piety." And this
is noe *detractio, sed attractio; impius in tenebris latet,* he holds his peace,
but Lord open thou our lips, and our mouth shall shewe forth thy prayse;
Paratum est cor meum, My heart is ready, my heart is ready, &c.

                                                           fo. 117.
It was bruited that the Lord Beauchamp, the Earl of Hartfords   27 Marche.

28.

sonne, is up in armes,[1] and some say 10,000 strong. Mr. Hadsor told me the Lords sate about it upon Satterday night, and have dispatcht a messenger to entreat him to come unto them, or els to be in danger of proclamacion of treason. An other bruit, that Portsmout is holden for him, that the Frenche purpose against us, that the Papists are like to rise with Beauchamp; they may trouble us, but I hope shall not prevaile.

" He is up," said one. " He is risen," said an other. " True, I thinke," said I, " he rose in the morning, and meanes to goe to bed at night."

Ch. Davers said he could tell the King what he were best to doe; not to chaunge his officers. "Nay then, it were best to choose you first for a counsellor," said I.

I sawe this afternoone a Scottishe Lady at Mr. Fleetes in Loathebury; shee was sister to Earl Gowre, a gallant tale gent., somewhat long visage, a lisping fumbling language. Peter Saltingstone came to visit hir.

29.

I askt Mr. Leydall whether he argued a case according to his opinion. He said, noe! but he sett a good colour upon it.. I told him, he might well doe soe, for he never wants a good colour; he is Rufus.

Mr. Rudyerd tels that to muster men in these tymes is as good a colour for sedicion, as a maske to robbe a house, which is excellent for that purpose.

[1] The way in which the exuberance of Lord Beauchamp's loyalty occasioned this report will appear in a subsequent entry. This Lord Beauchamp was the father, as our readers will be aware, of the Marquess of Hertford, who was the faithful servant of Charles I., faithful even to death, and after the Restoration was created Duke of Somerset.

Mr. Rous said that the Queene began hir raigne in the fall, and ended in the spring of the leafe. " Soe shee did but turne over a leafe," said B. Rudyerd.

Was reported that the King had sent for some 5,000*l.* to bring him into England; it is said the Queenes jewes [jewels] shee left were worth 4 millions [?], *i. e.* 400,000*l.*; in treasury present 50,000*l.*, noe soe much this long tyme.

The Kings booke Basi[li]con Doron came forth with an Epistle to the reader apologeticell.

A man may do another a good turne though he cannot performe it for himselfe, as the barber cannot trimme himselfe though he can others. (*Pim.*)

It was sayd our King is proclaymed nowe Duke of Gelderland.

Jo. Grant told me that the King useth in walking amongst his nobles often tymes to leane upon their shoulders in a speciall favour, and in disgrace to neglect some in that kindenes.

It is sayd Sir Robert Cary, that went against the Counsells directions in post toward the King to bring the first newes of the Queenes death, made more haste then speede, he was soe hurt with a fall from his horse that an other prevented his purpose, and was with the King before him; this Cary had an office in the Jewell house.[1]

---

[1] The particulars of Cary's wonderful ride are related by himself in his Memoirs. " He took horse," apparently at the lodging of the Knight Marshal at Charing Cross (probably at the old Mews), "between nine and ten o'clock," on the morning of Thursday the 24th of March, "and that night rode to Doncaster," about 160 miles. On Friday night he came to his own house at Widdrington, about another 135 miles. " Very early

31.

This night there came a messenger from the Kinges Majestie with letters directed to the Nobles and Counsellors of his late sister the deceased Queen, all to continue their places and keepe house and order matters according to their discretion till he came. (*Isam.*)

A puritane is such a one as loves God with all his soule, but hates his neighbour with all his heart. (*Mr. Wa. Curle.*)

fo. 118.
31 Mar. 1603.

Of a beggar that lay on the ground drunk.

He cannot goe, nor sitt, nor stand, the beggar cryes ;
Then, though he speake the truth, yet still he lyes.

I was in Mr. Nich. Hares companie at the Kings Head. A gallant young gentleman, like to be heir to much land: he is of a sweet behaviour, a good spirit, and a pleasing witty discourse.

It was soe darke a storme, that a man could never looke for day, unles God would have said againe *Fiat lux.*

*   *   *   *   *

A gentlemans nose fell a bleeding verry late in a night, and soe causing his boy to light him downe to a pumpe to washe the bloud away, he spied written upon the pump, that it was built at the proper cost and charges of a physician which lay nere the place, whom he presently sent for, to come to a lady that was dangerously sicke; but when he came he shewed that his nose was bloudy, that he went downe to have washt at the pompe, but espying it to be built at his proper costs and charges, he thought good manners to aske leave of him, before he would washe it. (*Mr. N. Hare.*)

on Saturday he was again on horseback and reached Norham on the Tweed about noon. This was about 50 more miles, and left only about another 50 miles, " so that," he says, " I might well have been with the King at supper time ; but I got a great fall by the way, and my horse, with one of his heels, gave me a great blow on the head, that made me shed much blood. It made me so weak that I was forced to ride a soft pace after, so that the King was newly gone to bed by the time that I knocked at the gate" [of Holyrood House.] (Memoirs of Robert Cary, Earl of Monmouth, ed. Edinb. 1808. pp. 126—128.

Dr. Some,[1] upon a tyme speaking of the Popes in a sermon, said fo. 118ᵇ. that Pius V. sent out his bulles against the Queene like a calfe as he 1 Aprill, 1603. was. (*Mr. Isam.*)

I heard that one Griffin, Queene Marys Attorney, purchased some 24 mannors togither; his sonne hath sold 10 of them, and yet is in debt; *male parta male dilabuntur.*

One Mr. Marrow, late Sherife of [Warwickshire], useth his wife verry hardly, would not allow hir mony nor clothes fit for hir, nor trust hir with any thing, but made hir daughter sole factres. (*Mr. Wagstaffe.*)

A covetous fellowe had hangd himselfe, and was angry with him that cutt the rope to save his life. A covetous man rather will loose his lyfe then his goods.

One when the house was on fyre, and himselfe ready to be burnt, fell a seeking for his girdle, amidst the fyre.

Homo impius quid aliud quam immortale pecus. (*Ludovicus Vives.*)

Felices essent artes, si nulli de eis judicarent nisi artifices. (*Mr. Maynard.*)

He thinks the statut of wills will be as greate a nurse of controversies as the statut of tayles and uses in common. The eggs are layd, and are nowe in hatching. (*Idem.*)

Wee are purged from our corruption, *non per gratiam naturæ*, fo. 119. *sed per naturam gratiæ.* (*Dr. Dod.*) 1 Aprill.

Wee worshipt noe Saints, but wee prayd to Ladyes, in the Queenes tyme. (*Mr. Curle.*) This superstition shall be abolished we hope in our Kings raigne.

---

[1] Dr. Ralph Some, Master of Peter House, Cambridge, elected 1589. (Hardy's Le Neve, iii. 668.)

*

One reading Horace happened upon that verse:

Virtus est vitium fugere, et sapientia prima
Stultitia caruisse.[1]

"Here is strange matter," said he, "*Virtus est vitium.*"   "Read on," said another.   "Nay first lett us examine this;" and would not goe a word further.   "Nay," said the other, "yf you gather such notes, I will find another as strange as that in the same verse, '*Et sapientia prima stultitia.*'"   (*T. Cranmer.*)

Natura brevium. (*Fitch.*)   The nature of pigmies (said *B. Rudyerd*).

3.

Dr. Spenser upon the 1 Mark, v. 29 to the 36.

Christs Sabboths dayes work, to cure the diseased; a miracle, a work of his mercy, that he would of his power that he could.

A man must take the tyme that Christ offereth himselfe: yf he was with Simon and Andrew at night, he parted into the wildernes in the morning. The feuer left hir, and shee ministred, v. 31, hence he collected the conveniency of church-going for women to give publique thanks for safe deliverance.

fo. 119ᵇ.
3 Aprill, 1603. In the afternoone Clapham.   He prayed for the King and his sonne Henry Frederick and Frederick Henry ; prayed for a further reformacion in our Churche.

Note : the 7 moneth amongst the Jewes, according to their civil computacion, was but the first in their ecclesiasticall.

Close fisted, that will give nothing to the ministers and musty doctors that lett learning mould and rust in them for want of use.

4.

Gluttony and lechery dwell togither, *Venter et genitalia sunt membra vicina.* (*Mr. Key.*)   As they are placed in that prayer, Ecclesiasticus xxiii. *v.* 6.   "Lett not the gredines of the belly, nor the lust of the flesh, hold me."   A great spender in leachery must be a great ravenor in glutony, to repayre what he looseth.

---

[1] Epist. lib. i. 41.

Dr. Parry told me the Countess Kildare assured him that the Queene caused the ring wherewith shee was wedded to the crowne, to be cutt from hir finger some 6 weekes before hir death, but wore a ring which the Earl of Essex gave hir unto the day of hir death.

*   *   *   *   *

I heard that Sir Robert Carewe lay in the Kinges chamber the first night he brought the newes of hir Majesties death, and there related the whole discourse; whereupon he was made one of his chamber, a place of confidence and means to preferment.[1]

fo. 120.
5 Aprill.

It is certaine the Queene was not embowelled, but wrapt up in cere cloth, and that verry il to, through the covetousnes of them that defrauded hir of the allowance of cloth was given them for that purpose.

There was a proclamacion published in the Kinges name conteining his thankefullnes to the people for continuance in their duty, in acknowledging him and receiving him as their rightfull successor, and a restraint of concurse unto him, especially such as were in office and had great place in their countryes, with a clause for continuing officers of justice in their place.[2]

6 April.

[1] The curious admixture of fact and fiction in our Diarist's memoranda relating to Sir Robert Cary will be observed by every one who turns to his Memoirs before referred to. The principal fact in this entry is that James was foolish enough to reward the bringer of good tidings with an appointment as gentleman of his bed-chamber. The thing was so silly, and so much in the nature of an affront to the English Council, that the over-delighted monarch was obliged to withdraw the appointment, much to Cary's annoyance. (Cary's Memoirs, ed. 1808, p. 132.)

[2] One of the reasons alleged in this proclamation for restraining that " earnest and longing desire in all his majesties subiects to enioy the sight of his royall person and presence " which had induced " very many of good degree and quality to hasten and take their iourneys unto his highnesse," was that the country whither such " over-much resort and concourse " was made, being " over-charged with multitude, scarcity and dearth was like ynough to proceed." (Book of Procs. fol. 1609, p. 5.) His Majesty left Edinburgh

A letter gratulatory to the Lord Maior, Aldermen, and Citizens, was read in their court, which letter came from his Majestie, dated at Halliroode House, 28 Martij, 1603; it conteined a promise of his favour, with an admonission to continue their course of government for matters of justice.[1]

DR. OVERALL, Deane of Paules, made a sermon at Whitehall this day, his text, "Watch and pray that ye enter not into temptation." He discoursed very scholastically upon the nature of temptations, their division, &c., fit for these tymes in this change, least wee be tempted to desyre innovacion, &c. He held that God permits many thinges to worke according to their nature, not forcing their actions by his decre, soe wee enter into temptacions unforced, of our owne accord, by his permission.

Mr. Timothy Wagstaffe and my self brought in a moote whereat Mr. Stevens, the next reader, and Mr. Curle sate.

I heard there had bin a foule jarr betwixt Sir Robert Cecile and the Lord Cobham, upon this occasion, because the Lords and late Counsell, upon the Queenes death, had thought good to appoint an other Captaine of the gard, because Sir Walter Rhaley was then absent, which the Lord Cobham tooke in foule dudgeon, as yf it had bin the devise of Sir Robert, and would have bin himselfe deputy to Sir Walter rather [than] any other. The Lord Cobham likewise at subscribing to the proclamacion tooke exception against the Earl of Clanricard, *inepte, intempestive,* but he is nowe gone to the King, they say.

The occasion of the bruite that was raysed of the Lord Beauchamps rising was but this; he had assembled divers of his followers

on the 5th April, the day on which this proclamation was published at Whitehall, and entered Berwick the day following.

[1] See it printed in Stowe's Annales, ed. Howes, p. 818.

and other gent. to goe with him to proclayme the King, which a good lady not understanding gave intelligence that he assembled his followers, but upon the effect hirself contradicted hir owne letter.

AT WHITE HALL.

Dr. MONTAGUE, Master of Sydney Colledge in Cambridge, made a sermon; his text Matt xviii. 11. " The Sonne of Man came to save that which was lost "

In his prayer: " Wee give ourselves to synn, without restraint in our conscience before, or remorse after." He considered 3 points: 1. The stile of Christ ; the Sonne of Man. 2. To whom he came ; to the lost. 3. The end of his coming ; to save. Where men come of an honourable parentage, or beare an office of dignity, it is their use to stile themselves in the name of their auncesters, as Solomon the sonne of David, &c. But where they have none, the Jewes call them Ben Adam, the sonne of man. Howe happens it then that Christ which is *Salvator mundi*, Σωτήρ, the best word that the Greekes have, that he takes upon him this stile of basenes? For two reasons : 1. Because the nearer he came to our nature, the nearer he came to our name; first before the lawe he was called *Semen mulieris*, then *Shilo*, after *Messias*, and nowe himselfe gives himselfe this name, the Sonne of Man, by speciall effect changing his name; when he was Silo wee were but servants, &c.

He layd downe his name to take up ours, that wee might for his sake lay downe our lives to take up his glory.

He would not have his glory upon earth : he would never suffer himselfe to be called God upon earth, nor suffer his miracles to be blazoned, he would have his fame spread by the inward persuasion of the spirit not the outward applause of the mouth. And hence he noted the difference betwixt the fame of a magistrat and of a minister; for from the outward action of the magistrat we come to an inward approbacion of his virtue ; but contrary in a minister, from our inward perswasion of his virtue to the outward approbacion of his actions.

Exinanition [Exaninition] of Christs glory on earth typified in the auncient Jewish manner of coronacion, and enthronizing their kings, when they powred a horne of oyle upon his head, to shewe that as the horne was emptied to annoint him, soe out of his fullnes he should enrich others. Oyle is taken for grace.

Second point; to those that were lost. The Rabbins devide all the people into three sorts, *Sapientes*, such were the Scribes and Pharises; 2. *Sapientum filij*, such as held nothing for opinion, nor did any thing for action, but that which was approved by the Pharisees; 3. *Terræ filij*, the children of the world, publicans and synners, reputed as lost sheepe: to these Christ came, and for conversing with these he

was obrayded; to teache men what a different course there is in the managing of heavenly and earthly things. The greate affayres of the world begin at the Prince, and soe are derived by a long course to the people, but the matters of heaven begin in the people, and soe rise up to the Prince. The first newes of Christs birth was brought but to a company of silly shepheards, from them to a poore city, Bethleem, from thence to Jerusalem, and soe by calculacion it was neere two yeares before it came to the Kings eare.

There are two Kingdomes in this world, a temporall and a spirituall or mysticall, eache needing other. Where the rich feeling their poverty in spirituell, come to the minister to be furnished in that commodity, and the minister feeling his wants in the riches of this lyfe, followeth great men, to be relieved in that necessity. *Communis indigentia est societatis vinculum*, mutuall necesity is the surcingle of the world.

Second reason; Christ came to these, as the fittest to receive his doctrine, and yet it is clapt in amongst his miracles that the poor beleeved. The promises of a kingdome in heaven is a greate matter which greate men according to their course in earth will hardly beleeve can be effected without greate meanes, and therefore a miracle yf princes receive Christ. Our

Prince did, and our King doth continue this miracle; for shee did, and he doth, hold and will maintaine the truth of the Gospell, "and this hath king'd him," said he.

Two conclusions; better to be a lost sheepe in the wild field, then put up safe in the fold of the Pharisees.

There have bin three great monarchies in the world, the first of Synn, the second of the Lawe, the third of Grace, and these had severall ends; the first was death, the next Christ, and the last is lyfe; and these were attained by severall meanes, for synn brought us to death by concealment of our faults, the lawe brought us to Christ by knowing our syn, by revealing our syn, and Christ by his grace leads us to everlasting lyfe. In each soule those three kingdomes have their succession yf it be saved. Though the lawe was delivered with thunder, yet there insued comfort in the first word, " I am thy God." The lawe like a bason of water with a glas by it, serves to discover, and scower away the filthines.

Second conclusion. Noe syn soe greate that should discourage us from comminge to Christ. Aesculapius, as the poets faine, dewised more remedys against poison out of a serpent than any other creature, yet the serpent more poisonous in it selfe then anie man. Soe from syn. Our confidence, *i. e.* from the nature of God, whoe regards not soe muche what a man hath bin, but what he is, and will bee. Whereas the judgment of man, on the contrary, is ground[ed] upon *vita anteacta*, and forepassed actions ; soe Ananias made conjecture of Paule. God more delights to pardon the synner, then to punish the synne.

fol. 123ᵇ.
Aprill 1603.

2. From the nature of Christ ; more mild and mercyfull than Moses: for Christ never executed any point of judgment. He is an intercessor, and shall be our judge: but that tyme is not come, soe our creede notes, " From thence He shall come to judge." And this seemes to be the reason, that under the lawe, yf anie strang syn had escaped the hand of the magistrat, yet it was usually punished by the hand of God : whereas nowe, yf offences slip the magistrat, they are seldome or neuer revenged from heaven.

Christ is not soe muche a remedy for easy synns, but even for such synners as even beginn to stink and rott in them, as Lazarus did in the grave. Shee that had hir issue 12 yeares was healed with the touch of his garment, &c. He is more ready to pardon a synner upon repentance then to punishe him upon perseverance.

3. The end : To save. *Christus salvat ; solutione debiti et applicatione remedij. Debitum nostrum* 2ᴬ; *Obedientiæ; Pœnæ.*

Woe must obey the lawe or indure the punishment. Christ by his lyfe hath payd the dett of our obedience, and by his death had cleered the debt of our punishment. Both were necessary to our plenary redemption: his life to ripe age to accomplishe our righteousnes ; his passion by death to meritt of [*sic*] our salvacion. Righteousnes of his lyfe. Merit of his passion.

fo. 124.
Aprill 1603.
The applicacion; by taking upon him our syns, and imputing unto us his righteousnes. In all synn, three things, *culpas, reatus, pœna,* and the remedy must have something contrary to the malignant quality of the disease : soe Christ cureth the fault by his obedience, the guilt by his innocency, and the punishment by his passion ; soe by applicacion all our synns are his. All his righteousnes is become ours. But heere surges a a doubt, howe it comes to passe that synce the imputacion of his merits makes us righteous, the imputacion of our synn cannot make him synfull. *Ferrum candens absorbet aquam,* and the drop of our synn cannot infect the ocean of his innocency; *finiti ad infinitum nulla proportio.* The applicacion of our syn to him is but a mere imputacion, but his merits, beside an imputacion, worke in us alsoe an inherent righteousnes. For applicacion; the commaundments are given in the second person ; and the bible written in fashion of a story, not precepts and rules, because it is more for practise then speculacion, and God would have us rather good Christians then good schollers. Without particular applicacion all is nothinge but like the rude chaos, for before the incubacion of the Spirit of God, there was noe separacion, noe vivificacion, noe animacion. In the sacrifice in the old lawe it was noe idle thing that they were to sprinkle the right eare, the right thombe, and the right foote too, to shewe the inward affection must be moved by the eare, and the action by the thomb and the toe.

fo. 124ᵇ.
Aprill 1603.
The Virgin liked the newes well which was brought hir, "but howe shall this come to passe," quoth shee ; soe it is welcome to every one to heere that he shall be the Sonne of God, but howe shall he knowe that? There is but thre wa[y]s of knowing himselfe to be the Sonne of God : 1. *Scientia unionis,* and soe Christ onely knowes himselfe to be the Sonne of God. 2. *Scientia visionis,* and soe the Saints. 3. *Scientia revelationis,* and soe every Christian. And this last is twofold, either by a descendant course, whereby Gods spirit comes downe to us, and this those knowe which have it. Philosophie sayth every lambe knowes his owne dame, *non per eundem sonum sed per eundem Spiritum :* as the uniting of the Father and the Sonne in the Trinity is *per communionem Spiritus.* "My sheepe heare my voyce," by inward perception. "Did not our harts glowe within us ?" The difference is knowne to them that have it. Samuel, before he was acquainted with it, thought it had bin the voyce of a man, but Ely could

discerne it. 2. Wee knowe by our Spirit ascending to God: the Spirit like fyre, still ascendeth, like a steele toucht with the magnet turnes northward, soe this heavenward. Wee are placed twixt heaven and earth ; like an iron betwixt two loadstones wee incline still to one of them.

fo. 125.

I heard the Queene left behinde hir in money, plate, and jewels, the value of 12,000,000l. whereof in gold is said, 400,000l.

8 Aprill 1603.

It was said for a truth that the Countes of Essex is married to the Earl of Clanricard, a goodly personable gentleman something resembling the late Earl of Essex.

The Lord Keeper Sir Thomas Egerton hath married his sonne, before the Queene dyed, to the Countes of Darbys daughter, his Ladys daughter; bloud-royall. *Superbe satis.*

This afternoone a servingman, one of the Earl of Northumberland, fought with swaggering Eps, and ran him through the care.

I heard that the King hath or will restore the Lord Latimer to the Earldome of Westmerland; some 3 or 4000l. per annum.

There came forth a proclamacion for making certaine Scottish coyne currant in England; as a peice of gold for 10s., and the sylver at 12d. ob. and this for the menaging of commerce betwixt these nations.[1]

fo. 125b.
9 Aprill 1603.

Mr. Barrowes called Seminaryes, Semminaries.

I heard that my Cosen Wingat is married to a riche widdowe in Kent.

10.

[1] See Book of Proclamations, fol. Lond. 1609, p. 6.

AT THE COURT AT WHITEHALL.

DR. THOMSON, Deane of Windsor,[1] made a sermon; he hath a sounding laboured artificiall pronounciacion; he regards that soe muche, that his speech hath no more matter then needes in it. His text 2 Psal. 10, 11. "Be wise nowe, O ye Kings; be learned, O ye Judges; serve the Lord with feare, and rejoyce unto him with reverence."

Be learned; *scientia conscientiæ* rather then *scientia experienciæ*. Serve the Lord: a straung doctrine that those whom all desyre to be servants unto, should be taught, that themselves must serve an other: yet this the highest point of their honour to serve God: for the excellency of man is in his soule, the glory of his soule in virtue, the height of virtue in relligion, and the ende of relligion to serve God. As strang to teach that they whom others feare, should feare an other.

fo. 126.
10 Aprill 1603, MR. LAYFEILD; his text. "Not preaching ourselves." Noo heretike ever preached himselfe directly, for they never can be heretikes except they professt Christ, and such as preach themselves for saviours deny Christ; but preaching them selves undirectly is when by preaching men stake their owne glory or advauncement, as the cheifest end of their preaching. "Labour not for meat;" that is, make not meate the chiefest end of labour, but the service of God in that vocation, and the benefit of the State; soe labour in all your trades as yf you laboured for God, making not the hyer the maine end, though it be an end alsoe.

Every man spends more then he can gett; untill thirty yeare commonly men doe nothing but spend, and then when they begynn to gaine, yet expenses runne on with their tyme.

Every manuary trade is called a mystery, because it hath some slight or subtlety of gayning that others cannot looke into. Every man cannot be a carpentour of his owne fortune. The faults of preachers in preaching themselves and false doctrine, like a physicion that poisoneth his medicines, or a mintmaister that adulterates the coine; he kils under pretence of safety, and this robbes all under pretext of honest gaine.

---

[1] Dr. Giles Thompson appointed 25th February 1602-3, elected Bishop of Gloucester in 1611, and held the Deanery *in commendam* until his death on 14 June 1612. (Hardy's Le Neve, iii. 374.)

Mr. Hill told me that Mr. Layfeild married a rich wife, worth above 1,000*l*. He speakes against covetousnes, but will exact the most of his dutyes in his parishe.

AT WHITEHALL IN THE AFTERNOONE IN THE CHAPPELL.

fo. 126ᵇ.
10 Aprill 1603.

DR. EATON,[1] BISHOP OF ELY. His text, " Come unto mee all yee that labour, and are heavy laden, and I will refreshe you;" *Ego reficiam*. " Come unto me;" God thy father hath given all power in heaven and earth unto Christ; therefore in our prayers to obtaine any thing wee must goe unto him, and in him wee may be sure to obteine : for this is hee in whom the father is well pleased. He consider[ed] the subject, " All yee," &c. the invitacion "Come unto me," and the promise, " I will ease you." " All yee" is heere specially limited to those that labour and are laden, which are [have ?] greate synnes and feele the waight of them. Noe synn soe dangerous to men, soe odious in the sight of God, as contempt of synn. Amongst manie synns which he mentioned as greivous and haynous offences not one word of sacriledge.

Synne makes a man turne from God' like a runagate that having committed some offence for which he feares punishment runnes away from his maister, but there is noe place, noe tyme, can hide him from the presence of God, but onely the wing of Jesus Christ his mercy. Adam was soe foolishe to thinke he might have hidden himselfe, but David sayth " Yf I goe into the wildernes, etc." *Qui recedit a facie irati* for synn, *accedat ad faciem placati* in the merit of Christ, in whom onely he is well pleased.

" Which labour, and are laden." All labour under synne, and all are laden with it, but such as have greivous synnes, and are greived for them, and almost pressed downe to despayre, lett them come. *Reficiam;* he will ease them; not take away the roote but *reatum*, for the old man will be in us as long as we live, and as fast as we rise by grace the fleshe is ready still to pull us downe againe to synn.

fo. 127.

* * * * *

[1] Dr. Martin Heton, Bishop from 1598 to 1609. (Hardy's Le Neve, i. 343.)

fo. 127ᵇ.   Jo. Davis [1] reports that he is sworne the Kings Man, that the
10 Aprill 1603. King shewed him greate favors. *Inepte.* (He slaunders·while he
praycs.)

There is a foolishe rime runnes up and downe in the Court of
Sir Henry Bromley, Lord Thomas Haward, Lord Cobham, and
the Deane of Canterbury, Dr. Nevil, that eache should goe to move
the King for what they like.

> Nevil for the Protestant, Lord Thomas for the Papist,
> Bromley for the Puritan, and Lord Cobham for the Atheist.
>   (*Mr. Ysam nar.*)

*   •   *   *   *

I heard that the Earl of Southampton and Sir Henry Nevill were
sett at large yesterday from the Tower; that Sir Henry Cock the
cofferer was sent for by the King, and is gone unto him.

Was with the Lady Barbara.[2] Shee saith the King will not
swear, but he will curse and ban at hunting, and wish the diuel
goe with them all.

In the Frenche Court, the guard is all of Scottishmen, and to
distinguishe betwixt a Frenche and a Scot in admitting anie to a
place of present spectacle, the[y] give the word "bread and chese,"
which the Frenche cannot pronounce; " bret and sheese."

fo. 123.   Mr. Thomas Overbury spake much against the Lord Buckhurst
11.   as a verry corrupt and unhonest person of body.

---

[1] Sir John Davies ; he was of the Middle Temple, but was expelled for some quarrel-
some misconduct. As Attorney-General of Ireland he obtained great favour at Court,
and would have been appointed an English Judge, but for his sudden death. He is now
principally known by his poem on the Immortality of the Soul. In a passage in this Diary
which we have omitted on account of its grossness, he is described as extremely awkward
in his gait ; waddling in most ungainly fashion and walking as if he carried a cloak-bag
behind him.

[2] Lady Barbara Ruthven, the sister of the Earl of Gowrie, mentioned at p. 156.

He spake bitterly against the Bishop of London. [1] That Darling   12.
whoe was censured for a slaunderous libellor in the Starre Chamber,
and had bin convict for a counterfaitour of passes [?] was a better
scholler then the Bishop: that the Bishop was a verry knave. I
contradicted.

He would not have the bishops to have anie temporalities, or   11.
temporall jurisdicion, but live upon tithes, and nothing but
preach, &c.

When I was mentioning howe dangerous and difficult a thing it
would be to restore appropriacions, he said *Fiat justicia et cœlum
ruat*, which applicacion I termed a doctrine of Jesuits.

He said Sir Robert Cecile followed the Earl of Essexes death,   12.
not with a good mynde.

This day the two Cheife Judges Sir John Popham and Sir
Edmund Anderson, with the rest of the judges, were sworne. I
sawe divers writs or commissions scaled by the Lord Keeper, with
the old seale of Queene Elizabeth. It is verry like wee shall have
a terme.

*   *   *   *   * [2]

Dr. Parry was sollicited by the Archebishop to make a kinde of   fo. 133.
funerall oracion for the Queene, to be published not pronounced,   13 Aprill 1603.
and hath given him instruccion: Mr. Savil [3] or he must doe it. Savil
fitter, for better acquaintance with the Queenes private accions and
reddier stile in that language; both scarse have leisure. Dr. Parry
warned to be provided of a sermon against the Kinges coming. He

---

[1] Bishop Bancroft from 1597 to 1604, when he was translated to the see of Canterbury.
(Hardy's Le Neve, ii. 302.)

[2] We have here omitted several pages of extracts from Sir John Hayward's Treatise on
the Succession in reply to Father Parsons, a book of great interest in its day. It is now
easily accessible to those who desire to refer to it. It was published Lond. 1603, 4to.

[3] The future Sir Henry, Editor of Chrysostom, and Provost of Eton.

told that the Bishop of Durrham[1] hath tendered his duty in all
humility, craving pardon for his opposicion heretofore, with promise
of faythfull service; hath preacht at Berwike before the King, and
said grace at his table twise or thrise.

The Queene nominated our King for hir successor: for being
demaunded whom shee would haue succede, hir answere was there
should noe rascals sitt in hir seate. "Who then?" "A King,"
said shee. "What King?" "Of Scotts," said shee, "for he hath
best right, and in the name of God lett him haue it."

The Papists verry lately put up a supplicacion to the King for a
tolleracion ; his aunswre was, Yf there were 40,000 of them in armes
should present such a petition, himselfe would rather dye in the
feild than condiscend to be false to God. Yet seemed he would not
use extremity, yf they continued in duty like subjects.

The Queene would sometymes speake freely of our King, but
could not endure to heare anie other use such language. The Lord
of Kenlosse,[2] a Scott, told our nobles, that they shall receive a verry
good, wise, and relligious King, yf wee can keepe him soe; yf wee
mar him not.

Lord Henry Howard[3] would come and continue at prayers when
the Queene came, but otherwise would not endure them, seeming to
performe the duty of a subject in attending on his prince at the one
tyme, and at the other using his conscience. He would runne out

[1] Dr. Matthew Hutton, Bishop from 1595 to 1606, when he was translated to York.
(Hardy's Le Neve, iii. 295.) The opposition alluded to was probably connected with
Border quarrels.

[2] Sir Edward Bruce, Lord Bruce of Kinloss, who came to England with the Earl of
Mar in 1601, ostensibly on a visit of congratulation to Queen Elizabeth, but really to effect
an understanding with Sir Robert Cecil, and pave the way, which he did most suc-
cessfully, for his master's succession. He was appointed Master of the Rolls in 1604, and
lies buried in the Rolls Chapel.

[3] The future Earl of Northampton.

of the Queenes chamber in hir sicknes when the chaplein went to prayer. Their prayer, for him, like a conjuracion for a spirit.

The Earl of Southampton must present himself with the nobles, and Sir Henry Nevill with the counsellors; like either shall be one of their rankes. ·

fo. 133ᵇ.

13 Aprill 1603·

It is a common bruit, yet false, that Sir Walter Rhaly is out of his Captainship of the Guard; *facile quod velint credunt, quod credunt loquuntur.*

Sir Amias Preston, an auncient knight, sent a challendge a while since to Sir Wa. Ra. which was not aunswered. Sir Ferdinand Gorge is out with him, as some say.[1]

He hath a good witt but it is carried by a foole, said Cobden of W. Burdett.

14 Aprill 1603.

Crue invited Cobden to a fyre, and there cald him foole; " It is one comfort," said Cobden, " that I am in a Crue of fooles."

Dr. Parry's note saith, the Queene was soe temperat in hir dyet from hir infancy, that hir brother King Edward VI. did usually call hir Dame Temper[ance.][2]

13.

Mr. Hemmings, sometyme of Trinity College in Cambridge, in a sermon at Paul's Crosse, speaking of women, said, Yf a man would marrie, it were 1,000 to one but he should light upon a bad one,

14.

---

[1] Raleigh on his trial alludes incidentally to Sir Amias Preston's challenge. Speaking of a book against the title of King James to succeed Elizabeth, which Cobham had stated that " he had " from Raleigh,—" I never gave it him," answered Raleigh, " he took it off my table. For I remember a little before that time I received a challenge from Sir Amias Preston, and, for that I did intend to answer it, I resolved to leave my estate settled, therefore laid out all my loose papers, amongst which was this book." (State Trials, ii. 21.) As to the relations between Sir Walter and Sir Ferdinando Gorges, see Archæologia, vol. xxxiii. p. 241.

[2] Camden is probably the original authority for this pleasant anecdote :—" *qui non alio nomine quam dulcis sororis Temperantiæ nomine salutavit* " are the words of his Introduction to the Annales of Elizabeth.

there were so many naught; and yf he should chaunce to find a good one, yet he were not suer to hold hir soe: for women are like a coule full of snakes amongst which there is one eele, a thousand to one yf a man happen upon the eele, and yet if he gett it in his hand, all that he hath gotten is but a wett eele by the tayle. (*Mr. Osborne.*)

'Tis certaine that Tyrone hath submitted absolutely, as to the late Queene, not knowing of hir death ; he is nowe at Dublin with the Lord Mountjoy, and Tirrell is come in with him.

APPENDIX.

Invocation of the Trinity.

I Richard Manningham, of the parish of East Malling, co. Kent, gent. being in tolerable health of body in regard of mine age and infirmities, but of perfect mind and memory, endued with all my senses, I laud and praise God therefore.

Will all written with mine own hand.

My body to be buried in the parish church of East Malling, by my first wife.

I give to the poor inhabitants of East Malling, 10*l.*

To the poor inhabitants of St. Alban's, where I was born, 10*l.*

To Edmund Manningham, my kinsman, 20*l.* with forgiveness of a debt of 20*l.*

To William Manningham, son of Edmund, 5*l.*

To Marion Manningham, daughter of Edmund, 5 marks.

To William Manningham, brother of Edmund, 40*l.*

To Charles Manningham, brother of William, 30*l.*

To Anna, Marie, and Elizabeth, sisters of Charles, 10*l.* a piece.

To Elizabeth Houghton and Mary Cleyton, daughters of my late half-brother Robert Kent, 10*l.* a piece.

To the widow of Drewe Kent, one of the sons of the said Robert, 5*l.*

To Gregory Arnold, eldest son of my late half-sister Elizabeth Arnold, 10*l.*

To Marie Lawrence and Sara Peters, daughters of the said Elizabeth Arnold, 10*l.* a piece.

To the four daughters of Marie Lawrence, 10*l.* a piece.

To Susan Hardy, daughter of my other half-sister Marie, 10*l.*

To Janeken Vermeren, daughter of my first wife's sister, 20*l*.

To the only daughter of George Herne, late painter, of London, 10*l*.

To James Ashpoole, my tailor, 10*l*.

To John Demua and Isabell his wife, sometime my servants, 5*l*. a piece.

To Thomas Whithead, my late servant, 5*l*.

To poor Joan Hawkyns, the like, 40*s*.

To Jane Owen, my maid servant, 20 marks.

To Arthur Wise, my husbandman, 5 marks.

To John Haslet, my man, and to Edmond Gibson, my boy, 40*s*. a-piece.

To my two maid servants, Katherine and Annis Wood, 5 marks a-piece.

To my other maid-servant, Ales, 40*s*.

To William Short, late servant to my cousin John Manningham, 5*l*.

To the Master, Wardens, and Livery of the Company of the Mercers of London, whereof I am, 25*l*. to make them a dinner.

To my honest water-bearer of London, Goodman Pigeon, 20*s*.

To my two poor labourers Edmond Gibson and Thomas Rogers, 40*s*. a-piece.

To my kinsman William Cranmer, the merchant, 5*l*.

I remit all moneys owing to me by William Kent, John Kent, Roger Kent, Nicholas Kent, Drewe Kent, and Stephen Kent, all sons of my aforesaid half-brother Robert Kent; and by George Arnold, Barnaby Lawrence and Jacob Peters, sons-in-law of my late half-sister Elizabeth Arnold; by William Pawley and Thomas Pawley; by Thomas Whithead, James Ashpoole, Alexander Brickenden, and Edmond Pierson.

Also to Arnold Verbeck, Abraham Verbeck, and Goris Besselles, merchant-strangers, kinsmen to my first wife, 400*l*. which I lent them at my said wife's request and for her sake, in 1595, upon condition that they pay to the two daughters of the said Arnold Verbeck, Margarita and Susanna, and to their nicht [niece] Janeken Vermeren, 40*l*. a-piece within a year after my executor shall have given them intimation so to do.

I nominate my kinsman and son-in-love, John Manningham, gentleman, of the Middle Temple of London, executor of this my will, and my good friend Emanuell Drom of London, merchant, overseer of the same, unto whom I give for his pains therein 10*l*.

The residue I give to my executor, and I require, charge, and adjure him by all the love and duty which he oweth me, for all my love and liberality which I have always borne him and his heretofore, but chiefly in this my will, that he perform and pay all and every legacy in this my last will given within six months at the farthest after my death, those excepted that are appointed to be paid at certain days limited, and those also to be duly paid at their days appointed and limited, all according to my true intent and meaning, as my trust is in him, and as he will answer afore God and me at the latter day.

If it be needful, I confirm to my executor the grant and gift formerly by me unto him made of all this my mansion house called Bradborne with my lands situate in East Malling, except as in the same gift is excepted, in which said grant I have reserved to myself a power to dispose of the premises, by will or otherwise, to what persons I list for the space of five years after my decease, as by the said deed dated 3rd January in the 7th year of the King that now is appears. I renounce the said power, and leave the premises to John Manningham and his heirs for ever immediately after my death.

I give to the said John Manningham all other my lands in East Malling, and to his heirs for ever, except one tenement lately purchased of John Goldsmyth, now in the occupation of Harry Metcalfe, and that other tenement in Melstreet [Mill street ?] called Hackstables, lately purchased of John Dowle, both which tenements I give to my bailiff Thomas Rayner and to his heirs for ever ; and also excepting to my poor servant Thomas Whithead his dwelling use and profit of that cottage called Poor John's during his life.

I give to the said John Manningham all my lands in Cranbrook, to him and his heirs for ever.

Lastly, I give to my kinsman John Arnold of St. Alban's, and to my kinsman Richard Lawrence of Maidstone, and to my maid-servant Annis Hull, and to their heirs for ever, my thirty acres of land called Larkhall in Hadlow or elsewhere in Kent, lately purchased of Thomas Tutsom, now in the occupation of John Bredger, to be equally divided between them, and I give to each of them 20 nobles in money.

Having thus, I thank God, finished this my last will and testament, and set an order in my worldly affairs, I will now henceforward await God's

merciful will and pleasure, to depart hence in peace when his blessed will
shall be to call for me, most humbly beseeching him of his infinite
goodness and mercy that when the final day of my dissolution shall be
come I may by his grace be armed with a true and lively faith, firm hope,
and constant patience against all the assaults and temptations of my
ghostly enemy the Devil, and to be willing and ready to forsake all to go
to my blessed Saviour and Redeemer Jesus Christ. Amen, good Lord.

Will all written with mine owne hand in five whole pages and eight
lines of the sixth page fastened together with my seal in merchants' wax.

Attestation states the length of the will, and that, in the presence of
the witnesses, the testator fastened all the pages together with his seal
in merchants' and hard wax.

Witnesses: William Prew, rector de Ditton; Richard Brewer; Matthew
Crowhurst; William Whiller.

Proved in the Prerogative Court of Canterbury before Dr. Thomas
Edwardes on the first May 1612, by John Manningham, the executor.
Registered in Fenner, 38.

II.—Inscription on Monument to Richard Manningham in East'
Malling Church.[1]

Richardus Mannyngham, honesta natus familia, mercaturam juvenis
exercuit satis copiosam; ætate provectiore ruri vacavit literis et valetudini,
in studiis tam divinis quam humanis eruditus; Latine, Gallice, Belgice
dixit, scripsit, eleganter et proprie; nec alieni appetens nec profusus sui,
amicos habuit fideliter et benigne, pauperes fortunis suis sublevavit,
affines et consanguineos auxit; animi candore, vultus suavitate et gravitate
conspicuus; sobrie prudens, et sincere pius. Languido tandem confectus
morbo, fide Deum amplexus orthodoxâ, expiravit 25° die Aprilis, anno
salutis 1611 et ætatis suæ 72° Desideratus suis, maxime Johanni
Mannyngham hæredi, qui monumentum hoc memor mœrensque posuit.

[1] The monument stands on the north side of the chancel, in a niche, over which is in-
scribed "*Redemptor meus vivit.*"

III.—Abstract of Will of John Manningham, dated 21st January
1621-2 ; 19th James I.

I John Manningham of East Malling co. Kent, esquire, being in
reasonable good health of body and in perfect and sound memory, God be
thanked !

I give to the poor inhabitants of East Malling, 5l. to be paid on the
day of my funeral.

To the like of Fenny Drayton, co. Cambridge, 5l.

Rings of gold of the value of 20s. a piece to be given to every one of
my servants, to each one, as a remembrance of me.

To my daughter Susan 300l.

To my daughter Elizabeth 250l.

To my son Walter 100l.

If Susan or Elizabeth die before accomplishing her age of 18 her
portion to be divided amongst my younger sons John and Walter and my
daughters that shall survive, and if Walter die before 21, his legacy to
be divided amongst his sisters and brother John, or such of them as shall
then be living.

My executors to employ the children's legacies, and out of the profits
to make an allowance for their maintenance.

I give to mine executors 20 nobles a-piece.

The residue of my goods and chattels I give to my dear and well-
beloved wife Anne Manningham and to my son Richard, equally to be
divided between them.

I appoint my loving brother-in-law Walter Curle, D.D. and Dean of
Lichfield, and my very loving cousin William Robardes of Enfield, D.D.
executors.

A fine having been levied in Michaelmas Term, 10th James, between
Edward Curll of the Middle Temple, esquire, now deceased, and my cousin
Beckingham Boteler of Tewing, co. Hertford, esquire, and myself John
Manningham, Edmund Manningham, William Manningham, and Charles
Manningham, of all my lands in Kent, the same are settled to the use of
me and my heirs and assigns until by will or deed I appoint the same.
Now as to my capital messuage and mansion-house called Bradborne
in East Malling and all lands in the same parish which my late dear cousin

and father in love Richard Manningham purchased of George Catlin, John Pathill, and Nicholas Miller, I appoint the same to the use of my wife for life, and after her decease to the use of my son Richard Manningham in tail male, and for want of such heirs of his body to the use of my right heirs for ever.

And as to my two messuages or farms in Well Street, East Malling, in the occupation of Thomas Pennyall, Moses Watts, and Nicholas Beeching, I appoint the same to the use of my son John in tail male, with remainder to the use of my son Walter in like manner, with remainder to my own right heirs.

And as to my lands in Detling and Thurnham in Kent, I appoint the same to the use of my son Walter in tail, remainder to the use of my son John in like manner, remainder to the use of my son Richard in tail, remainder to the use of my own right heirs for ever.

And as to all that capital messuage and lands which my late dear cousin and father in love Richard Manningham (who for ever is gratefully to be remembered by me and mine) purchased of Sir William Gratewick deceased, and of Edmund Catlin deceased, and all other my hereditaments in Kent not before disposed of, I appoint the same to the use of my son Richard in tail male, with remainder to each of my sons John and Walter in like manner in succession, and with an ultimate remainder to my right heirs for ever.

I appoint my wife guardian to my son Richard and the rest of my children.

Will written with my own hand, in three sheets of paper fixed together with a label. Executed on 20th February, 1621-2. Attested by Sackville Pope, Richard Butler, John Roberts, John Gwy.

Proved before Sir William Byrde, in the Prerogative Court of Canterbury on 4th December, 1622, by Dr. Walter Curle, Dr. William Robartes having renounced. Registered in Saville, 112.

ADDENDA AND CORRIGENDA.

Introd. p. **x.**—Although born in Hampshire, there is reason to believe, from a similarity of arms, that Thomas Manningham, Bishop of Chichester, was descended from the Cambridgeshire branch of our Diarist's family. He was educated at Winchester and New College, Oxford. His principal preferments in the church were the Preachership at the Rolls, the Lectureship at the Temple, and the Rectory of St. Andrew's Holborn, to which last he was presented by the Crown in 1691; he also held a royal chaplaincy, and the Deanery of Windsor, to which he was appointed in 1708. He kept his Deanery *in commendam* with his Bishopric.[1] Many of his sermons were published; one preached at St. Andrew's on the death of Queen Mary, 4to. London, 1695, passed through at any event three editions, and has an interest from the preacher's delineation of the amiable character of his royal mistress.

Sir Richard Manningham published, besides certain more strictly professional works, "An Exact Diary" (another Manningham's Diary) "of what was observ'd during a close attendance upon Mary Toft, the pretended Rabbet-Breeder of Godalming in Surrey, from Monday Nov. 28 to Wednesday Dec. 7 following. Together with an account of her confession of the Fraud. By Sir Richard Manningham, Kt. Fellow of the Royal Society, and of the College of Physicians, London." (Lond. 8vo. 1726.) Another of Sir Richard's good deeds was the erection of the well-known Park Chapel, Chelsea.[2] He died on the 11th May 1759, and was buried at Chelsea.

P. 13. *l.* 11. *For* Dene, *read* Drewe.

---

[1] See Wood's Athenæ, iv. 555 ; and Dallaway's Sussex, i. 94.

[2] In Munk's Roll of the Royal College of Physicians, ii. 67, an excellent work of reference, to which I am indebted for most of these particulars, "Chelsea" is misprinted, in this instance, "Cheltenham."

P. 16, l. 4.—The anagram upon the name " Davis," here attributed to "Martin," should have had a note to point out that the combination of these two names leads one to suppose that the Davis alluded to was probably the future Sir John Davies, and that the Martin to whom this saucy witticism is attributed, may have been the Richard Martin commemorated by Ben Jonson, and the person for a scandalous attack upon whom Davies was temporarily struck off the books of the Middle Temple, as mentioned at p. 168. The outrage occurred on the 9th February 1597-8. Davies was restored to his membership of the Inn on the 30th October 1601. The late Lord Stowell, in his communication to the Society of Antiquaries on this subject (Archæologia, xxi. 108,) somewhat favours a suggestion of Alexander Chalmers that a rivalry between Martin and Davies in colloquial wit may have led to Davies's misconduct. The peculiarity in Sir John's gait noticed at p. 168, and which would attract more attention among young students than it deserved, was probably not unique. Sir Walter Scott, who no doubt drew from an original, describes something very like it in the instance of Baillie Macwheeble, who waddled across the court-yard of the manor-house of Tully Veolan, like a turnspit walking upon its hind legs.

P. 23, last line but one,—for Bradbourne, *read* Brabourne.

P. 40, n. 2,—for whose Autobiography, *read* whose son's Autobiography.

P. 85, third line from the bottom.—These remarks may perhaps be a young man's judgment upon the works of the celebrated Dr. John Reynolds, president of Corpus Christi College, Oxford. Bishop Hall spoke of him in other terms :—" He alone was a well-furnished library, full of all faculties, of all studies, of all learning ; the memory and reading of that man were near to a miracle." The opinion of all his most distinguished contemporaries agreed with that of Bishop Hall. (Wood's Athenæ, ii. 11.)

P. 117, last line, for Sing, *read* Snig.

INDEX.

2 B